PRAISE FOR LOU ARONICA'S #1 BESTSELLER

The Forever Year

"*The Forever Year* is pure pleasure from beginning to end, beautifully written and emotionally rich."
— Susan Elizabeth Phillips,
New York Times bestselling author

"*The Forever Year* is a wry, tender, beautifully written novel …. Once I started, I couldn't put it down."
— Lisa Kleypas,
New York Times bestselling author

"Better than Nicholas Sparks's best. There's more wit, more wisdom, and yes, there are tears."
— John R. Maxim,
New York Times bestselling author

"*The Forever Year* is a warm, engaging story with a valuable contemporary lesson inside — it is well structured and funny and keeps you turning the pages till the very end to find out what happens. It may even make you rethink your own attitude toward love! I really enjoyed it."
— Suzanne Vega,
multiplatinum recording artist

"An enduring story that should be read by all. This is a story that will have you seeing your parents differently, wondering how your own children see you, and falling in love again. An emotional read! Heartwarming! A love story on many levels. Strongly recommend!"

– CMash Reads

"The love story that is told is so touching, and really made me evaluate my own relationship and understand how special it really is. I fell for this book, and I hope you will too!"

– Chick Lit Plus

"*Blue* is enriched with great characters, a moving story line, and an author who will have you want to read more of his work. I could feel the anguish Chris felt for his daughter and wanting to spend as much time with her as he possibly could. The world of Tamarisk is full of intriguing people, who are almost as real as Becky. *Blue* is a five star read in my books!"

– Cheryl's Book Nook

flash
AND
dazzle

flash
AND
dazzle

A NOVEL BY

lou aronica

THE
STORY PLANT

The Story Plant
Studio Digital CT, LLC
PO Box 4331
Stamford, CT 06907

Print ISBN-13: 978-1-61188-069-4
E-book ISBN-13: 978-1-61188-070-0

Visit our website at www.fictionstudiobooks.com
Visit the author's website at www.louaronica.com

Originally published under the name Ronald Anthony
Original Forge Books paperback publication: January 2007
First Story Plant Paperback Printing: November 2013

Printed in the United States of America

FICTION BY LOU ARONICA

The Forever Year
Flash and Dazzle
Blue
Until Again
Differential Equations (with Julian Iragorri)

NONFICTION BY LOU ARONICA

The Culture Code (with Clotaire Rapaille)
Miraculous Health (with Dr. Rick Levy)
The Element (with Ken Robinson)
Finding Your Element (with Ken Robinson)
The 5 Essentials (with Bob Deutsch)

For David.

The fact that you know so much of what's in this novel already makes me deeply proud.

ACKNOWLEDGMENTS

I'd like to thank my family – my wife Kelly, and my children Molly, David, Abigail, and Tigist – for providing me with the greatest benefits of the writer's life.

My agent, Danny Baror, has been a stalwart supporter even when conventional wisdom suggests throwing in the towel. I greatly appreciate that.

Jennifer Hershey was the first person to read the 2007 version of this novel and her advice spurred me on. I always knew she was great at what she did, and it was a pleasure to benefit from it firsthand from this perspective.

Terry Banker and I spent a considerable amount of time batting this idea around. I appreciate his insights and his passion.

Thanks to my editor for the 2007 edition, Melissa Singer, for her enthusiasm and good editorial recommendations.

Tom Avitabile gave me much-needed screenplay advice and a few tips on the advertising world. Thanks, Tom.

Thanks to Barbara Aronica Buck for the sensational work she always does on my book covers.

Thanks to Sue Rasmussen for the copyediting help she has given me and many Story Plant authors.

And special thanks to the many readers of my other novels who have written to tell me how much my work has moved them. Those kind words have inspired me at levels I never could have imagined.

The chapter about Daz
(well, I guess they all are)

I never was the kind of guy who was big on outward expressions of emotion. When you grow up in Ice Land (which in this case is a pejorative for the household I was raised in, not the place where Bjork comes from), you're trained that way. But in the time since Daz died, I find that just about anything can bring me to the verge of tears. The outreached hand of someone I'm meeting, a television commercial advertising baby food, the guy who plays the steel drum at the entrance to Central Park (especially if he's playing *Ode to Joy*, which I realize is like getting choked up over Barry Manilow, but it just *happens*). And the reminders, of course. There's a city, a country, a universe full of them, any one of which could inspire another bout of melancholy.

Daz would laugh if he saw me this way. Maybe even say something to make me feel ridiculous about it. At the same time, though, I know (at least *now* I know) that he'd appreciate it.

I suppose at some point his passing will be easier for me to take, that I'll adjust to the ache I feel whenever I realize for the thousandth time that he isn't here any-more. Even though the idea is just this side of inconceiv-able right now, it has to happen, I suppose. I really hope it doesn't, though. I'm not sure what I'd do if the hurt was gone too.

I guess you always find out eventually that when everything is going according to plan this probably means your plan wasn't a very good one. Still, in the spring of '13, the plan seemed awfully sweet. It went like this: throw together a huge bash for our twenty-eighth birthdays (a week apart in April), pick up a couple of Clios for the BlisterSnax campaign, accept lots of kudos while feigning humility, do a snappy and witty interview in *Ad Week*, impress the pants (literally) off of Carnie Brinks and Michelle Dancer, and get our own agency up and running and doing major billing by the time we were thirty. Tough in the current market, maybe, but all of it entirely reachable with the right level of dedication, the prodigious application of imagination, and the genuine commitment to make it happen.

Frankly, it didn't seem daunting to us in the least. I don't know, maybe it was just me who didn't find it daunting. Or even consider it particularly important. That was one of the hundreds of things I never found out, though I can at least credit myself with making the effort in the end. I'm sure the subject would have come up if we hadn't run out of time, but there were so many other things in line ahead of it. To tell you the truth, "the plan" didn't really enter my mind at all during those final weeks.

Daz and I had been running buddies since right before our freshman year at college at the University of Michigan. I'd arrived from the Gold Card nurturance of Scarsdale, NY, an upper-middle-class neighborhood in Westchester where my parents settled when I was a little kid. He got to school on a soccer scholarship from

Manhattan, Kansas, home of Kansas State University and maybe forty or fifty other people. He was long and wiry, accustomed to hours and hours of running on the pitch, a word that, before we met, I had no idea referred to a soccer field. I managed to pack all of my energy into a compact sixty-six inches and, while college-level organized sports eluded me, I stayed at least relatively trim through three or four days a week in the weight room to offset what had always been a considerable appetite.

We met at one of those initiation weekends where they threw a bunch of us together so we could bond and feel like we knew someone before stepping foot on campus. They sent us to a KOA campground in Ypsilanti (a word that I discovered Daz found curiously funny) and stuck us in four-person tents based on no criterion we could identify other than gender. After that weekend, I never again saw the two other guys who'd been assigned to camp with us. One was named Don, but Daz and I quickly took to calling him "Juan" because from the moment the bus dropped us off, he was in search of softer and decidedly feminine sleeping arrangements. I can't remember the other guy's name, but we nicknamed him "The Inebriator" because of his seemingly monomaniacal desire to get as drunk as possible as quickly as possible. I'm definitely not a teetotaler, but it was a little frightening to watch this guy go at it. He snatched drinks from whomever he could with absolutely no concern for what the combination did to his body other than the obvious.

The weekend started innocuously enough. Daz was kicking a soccer ball around with a few guys when I approached and suggested we turn to a "real game" like football. This being the University of Michigan, others took me up on this suggestion quickly, and we walked off to get something going together. As I turned, Daz kicked the soccer ball at my head, not hard enough to hurt, but definitely hard enough to attract my attention. I looked back at him, throwing him my *what the hell?* face as I did.

"Thanks for breaking up my game," he said sharply.

"You don't play football?"

"I can kick your ass in football but I was *playing* soccer."

That seemed a little intense. "Feel free to continue," I said, shaking my head and going to catch up with the other guys. As I turned away, the ball struck me in the head again, this time just a tiny bit harder.

"You're gonna have to stop doing that," I said, a bit miffed, throwing the ball back at him.

"Just wanted you to know I could."

What was that supposed to mean? At this point, I was a little concerned about spending the night in the same tent as this guy. I began to wonder if Juan had found someone with a friend.

"I'm impressed," I said sarcastically. "Do you know any other tricks?"

Daz smiled, which totally changed his expression, and did a back flip before bicycle-kicking the ball straight at my gut. I caught the ball before it did any damage, but the entire exercise made me laugh. And I had to admit that I was a little impressed.

"That was pretty good," I said.

Daz chuckled. He seemed to be having a very good time with this. "Thanks. I can also eat an entire cherry pie in a minute and twenty seconds."

I had definitely never had a conversation like this before.

I threw my hands out at my sides. "I'm humbled."

"Don't be," he said casually. "I'm sure there's something you're really good at, too."

"Yeah, something." I heard some of the other guys joking with each other in the distance. "So listen, are you coming to play football with us or what?"

Daz shook his head. "Nah. I heard some girls were going to be singing around a campfire pretty soon. Possibilities, you know?"

I looked off toward where the football game was gathering and shrugged. "Campfire sounds cool."

Anyway, by midnight that night we were back in our tent, having gained nothing from our campfire experience beyond a deeper appreciation of the Joni Mitchell songbook. Juan presumably was sharing a sleeping bag with someone who'd bought his act, and The Inebriator was completely passed out on the other side of the tent, occasionally twitching.

"You don't think he needs medical attention, do you?" Daz said.

"There's nothing a doctor can do for this guy. I hope the infirmary is well-stocked with Tylenol, though. He's gonna need a whole bottle of the stuff tomorrow morning."

The Inebriator rolled over, belched loudly – which caused both of us to retreat to the furthest corner of the tent – and then stopped moving again. Daz and I just looked at each other and laughed.

We hung out together the rest of the night. We'd already shared an affinity for burnt hot dogs and a disdain for girls whose singing voices were completely different from their speaking voices. Now we kicked back with a couple of beers (they were Coronas because we

thought that was the brew of champions at the time)
and we talked about a lot of things: music (he liked John
Mellencamp and Willie Nelson, which I forgave because
he also liked Radiohead and Death Cab for Cutie), girls
(he had a thing for tall, lanky blondes; back then I was
an absolute sucker for the dark Mediterranean look),
sports (he was okay with the fact that I liked watching
baseball even though he thought it was too slow – which
I thought was hilarious coming from a *soccer* player; I
was okay with the fact that he liked the Dallas Cowboys,
even though it went against every instinct I had as a
Giants fan) and then some more about girls.

"Met anyone you want to date yet?" I said.

"I'm a pretty picky guy."

"Yeah, me too."

"There are a lot of really good looking women on
campus, though."

"Kind of an amazing number, actually."

"It's good to be picky, though."

"I totally agree with you."

Daz took a pull on his beer and laughed. "Especially
when none of them have shown any interest in
me whatsoever."

"Yeah, I know what you mean."

I think I spent the next twenty minutes trying
to explain to him how exciting baseball could be if
you knew how to watch it. A few beers later – these
scammed off the people in the next tent because we
were out – things got quiet for a few moments. That
made me think about the way I'd left home the week
before, something that kept creeping back into my mind.

"Do you know that my mother didn't bother to come
with me to the airport before I flew out here? She gave

me this leather backpack and told me she had a lunch date she couldn't break. Of course that was a freaking love-fest compared to what my older sister did. I tried to get together with her before I left and she couldn't find the time to fit me in her schedule. Not a single minute to say goodbye to me until Christmas."

I shook my head thinking about it and looked over at Daz. He just screwed up his face and said, "Aw man, families *suck*."

Exactly what I was thinking, even though I'd never quite phrased it that way. "You got that right," I said. We clinked beer bottles and moved on to more interesting topics. I don't remember what exactly. Probably something to do with all-girl sports bands. The weird thing was that Daz's offhand comment had made me feel better. Maybe it was his expression when he said it. Maybe it was the seven beers. Or maybe it was the way it just cut to the heart of what I was feeling. Regardless, I didn't think about my mother or sister again the rest of the night.

Daz and I didn't have any classes together that first year and we lived in dorms far away from each other, but we stayed in touch. As the second semester drew on, we started going out drinking more and even pulled all-nighters together at the library during midterms. It wasn't easy to keep Daz focused on studying, and sometimes his distraction could be a little distracting, but for whatever reason, I found that I worked harder when he was around. It was probably because if I did an efficient job of studying we could grab a couple of beers and play a round or two of foosball before crashing.

It was during this time that we decided to apply to be roommates for our sophomore year. I was living with

two guys, one of whom had an all-too-unhealthy fascination with controlled substances and the other who had
an all-too-unhealthy aversion to showers. Daz got along
fine with his roommates, but was certain that one of
them would wind up in maximum security before the
year was up. Rooming together was not only the prudent
thing to do, but I think we both knew we'd have a great
time doing it.

And we did. Whether it was playing practical jokes
on the girls down the hall, taking on all comers in an air
hockey tournament, or starting unthinkable line dances
at a local pub, we were just about inseparable after that.
Daz majored in Commercial Art and I headed toward
a degree in Marketing. In the middle of our sophomore
year, we volunteered to do some posters for the spring
blood drive and the job sort of took on a life of its own.
Daz drew a picture of a guy staggering off of a table
after giving blood and I paired it with a line that read
"Get High for Free!" Then Daz drew a picture of a girl
with four IVs sticking out of her arms and I gave it the
headline, "What the Hell Do You Need Five Quarts
of the Stuff for Anyway?" We did a few more like that
and when we delivered them, the woman who assigned
us the project seemed a little freaked. I don't think this
was at all what the school had in mind. Somehow we
fast-talked her into using them, though – and they got
thirty-four percent more blood donors than they'd ever
gotten before. From that point on, we became the unofficial promo people for more than a dozen school organizations, which got us invited to an awful lot of parties.

Kelsey Bonham, who commissioned us to do the
cover of the literary magazine, was the one who dubbed
us "Flash and Dazzle." She threw it out when she passed

us on campus one day and Daz turned to me and said, "We should have thought of that ourselves, you know." How these things make their way around, I'll never quite understand (it was the first thing I blamed on social media), but soon after, it seemed that everyone we knew was calling us by that nickname. By this point, we'd also adopted it ourselves. We carried it from Ann Arbor to Alphabet City in Manhattan to our fabulous co-ops on the Upper West Side to those days in late March 2013 when everything seemed to be going according to plan.

Rich Flaster and Eric Dazman. Flash and Dazzle. Flaccid and Spazman on our bad days. Strutting down the road to (benevolent, of course) world domination.

We never once thought about stumbling.

I certainly never expected to be sitting here by myself wondering how this could have happened while just about anything could bring tears to my eyes.

Daz was gone. And I missed him like crazy.

The chapter about trying to get Daz to the office (also known as the daily Sisyphean struggle)

It wouldn't be fair to call Daz a slug. After all, he had been a third team all-conference striker in college, and he was still slim and fleet. However, getting him out of his apartment in the morning had always been a considerable task. There was the *ringing the doorbell seven times before going in with my key* part. There was the *don't you remember we have that meeting at 9:30* part. There was the, *I really don't give a shit what your hair looks like* part. Then there were the inevitable battles with toothpaste choices (Daz was the only person I ever met who kept multiple flavors of toothpaste in his bathroom), Cap'n Crunch (the only thing he deigned to eat for breakfast), and *Power Rangers* (which appeared on ABC Family at 8:30 every morning and from which Daz took surprising delight for someone his age).

On most days, by the time I got to his place to pick him up, I'd already read the relevant sections of the *Times* and the *Journal* and surfed three or four entertainment, media and business sites on the web. About a year ago, it finally dawned on me that I could sleep fifteen minutes later in the morning if I brought my bagel and coffee with me so I could have breakfast while I waited for Daz to get ready. On certain days I thought it might be smart to bring a lunch as well.

It was this way from our first days in the City. The only difference at the beginning was that we were in the same apartment and Daz sometimes dragged himself out of bed earlier if I made enough noise or if I did something like flick water on his face after my shower.

The other difference was the nature of our living quarters. The place on Avenue B had been only moderately better than sleeping on the street. The lobby was tastefully adorned in crack vials, hypodermic needles, and spent condoms, and our "doorman" was a sixty-something guy with more jackets than teeth who squatted in front of our building. My mother came to visit exactly once, sneered at my decision to live here rather than commuting from a garden apartment in Hastings, and told me that if I wanted to see her in the future, I knew the Metro-North schedule. She didn't even give me her little faux kiss on the cheek on her way out the door. This irked me until I thought about the possibility of her being propositioned by a male prostitute before she could get a cab out of the neighborhood. I imagined her scandalized expression and smiled.

A year later, when we were recruited as a team by The Creative Shop, we made our first "big move." It was a walkup in Hell's Kitchen – not exactly Fifth Avenue, though a huge improvement over what it had been only a few years earlier – but the space was a lot better and a much higher grade of junkie and hooker hung around outside. When we got our first major bonus checks – one of several to come our way in the past few years – we knew it was time to find someplace a little more respectable, someplace where we could have a party and not worry if our guests could make it in and out of the building alive.

It was my father's accountant who first suggested we consider buying. The thought had never even crossed my mind, though admittedly we did a terrible job of managing the money we made and got brutalized on our 2011 tax returns. He also told us that if we bought, we had to buy *separately* to get the most bang for our tax deduction bucks. It was an odd thing to think about. We had lived together for eight years at that point and while we knew we'd eventually find romantic partners to move in with, the notion of no longer being roommates for *financial* reasons seemed incongruous. In the end, though, it really did make the most sense. And with Daz at 89th and Broadway and me at 91st and West End, we were nearly roommates anyway.

"Who do we have a meeting with this morning?" he said, coming out of the bathroom with a toothbrush in his mouth. He had different colored toothbrushes for the different flavors. The gray brush meant fennel.

"It's just us."

"Us? Like you and me?" He returned to the bathroom to spit.

"And Michelle and Carnie and Brad and Chess."

"Sounds like the *meeting* we had at Terminal 5 last night."

We'd all gone there to see Beam, an incredible British trance rock band.

"Except this time we're going to have a serious business conversation and it won't look as cool if your head lolls back and forth."

"And what will we be talking about again?" He asked this question from his bedroom, where he was almost certainly trying to decide if it was a *red* flannel shirt day or a *blue* flannel shirt day.

"The Koreans."

"Motorcycles, right?" he said, sticking his face out the door.

"Cars. Affordable luxury for twenty-somethings."

"Twenty-somethings want luxury?"

"They do if it's affordable."

"That's why you're the word guy and I'm the picture guy. I wouldn't have a clue how to pitch this."

"Good thing I'm around then, huh?"

He disappeared back into the bathroom, meaning we were somewhere between eight and fifteen minutes of departure time, assuming I kept him away from the Power Rangers.

I finished my bagel and scrolled through my Twitter feed. Not finding anything to capture my attention, I stood up and walked around the apartment. The morning crowbar exercise notwithstanding, we spent much less time in Daz's place than we did in mine. This was primarily because I had the better toys – the sixty-inch TV, the foosball table, the multiple gaming systems, the Bang and Olufsen stereo with full theatre sound (the potential of which I never got to exploit because of the co-op rules) – and also because I actually kept food in the place. Daz hadn't done particularly much with his home space. The obligatory Crate and Barrel couch and coffee table, the Mondrian print squaring off against the Dave Matthews Band poster, the formal dining table that he never explained why he bought (I don't know; maybe he wanted me to have my bagel and coffee in comfort), the airbed he propped up against the wall next to the couch rather than deflating, and not a hell of a lot else.

Other than the air hockey table. And the massage chair. The latter was Daz's first significant purchase once he bought his place. I asked him why he wanted one – he never seemed *in need* of a massage – and he gestured toward the chair to suggest that I give it a try. Once I did, I understood immediately.

I sat there now and set the chair to *knead*. I would have loved to have one of these in my office, but one of the unspoken deals Daz and I had was that we wouldn't spend a lot of money on something the other guy already owned. What was the point? I kicked the massage level up to *medium* and switched from kneading to tapping. I thought about taking my shoes off to use the foot massager and then checked the time on my phone instead.

"I mentioned that the meeting was today and not in August, right?" I said, my voice vibrating from the thumping my back was receiving.

"I'm done," he said, walking over to stand in front of me in blue flannel. "Just a quick one-on-one with the Cap'n and we'll be out of here."

I turned off the chair and got up. Daz opened the box of cereal and poured it directly into his mouth. "Let's go," he said, taking a swig from a milk carton and grabbing his keys.

I gathered my stuff and we made our way out the door. Daz locked the two deadbolts and my eye fell on his keychain – a plastic hot dog that he'd burned with a cigarette lighter in honor of our first (and only) camping trip. He'd toted that thing around for the last ten years.

"I think Michelle and I had a little thing last night," he said as we walked out onto Broadway to begin our search for a cab.

I laughed. "I was with the two of you the entire time. You didn't have a thing."

"No, I think we might have. It was an *eye* thing."

"An eye thing as in she saw you and said hi?"

"Don't be a schmuck. I *can* tell the difference, you know. I think she kinda likes me."

"Daz, everyone kinda likes you. See that woman who just stepped in front of us to steal our cab? I'll bet she likes you. You're a likable guy. I just wouldn't get my hopes up about Michelle if I were you."

"She came to my office just to see *my drawings* the other day. She's never done that before."

"Daz, reachable goals, remember? Reachable goals."

"I think you might be surprised here."

"Surprised wouldn't begin to describe it. Stunned speechless maybe. Or shocked to the point where I needed a defibrillator."

He regarded me sternly. "Why do you think I couldn't get a woman like Michelle?"

"Did I say that?"

"Pretty much exactly that."

"You're misunderstanding me. I'm speaking specifically about Michelle. A woman *like* Michelle – you know, gorgeous, smart, clever, burgeoning career – you could get a woman like that. Anytime you wanted, probably."

"But not Michelle specifically. Translation, please."

"A translation isn't necessary. Right now, the only thing that's important is that we find some way to get the hell downtown."

Eventually we took a gypsy cab, one of those out-of-town car services that roamed around the City skimming off fares from Yellow cabs during rush hours. I hated doing this – I was *very* loyal to my city – but at 9:05 on a weekday, it really was the best we could do.

"If we left earlier, we wouldn't be riding in a fifteen-year-old Impala right now, you know," I said.

"If we left *later*, we wouldn't be doing this either."

"You know, it's a good thing you're an artistic genius. Otherwise you'd be working at Burger King. No, you'd lose your job at Burger King because you'd always be showing up late. Then you'd be out on the street collecting bottles to exchange for cheap liquor."

"Never happen."

"You don't think so?"

"Nope. Cause you'd be around to drag my ass out of bed so I could keep my job making french fries."

"Don't be so sure."

"Of course you would."

Yeah, of course I would. If I could be relied upon for anything, it would be making sure that Daz got to work at a reasonable hour. Beyond that, as it turns out, I was lacking in an entire suite of skills best friends were supposed to have. However, he would never be homeless as long as I was around.

We rode in silence for a couple of minutes, bucking and stopping every eight seconds or so as traffic dictated. Then something caught Daz's eye and he pulled out the sketch-pad he always carried in his backpack and started drawing.

"What are you doing?"

"That jogger we passed gave me an idea."

I hadn't even noticed a jogger. "An idea for what?"

"For the Space Available campaign."

Space Available was a custom-built closet company whose account we recently acquired. How a jogger related to this escaped me.

"Let me see," I said, leaning toward him in the seat.

He pulled the sketchpad back. "Not yet." He smiled over at me. "I want to show it to *Michelle* first."

"She'll never love you like I love you, Daz."

"There's another thing we can all be thankful for."

He drew for a bit longer, and while I knew there was a very good chance this brainstorm of his wouldn't produce anything – so many of our ideas didn't – I was curious. I tried to angle my eyes over without appearing too obvious, but Daz was doing a great job of blocking my view. Finally, he closed the sketchbook and returned it to his backpack, glancing out at the street as though there was nothing to this.

"Traffic's a bitch today," he said. "We really should have left earlier. You gotta get on the beam, Flaccid."

The chapter about imagination-starved clients and heroic solutions

The Creative Shop is a smallish agency (our president, Ron Isaacs, likes to call it "the biggest of the small agencies") that treats its staff like children. I mean this in the most complimentary way. Though I've never been privy to the planning sessions that guide the overall direction of the firm, it's obvious that the intention is to generate a playground atmosphere in the hopes that its mostly young staff will flourish. Cartoon and comic book characters adorn the walls, the break room includes arcade games and a stereo system playing everything from James Brown to the Rolling Stones to fun. to Jay-Z, and we're actually encouraged to download whatever we want from the Internet.

Which is not to suggest in any way that The Creative Shop doesn't take itself seriously. The account managers are in perpetual rainmaker mode, and I'm called on to do a headstand for one potential client or another on just about a weekly basis. This on top of the dozen or so clients I regularly serve and the occasional pitch I do myself in an attempt to keep extending my range of employable talents.

Six years ago, I was brought on board as a senior copywriter at the same time as Daz was hired as an art director. In the kind of blind-to-the-consequences move that typified business life in 2007 and would be unthinkable now, we brought our digital portfolios to a bevy of small and mid-size agencies and auctioned ourselves off as a package deal. A few of these agencies bit. By that time, Daz and I had done some memorable campaigns – especially those focused on the teen and college markets – and had a little bit of a reputation.

Ultimately, it was the Maximum Speed game that decided our new work home for us. On our third interview, Steve Rupert, the Creative Director at The Shop took us to the break room and while I told him I was impressed that Jonny Lang was playing on the stereo, Daz veered over to the arcade games.

"You mean this is here all the time?" he said, grinning in the way he usually only did when Pop Tarts came out with a new flavor.

"All the time," Rupert said.

"And we can play it whenever we want?"

"We'd prefer it if you didn't leave a client meeting to play but just about any other time."

Daz rolled his eyes to the ceiling. And when he looked at me, I knew it was going to be nearly impossible to get him to consider working anyplace else.

Whether the decision was made for the best reasons or not, it turned out to be a very good one for both of us. Daz and I got to work on some great campaigns together and we quickly became the go-to guys for anything in the tween, teen, and new adult demographics. We did national campaigns for breakfast cereals, sporting equipment, and vacation destinations and we did local campaigns for soft drinks, clothing stores, and a small chain of Mexican restaurants.

Our signature gig so far was BlisterSnax, a bite-size candy that was hot, sweet, and sour at the same time. Daz and I did their very first print campaign when the company (started by a couple of guys on the inheritance from one of their grandmothers) was tiny and distributed only in the tri-state area. Six months later, their early success led to a major expansion, and we launched them nationally with a TV, radio, and web campaign, which included the legendary BlisterSnax anthem, the lyrics to which I wrote. It was my first hit song – I mean kids actually *sang* my words, and the video we did for it was downloaded on YouTube four and a half million times. The launch was hugely successful and the campaign became a blitz, which brought a significant amount of billing to The Creative Shop – and some hefty bonus checks and big promotions to Flash and Dazzle. I was now Associate Creative Director for the entire firm and Daz had a staff of six art directors working underneath him. It meant that both of us had to deal with a modicum of administrative work, but the core of every day – and the thing that got me out of bed every morning – was still the campaigns. I could deal with budget meetings, employee reviews and the occasional tiffs that flared up among members of my staff as long as Daz and I spent several hours every day just doing ads.

I love this stuff. I really do. It certainly isn't fine art, it might not have any edifying social significance, and it probably isn't the kind of work that any real adult should do, but I love creating ads. I love throwing ideas around until one sticks. I love joining words and images in incongruous ways that make people laugh or cringe or just take notice. I love the brashness of the form. And I love the fact that if I do my job well enough, people might tell someone else about my ad the day after they see it instead of reaching for the remote to change channels.

The nine-thirty meeting that day didn't happen until eleven. Not because Daz couldn't get out of his apartment or because the traffic down Broadway was tortuous, but because the second we stepped off the elevator we were told to go to Steve Rupert's office to deal with the day's first hassle.

"SparkleBean doesn't like the angle you guys are taking," he said as we walked in. Rupert was the only guy in the entire place who wore a tie every day and it was usually a truly awful one. I couldn't tell if this was his version of "dressing down" (maybe he had a whole drawer of Versace and Hermes at home but wore these because it made him fit in more) or if he truly had such horrendous taste that these street corner specials appealed to him. Certainly, it wasn't because of the money. He wasn't rich – no one who worked at an agency this size made gigantic salaries, even with bonuses – but he could definitely afford better duds.

"What don't they like about it?" I said, feeling peeved instantly. It wasn't that I didn't understand that the client had the final call on all campaigns. I came into the business with a very clear sense that my job was to serve someone else's needs. Still, I hated it when good work got questioned.

"They don't think you're being reverential enough."

I narrowed my eyes to slits. "They want us to sell cream soda to fourteen-year-olds by being reverential?"

"Their marketing director kept talking about a hundred and seven years of history and how they're still using the same recipe that the original Mr. Hanson used from the very beginning."

"All of which is very appealing to kids," I said.

Daz shook his head. "Assholes."

We went about as far from reverential with this campaign as we could, storyboarding a thirty-second TV spot that featured a teenager in a convenience store buying a can of the stuff, taking a gulp and being propelled to amazing places on a stream of carbonation. Our tagline was, "Be the Bean." Not a single mention of – jeez – history.

"They really want us to talk about tradition and hand-crafting and all of that crap?" I said.

Rupert threw up his hands. "Look, I'm not saying I agree with them."

I knew that was true. Whatever Steve Rupert lacked in taste in clothing he made up with his eye for advertising. I also knew that if he loved a campaign – and he'd made it very clear that he loved this one – he would try everything at his disposal to drive it home with the client. The fact that he'd struck out meant we had no chance of winning the argument we weren't going to have anyway.

"What did the original Mr. Hanson look like?" Daz said.

Rupert shook his head. "I don't have a clue."

"Is it on their website?"

"Who knows? Probably, considering what a big deal they're making about it."

Though I had no idea why we were doing so, we called up the site on Rupert's computer. Sure enough, against the umber and sepia tones of their home page, there was a shot of Alexander Hanson, a year off of the boat, sitting on a crate of "Hanson's Original SparkleBean," and flashing us a sly smile.

Daz leaned toward the screen to give it a closer look. "What do you think he's smiling about?"

"Probably just made his first buck," Rupert said.

"Yeah, but it looks like he's goofing," Daz said. "Something tells me this guy wasn't nearly as hung up about tradition as the new Hansons are."

I slapped Daz on the back. "That's our campaign," I said, kissing him on the temple. He reached up to his head and then looked down at his fingers like he was expecting to see blood. "We start with a slow zoom in on this picture with soft orchestral music in the background and a voice over that says something like, 'A hundred and seven years ago Alexander Hanson crafted the very first bottles of SparkleBean out of the finest vanilla, sweetest cane sugar, and purest spring water. People said he was crazy to care so much about his soda. Some even called him a renegade, but you can still taste that dedication today.'"

Daz lay down on the carpet in Rupert's office and said, "At which point every kid in America will be doing this," and he started to snore.

"Wrong," I said. "Because right then, we cut to some guy standing on a box of SparkleBean and holding up a can and he says, 'Who cares about dedication? Just give me the taste.' And then he takes a drink and the colors get really hot and the music changes to speed metal and it's obvious that the kid never drank anything this good in his entire life. And we tag it with a line like, 'SparkleBean. Taste the renegade'."

Daz sat up on the floor. "Everything is sepia except for the kid and the can, which we do in a color wash. And then when he drinks, the whole screen comes alive in incredibly vivid colors."

"Right," I said, "of course." I turned toward Rupert.

"It's pretty good," he said. "Needs a little work but it's pretty good."

"Good enough to get past the automatons running the company?"

"Hard to say."

"Say."

Rupert looked at Daz. "You on board with this?"

Daz stood up and glanced over at the computer again. "There was something in that guy's face. I *know* the old man would have loved it. The new guys? Who knows? But yeah, I'm on board."

"Then let's try to sell it. Do up the storyboards and I'll try to get an appointment to see them on Thursday."

I nodded toward Rupert and then gestured toward Daz. "Come on; let's go be brilliant."

"I thought we were already being brilliant."

"*More* brilliant."

"Thanks guys," Rupert said. "I figured you were going to mope for at least half a day about this one."

"Put it on our account."

He chuckled and waved at us. Daz and I headed toward our individual offices, which were within shouting distance of one another.

"That was a pretty nice little save you made over there," Daz said as we walked.

"It was your idea."

"Right. I'm so great at what I do that I don't even know when I'm doing it."

I smiled at him. I really never would have come up with the new pitch if Daz hadn't suggested looking at old man Hanson's picture. "Give me ten minutes to see what's happening in my office and then come by and we'll start pounding out the storyboard before we meet with the team."

"You got it."

I stopped by my assistant Gibb's desk and he handed me three pink message slips. I booted up my desktop machine and grabbed a cup of coffee, then browsed through the e-mail that had come in since I last checked in the cab. I had twenty-four new messages. Some of them (and one of the phone calls) were easily dismissed, but a few required some real attention. It was obvious this was going to be an insane day. I groaned inwardly, but the truth was that this was exactly the kind of professional life I'd hoped for.

I'd gotten my first taste of this in college, where I graduated Magna Cum Laude and received a couple of small-time awards. Then my first job at Tyler, Hope and Pitt allowed me a few moments to shine. However, The Creative Shop was the first place to give me the opportunity to show what I could become profession-ally, and I loved the place because of it. If I was going to work for someone else – and I definitely didn't want to do that much longer; we really needed to start our own agency – these were the guys I wanted to work for. Until Daz and I were ready to strike out into the world, these cartoon-laden walls were home for me.

"Hey, are we meeting today?" Carnie Brinks said, popping her head into my office.

"Eventually, yeah. The Bean Brains have us redoing their campaign."

"They didn't like 'Be the Bean?'"

"Can you believe it?"

"Assholes."

"Yeah, that's what Daz called them."

Carnie walked in and sat down, propping her legs under her. Though she worked for me as a copywriter, "employee" was not the first thing I thought when I looked at her. Carnie graduated from Swarthmore, got a Masters at Columbia, and was decidedly on the fast track at The Shop. She was also 5'4", olive-skinned, black-ringleted, aquamarine-eyed, and in sensational shape. I truly believed that I never let her charms – physical and otherwise – affect me professionally, but I had a crush on her within five minutes of our first meeting. At the same time, I was convinced that I'd never do anything about it. Office romances were rarely a good idea and employee/employer romances seemed *especially* ill-advised.

"I've got some ideas about the BlisterSnax Max video," she said. The BlisterSnax people had developed a sourer version of the candy and they were presenting it to their distributors next month. They asked us to put together a five-minute promotional video for the event. "I want to introduce the distributors to Max."

"Well, yeah, that's sort of the point, isn't it?"

"No, not Max the candy, Max the guy. You know, BlisterSnax *Max*?"

"Is that something like Yosemite Sam?"

"Almost nothing like that at all. I'm thinking he's this really nerdy kid who pops one of these things and his glasses fling off and his hair flies into something more stylish and his clothes for some reason I haven't figured out yet turn into something much cooler."

I nodded. "Could work." Carnie was definitely a kindred spirit, and I appreciated how enthusiastically she took to her job. "Listen; let's talk about this after the meeting. I'd love to do it now, but the day is already backing up on me."

"Got it." She stood up. "Beam was great last night, weren't they?"

"They definitely were."

"I think they sent Michelle into some kind of dream state. She spoke in these loopy sentences the entire cab ride home."

I remembered Daz talking about the "thing" that had passed between him and Michelle, but I doubted it was their imaginary encounter that had made her loopy. "It was a really good show. We'll have to catch them again the next time they come to town."

"Definitely." She smiled and tilted her head. She really was stunning. "So I'll hang back after the meeting, okay?"

"Yeah."

"And when, exactly, *is* the meeting?"

"Maybe an hour or so from now. Stay tuned for more."

She left and I was still staring at the spot where she last stood when Daz walked in. He looked down the hall at Carnie, then back to me. "Why don't you just deal with it already?"

"Deal with what?"

"Your burgeoning lust."

"It would be unhealthy."

"Ignoring the urge is unhealthy."

"Yeah, like you should talk."

"Do as I say, Flaccid, not as I do."

I looked off in the direction in which Carnie had gone, though there was a wall preventing my view. "Nah, not a chance."

"There's always a chance."

Of course there was a chance. That wasn't the point, though.

I looked at Daz. "Let's get to work."

The chapter about
fools and foolishness

At The Creative Shop, April Fool's Day is right up there
with Christmas. Everyone gets into the act. The recep-
tionist routes calls to the wrong people (not the important calls, of course. In preparation for the event, Ron
Isaacs sends out a memo to the entire staff the day before
describing "business that cannot be screwed with");
someone always quits (sometimes several people if the
efforts aren't properly coordinated); someone deletes all
the playlists and replaces them with Lawrence Welk and
Liberace (this year we also got Johnny Mathis, which to
some of us was okay); and at least one wall in the lobby is
painted over, the images of Wolverine or the Tasmanian
Devil replaced by a photograph of Richard Nixon. Even
the accounts have gotten involved. Two years ago, Daz
and I spent an entire morning scrambling to come up
with a new pitch for the irate CEO of a hugely important
client before getting a call from his secretary saying he
was only kidding.

The feature event every year, though, is the April
Fool's Day party Daz throws in the designers' bullpen
outside his office. It has on occasion involved formal
business attire (hence providing the only suit in Daz's
closet), plastic food (it's amazing how much some of

that stuff looks like the real thing), kegs of alcohol-free beer (which created an amusing variety of alcohol-free buzzes), and fire drills. There are always donuts, though Daz has steadfastly refused to explain why. And a cardboard cutout of some random guy is always propped up on one of the counters to preside over the proceedings with the man's dour expression. Each party has a theme, though Daz won't tell us what it is ahead of time and it is never easily discernible. I usually need to ask him about it at the end of the day, though on occasion someone has guessed. Even I got it right once, which made me inordinately proud. Though Steve Rupert volunteered to have the company pay for the party after the first one was such a huge success with the staff – this was, after all, exactly what management had in mind when creating the work environment – Daz has always insisted on footing the bill himself.

"Why should the Shop pay for it?" he said once when I asked him about it. "It was my idea."

"Your *ideas* make the Shop a lot of money. If they volunteer, you should take them up on it."

"Nah. Then it wouldn't be my party anymore. And they'd probably want to get involved in the details."

Daz was big on parties. In addition to this one, we probably threw a half-dozen of them a year at various levels of excess. The biggest of all was our birthday party, which could extend in one way or another for the entire six days separating our two birthdays. But Daz was capable of dropping a party on us at a moment's notice, suddenly inviting twenty or thirty people to his place (or, if it were essential that the party involve video games, *my* place), buying a case of tequila and "letting things happen." And he prided himself on his ability to "conceptualize" parties. Even the most casual ones had motifs. He's never confirmed this for me, but I'm guessing he had matching paper plates, cups, tablecloths, and goody bags at his parties when he was a kid.

This year, Daz ordered prodigious amounts of Chinese food, decorated the bullpen with air fresheners, provided a soundtrack made up exclusively of one-hit wonders, and gave us T-shirts to wear featuring various cast members from "Undeclared," the Judd Apatow TV show that Daz loved and whose one truncated season he still watches regularly on DVD.

I came out of my office about twenty minutes before the party started to survey the backdrop. Daz had just put the Dour Man on top of a bank of filing cabinets. The guy looked especially unpleasant to me this year, though I was fairly sure the cutout was the same one Daz always used. I had no idea why Daz was so fascinated with the Dour Man. With the food and drink table just below, he would peer over all of us throughout the day. I always thought it was a little creepy, but the one time I said this to Daz, he gave me an unusually clipped response. The kind that said I should just leave it a mystery.

"You've figured it out already," he said when he saw me.

I shook my head, smiling. It tickled me that he got so caught up in this stuff – which of course meant that I got all caught up in it as well. "I'm gonna need a little more time."

He walked over and handed me a T-shirt. "Got it now?"

I held the shirt in my hands and examined it, then glanced around the room again. "Not a clue."

He laughed and walked away. "And I was being *ridiculously* obvious this year."

This humbled me. I wondered if Daz somehow thought less of me because I was so ineffective at decoding his themes. I put the shirt on and went back to my office, determined to come out a half hour later with the answer. In spite of my best efforts, though, I failed.

Not long after, the party was in full swing. This was the kind of event that people showed up early for. Of course, anything that got you out of work was a draw. But with Daz's parties, "fashionably late" often meant showing up on time. Even for The Shop, this was an opportunity to cut loose. Everyone got just a little bit louder, a little bit crazier, a little bit less inhibited.

About an hour into the festivities, Daz danced with Carl from the mailroom to "Tubthumping" by Chumbawumba, and Michelle sidled over to me. She carried two beers (alcoholic this year, as far as I could tell) and handed one to me. Michelle was the most beautiful light-haired woman I ever met in person. Where Carnie's beauty drew you into its depths, Michelle's emanated. She truly did brighten a room when she entered it. Since Michelle was the main media buyer on my team, we worked closely on a daily basis. That she and Carnie were both in my orbit was one of the true fringe benefits of working at The Creative Shop.

"Did you get any of the XO chicken?" she said. "It was great."

"No, I haven't made it as far as the food yet."

She nodded in the direction of the Dour Man. "Want me to get you some?"

This question somehow made me a little uncomfortable. "No, thanks, really. I'll get there eventually." I glanced out at the dance floor. "Hey, if Daz plays 'Sexy and I Know It,' you and I are going out there."

She smiled. "You're on." Her body swayed slightly to the rhythm of the music. "Figured out the theme yet?"

"No, not yet," I said, genuinely chagrined. "I'm working on it. I'm determined to get it this year without begging the answer out of Daz."

Michelle laughed to herself and said, "Maybe there *isn't* one this year. It would be just like Daz to have us all racking our brains and then say, 'April Fool's.'"

"I hadn't thought of that," I said, surprised. "Now I'm kinda wondering why *Daz* hadn't thought of that before."

"Maybe he has. Maybe he's fooled us all into thinking there were themes to his other parties when there really weren't."

I glanced over at Daz, who was getting "knocked down / but I get up again" in ridiculous ways with Carl. "I don't think so. Daz is a clever guy but he's not that clever. And he'd never be able to keep it from me. I'd know."

"Yeah, I guess you would." Michelle's movements intensified. I wondered if she wanted me to ask her to dance. We'd done so several times at clubs, and I always liked dancing with her. She was nearly as graceful as she was gorgeous. I was about to say something when she leaned toward me and said, "Listen, I was wondering if you and I could maybe go out for a drink sometime. There's some stuff I want to talk to you about."

"Yeah, sure," I said, a little thrown off by the request.

She laughed. "You just got a really funny expression on your face. It's nothing major; just some things I don't want to talk about in the office."

I tried to adjust my posture to seem more casual. "I get it. This isn't always the best environment for a conversation." I immediately chastised myself for saying something so officious. I thought about suggesting we retreat to a quieter corner, but that would be difficult to find today. Throw a client into this room and everyone here would revert instantly into top-flight professionals. With no clients around, though, it was part bacchanal and part playground.

Just then, Gibb, who insisted on staying at his desk even though the party was practically swirling around him, came up to me. "Rich, you have a call. The guy seemed pretty insistent."

Obviously someone who didn't know about this Shop ritual. "Okay, thanks, I'll be right there."

I looked at Michelle, who seemed to be watching the exploits of her colleagues with a bit of remove. She was definitely thinking about something. I touched her on the arm. "You okay?"

She turned and smiled at me. I didn't take my hand from her arm right away. "Yeah, I'm fine."

"You looked like you were somewhere else."

"Nope, right here. I was just thinking about whether I should go out on the dance floor."

She really didn't look like she was in the mood for dancing anymore. "We can have that drink anytime you want."

She nodded. "Thanks. We'll set something up later. Go take your phone call."

I went back to the office and picked up the phone. It was only then that I realized Gibb hadn't told me who was on the line.

"Hello?" I said tentatively.

"Rich, this is Noel Keane from Kander and Craft." Kander and Craft was the fifth largest ad agency in the country. "Do you have a few minutes?"

I snapped instantly out of party mode. "Sure."

"How are things going for you over there?" Keane had an Australian accent, though it sounded like one processed by numerous years in New York.

"Great," I said, settling into my chair. "Never better, really."

"That's good to hear, even if it might make this call pointless. I was hoping we could get together for lunch sometime soon."

I excused myself for a second to close the door, which also allowed me another moment or so to get my bearings. "I'm sorry, what were you saying?"

"I'd like to get together with you if possible. Something has come up in our downtown office that might be of interest to you."

I was a little stunned that Kander and Craft was calling for me. I hadn't expected to show up on their radar screen for another couple of years. That's when it dawned on me that this could be a joke. After all, the Australian accent did seem a little put on.

"Listen, why don't you call me on April *second* and we'll see if it's still interesting then."

"Excuse me?" The way Keane said that left little reason for me to believe that he was kidding. I felt like a moron.

"You were serious about that, weren't you?"

"Is this a bad time to call?" he said, with just enough of an inflection to make it clear that people *never* considered it to be a bad time to get a call from him.

"No, no, I'm sorry. Lunch would be great. I'd love to hear what's going on with your firm. Just tell me when you want to do it."

"I happen to be free tomorrow if that works for you," he said quickly.

Tomorrow? I looked down at my calendar. I had a client lunch that I could definitely reschedule. "Yeah, I can make that work."

"Good. Is DB at one o'clock okay with you?"

DB Bistro Moderne. The man knew a little something about recruiting. "That sounds good to me. Is there anything you want me to bring along?"

"Just bring yourself," Keane said with a little chuckle I couldn't quite interpret. "That's all that matters."

"I'll do that. Thanks for calling."

"I look forward to meeting you, Rich. I'm sure we'll have a nice lunch."

After we hung up, I sat at my desk behind my closed office door for a short while before returning to the party. I felt kinetic and riveted to my chair at the same time. I'd never been approached like this before, though we certainly had some people come after us when we put ourselves on the market before joining The Shop. I had to admit that I liked the way it felt. This must have been what it was like for Michelle to enter a bar. Even if nothing came of this – and it was hard to believe that anything would – it was kinda sexy.

I decided to check out Noel Keane on the web. I was shocked to discover that he was the Executive Vice President, Global Operations at Kander and Craft. He was the guy who made the firm run – the entire firm, all twelve offices worldwide. And he was coming after me. He must have a kid who loved BlisterSnax.

If you were serious about a career in advertising, you had to have at least a little bit of interest in Kander and Craft. They weren't the largest firm in the field, but they were perhaps the most visible. Their ads had a discernible crispness to them, and they always scored big at awards time. The odds were good that if you remembered an ad you saw on TV last night, it was done by K&C. They were the gold standard. And they wanted to talk to me about something happening in their downtown office.

My head spinning with this new piece of information, I eventually opened my door and headed out. Daz was standing only fifteen feet or so away, and when I came out of my office, he walked over to me.

"Everything all right?"

I smiled and looked over at the Dour Man. "Yeah, I'm fine, why?"

"The closed door thing and the *Invasion of the Body Snatchers* thing happening in your eyes right now."

I shook my head briskly. "Nothing. Stupid client tricks." I made the decision in that moment not to mention the call to Daz, though keeping a secret from him felt very strange. I guess I didn't want him to think that I even considered breaking up the act – especially since I had no intention of doing so. It was just so much easier to avoid the whole topic rather than worry him about something he had no need to worry about.

"I thought you had all of our clients trained to provide a hassle-free environment during parties."

I shrugged. "Me too. Guess I need to crack the whip a little harder, huh?" I realized I left the beer Michelle gave me in my office and thought about going back to retrieve it.

"You missed the Macarena," Daz said.

"There's something that'll keep me up nights."

"You missed *Michelle* dancing the Macarena. That's something you should regret for the rest of your life."

I nodded sadly and then looked around. "Good party this year. Everyone seems to be enjoying themselves.

Although given the day, they could just be *pretending* to be enjoying themselves."

"Nah, you can tell the difference. People don't spontaneously start a kick line when they're faking it."

"Yeah, good point."

Just then, Chess came over and handed me a bottle. "You look like you need a drink," he said.

Was that because I didn't have one or because I still looked dazed from my conversation with Keane? "Thanks," I said, clinking bottles with him and taking a long drink.

I turned to Daz. "All right, I give up. What's the theme?"

"You really can't figure it out?"

"Tried and fell flat on my face. I really, really tried. You beat me again."

He patted me on the shoulder to let me know he wouldn't hold this against me. "Think about it. Chinese food. One-hit wonders." He pointed to his T-shirt. "This great show."

"I don't know, stuff that you like way more than most people do?"

"*Things that don't last!*" he said definitively.

"Chinese food doesn't last? It's been around as long as the Chinese have."

"But an hour later you feel hungry again."

I shook my head in mock disapproval of the mildly racist comment that I knew held no trace of racism coming from Daz. "I should've seen that coming."

He smiled, obviously proud of himself, and then put a hand on my shoulder. "Come on; let's get back into the fray. If you're really lucky, I'll put on '99 Luftballoons.'"

Daz bopped off into the crowd and I followed behind him. As I did, I looked at the faces of my colleagues, several of whom I'd known for six years and many of whom I genuinely liked. How could any place be better to work than this? The Creative Shop had gotten under my skin, become part of me, provided me with a safe harbor. There was no way I would leave this place until Daz and I were totally ready to strike out on our own.

April Fool's.

The chapter about expensive things and things that shouldn't cost so much

DB is a study in contradictions. It's elegant and casual. Its menu sports the familiar in unfamiliar ways. And these menu items – many of which appear in different forms on other menus all over the City – cost much more here than they do in most other places. In fact, price seems to be part of the atmosphere, as though the numbers on the menu are an essential bit of decoration. The times I'd eaten there before, I loved it. Eating variations on chicken salad and steak frites and then signing a credit card bill for more than $150 (to be reimbursed by The Shop, of course) made me feel privileged. Yeah, I know it's stupid.

The place was one of several run by the legendary chef Daniel Boulud and I'd been to each of the New York ones. It was hard to say you had your finger on the pulse of the City dining scene without doing so. And I really loved being plugged in like this. One of the huge upsides to a job like mine was that you often needed to take clients to lunch. And it was *never* for a slice of pizza. I made sure to stay on top of the latest, the hottest, and the best, a task I took to with tremendous enthusiasm. I loved eating in great restaurants of every stripe and variety. This was one of the few things my parents instilled in me that I took with me to my adult life. We went out to eat at least twice a week when I was growing up, and I found the exercise even more fulfilling when expanded to cover most days – and especially satisfying since my mother and father were no longer part of the package. Eating out this often was a bit of a challenge to my waistline, but I gladly maintained a strict workout regimen to keep it going. To me, an hour on a cross-trainer and another half-hour on weight machines three or four times a week was a perfectly fair tradeoff.

This was one of the few things that Daz and I absolutely did not connect on. I could drag him to a steakhouse or for ethnic food, but if the place had white tablecloths, used an immersion circulator, or had any relationship at all with microgreens, he recoiled. He literally could have popcorn or Doritos or his old standby Cap'n Crunch for dinner. I had to have a real meal, even if it was prepared at a cleverly disguised dive. This never turned into too much of a hassle, and I knew that if I compromised with him one night, I could often make it up on a date the next night – and usually make it up with a client the next afternoon.

I got to the restaurant five minutes early, but Keane was still there before me. His photograph on the Kander and Craft website didn't do him justice. Where he appeared graying and doughy on the computer screen, he seemed fit and vigorous in real life. I put his age at somewhere in his early fifties, though I think he might have been a little older and simply trying to stay young. As I approached the table, he rose to shake my hand.

"Sorry to keep you waiting," I said.

"Not a problem. I was on the phone until just a moment ago. Sometimes it's just easier to make calls when I'm out of the office." He appraised me for a moment. "I'm glad to make your acquaintance," he said after a pause.

A waiter came over and I ordered a bottle of sparkling water. Keane was drinking a glass of red wine. I had never been able to drink during the day, feeling like it took too much of my edge away. I often heard stories about the three-martini lunches of earlier days and wondered how anyone got any business done in the afternoon. Maybe that wasn't the point.

"I've seen some of your work, Rich," Keane said as he took a sip of his drink. "A lot of it is very impressive."

"Thanks." I knew he was here to recruit me and that part of the process was flattery, but I still felt warmed by a compliment like this.

"The latest BlisterSnax campaign is truly inspired. And those fifteen-second spots you did for Smack Racquets were hilarious."

I smiled, thinking back on them. "That was the result of a particularly intense creative session." Daz and I came up with the idea at three in the morning in my apartment after hours of video game tennis "to get in the mood."

"Well, it bore fruit. And I'm sure I'm not the first to tell you so."

I guess the difference between hollow praise and the real thing is how the person doing the praising backs it up. Whether Keane had good taste or not was still to be decided, but he left me with little doubt that he meant what he said. I started to find the prospects for this conversation just a little more interesting.

My water came and I took a drink. We took a quick look at the menus, though I already knew I was having the DB burger. I'm not sure that anyone would have been able to convince me that a hamburger was worth more than thirty dollars, even if someone else was paying, but I ordered one on a lark once and was absolutely knocked over. The burger – ground sirloin stuffed with braised short ribs, foie gras and black truffles – was a singular experience. And the french fries were pretty great as well.

We ordered (Keane chose the skate) and then Keane took another sip of his wine and leaned forward in his seat. "The reason I asked to meet with you is because the Creative Director of our downtown office is moving to our London operation. I'd like to talk to you about the possibility of taking his spot."

Though hopefully none of this showed on my face, I was floored. I'd expected him to pitch me on a copywriting position, trying to sell me on taking a backward step to move up to a big agency. At most, I thought he'd offer me a lateral move (which would of course constitute a significant increase in salary). Creative Director of the downtown office was not even on my dreamscape.

K&C had two offices in New York. The midtown one was for their mainstream corporate clients and had been around for decades. Then, during the original Internet boom in the late nineties, they opened the downtown office to accommodate the looser, more frenetic style of this new business and to create an environment more conducive to the offbeat flavor of the advertising these clients desired. Since the bust and then the mainstreaming of Internet commerce, there were persistent rumors of K&C boarding up the second office and focusing exclusively on their more traditional base. They cycled staff for most of the past three years, and hanging on at K&C Downtown was like riding a bucking bronco at a rodeo. It wasn't a question of whether you'd be thrown off, only how long you could hold on before it happened and whether you got injured from the fall. There was more than a little bit of risk involved in getting involved with that operation – except that the K&C name looked great on a resume. When Keane mentioned the downtown office yesterday, none of this mattered particularly much to me since I assumed he was talking about a smaller job and I also assumed that this was only going to be a bit of meaningless flirtation anyway. The notion of a Creative Director's gig changed the parameters.

"I hadn't heard about the CD leaving," I said.

"We haven't announced it yet. We're shaking things up a little."

I nodded and didn't say anything.

"So is this something you're interested in talking about?" Keane said.

I took another drink of my water. "You know, I love it at The Creative Shop. The people there are great and I work on really good projects. It would take a lot to get me to leave." I smiled. "But we can certainly talk."

We did that for the next hour. While taking several opportunities to underscore the difference in scale between my current workplace and K&C, Keane outlined the nature of the downtown operation. He talked about the clients they had on board and spoke in broad terms about the clients they courted (some of whom I could identify because we'd courted them at The Shop as well). He talked about the resources the office had at its disposal and how they strove to give the place the feel of a small agency while at the same time backing it with the full power of their huge organization. He told me that they expected their creative directors to be precisely that – people who drove and directed creativity – and that they did their best to keep the administrative responsibilities of these people to a minimum. He was an excellent pitchman and it was difficult not to believe that K&C Downtown was a dream spot for a guy like me. Of course, I knew a thing or two about hype.

"This all sounds great," I said, "and the fact that you're even talking to me is very flattering. But I have a couple of nagging issues with this."

"Put them on the table."

"The first is the awful stuff I keep hearing about the downtown office. As I'm sure you know, the word on the street is that you guys are ten minutes away from shutting the whole thing down."

Keane chuckled with the easy assurance of someone who wasn't being challenged. "That's a bit of an exaggeration. Look, I'm not going to pretend that the office has been unaffected by the downturn in the market and the overall change in the advertising landscape. To be completely honest, our current CD is being moved to London because he's too valuable to let go. We have a much more stable client base there, and he's more suited to that kind of environment. But we aren't giving up on downtown. Not even close. In fact, we want to turn up the heat. The fact is, we need to get a little younger and a little fresher throughout the entire K&C organization, and we continue to be convinced that the downtown office can act as a pipeline feeding all twelve offices with this kind of talent."

I gestured to acknowledge his point and then said, "But things aren't exactly stable there."

He smiled at me and looked down at his hands, extending his fingers outward. "If you're looking for stable, you might want to seek a different profession." He glanced up and snared me with his eyes. "But let's look at the worst case scenario. You bomb out with us or we just decide to pull the plug on the whole office. In either case, you walk away with a hefty, pre-negotiated severance package. And it's not exactly a blight on your record to fail at K&C Downtown. Plenty of successful people have. Some might even consider it a rite of passage."

I nodded. "I can understand that."

Keane smiled. It was clear that he liked winning people over. "You said there were a couple of nagging issues. What's the other?"

For the first time, I took a more aggressive position in my chair. "The other thing is that I've kind of been part of a package deal my entire career. Eric Dazman is an amazing art director and we do our best work together. The prospect of making this move would be a whole lot more interesting if he came with me."

Keane stiffened at the mention of Daz. "Have you met Carleen Laster?" he said.

I shook my head to indicate that I hadn't.

"Carleen is the Executive Art Director of the downtown office. She's as good as they get. I'm afraid we don't have a place for your partner at this point. And if it means holding on to Carleen, I hope we never do."

He certainly didn't equivocate. I wasn't entirely sure what to say. Whether he intended it or not, Keane made me feel like I'd mentioned the unmentionable. To argue for K&C to bring Daz along with me assumed many things that I couldn't assume – including that I had any bargaining power. I looked down at the last french fry on my plate, picked it up and ate it.

"Do you have any other questions?" Keane said. His tone was a little brisk, his message clearly, *Don't bring up any subject even remotely close to the one you just brought up.*

"Not really, no."

The waiter took our plates and Keane asked me if I wanted coffee. As much as I probably should have just let the meeting end, I wound up ordering a double espresso.

I felt a little foolish, like I'd been offered a free ticket to a sold-out concert and my first response was to say, "Can I have one for my friend, too?" I was sure that speaking about Daz and me as a "package deal" tabbed me as a minor leaguer. I was the kind of guy who just didn't understand how big-time ad agencies worked, didn't understand the rare opportunity I was being offered, and therefore couldn't possibly have the constitution to take a major position at a huge shop. I was glad I mentioned Daz – I would have felt like a traitor if I hadn't even tried – but I still felt a bit like Keane had told me to go sit in the corner.

Keane was polite and asked me a number of questions about my personal interests, which I tried to answer as comprehensively as I could to give him a sense that I had at least a modicum of substance. I talked to him about restaurants and about books that I read and about cultural events I saw mention of in the *Times*. I went into spin mode, something I did when I felt I needed to put on a show for a client.

When we parted a short time later, though, I was relatively certain that he'd crossed me off his list. He certainly didn't say anything to suggest this, and he even told me that he enjoyed meeting me, but I couldn't erase from my mind the look of disapproval on his face when I mentioned Daz.

It was a funny thing. I went into the lunch assuming nothing would come of it and certain that nothing Keane suggested would divert Daz and me from our long-term plans. Knowing that the position was in the downtown office, I was skeptical right from the start, not understanding how it possibly made sense to take on an almost-certainly futile challenge like that, regardless of his assurances. Still, when I felt like I blew it, that I showed I wasn't ready for prime time, I found it upsetting that I wouldn't get this thing I didn't want in the first place.

I had been rejected by a woman I didn't really want to date. I had lost a race I wasn't all that interested in running. I had been turned away at a bar that I really didn't want to get into. It left me feeling a little humiliated.

At least the burger was good.

The chapter about
intimations of brilliance

The day after my lunch with Noel Keane, Daz and I held our first late-nighter on the Korean car campaign. We still had two weeks before the presentation to the account, so this wasn't a high-pressure session. Still, we liked to give ourselves a couple of opportunities to be truly awful before the stakes rose. Pizza with hot cherry peppers was often involved in our brainstorming, as we were aware of the mind-clearing qualities of spicy food and we both had a passion for Anthony's Oven, a pizzeria about four blocks from the office. Beer was also often involved, but only enough to wash down the peppers without dulling their awareness-heightening benefits.

Our meeting with the rest of the team, along with a conversation with Steve Rupert about basic direction, gave us a foundation to work from. Now it was time to just go where the ideas took us. This was unquestionably the way Daz and I worked best. We liked to get input from others, even creative suggestions from time to time, process all of it for a while, and then start churning.

"Explain this to me again," Daz said as he volleyed a soccer ball from foot to knee and back again. The ball skittered off a couple of times, which caused him to

mutter obscenities at himself before picking it up and trying again. "It's a luxury car for people in their twenties?"

"Luxury car is the wrong term," I said, somewhat
fixated on the motion of the ball and the fact that Daz
wasn't doing this as well as he usually did it. On his best
days, this kind of noodling was a form of performance
art. "It's a sedan. They've thrown in leather, wood trim,
a great sound system, and Bluetooth to make it seem
fancier than it really is. They're trying to distinguish
themselves. The price point is totally in the range of
other mid-size cars."

"I still don't get it. If I wanted a nice car, I'd get a
Jaguar or a BMW."

"That's because you can *afford* a Jaguar or a BMW.
Now imagine that you're one of the vast majority of
people who weren't lucky enough to hook up with a
genius sidekick and get a fistful of huge bonus checks.
Imagine that you're someone who's just on the way to
making it and want to appear like you're already there."

"Don't I get one of those mid-priced sports cars
instead?" He started taking shots against one of his office
walls. The primary reason we usually had these sessions
in his office was because Daz's drawing board and computer were there. A critical secondary reason was that I
didn't want him destroying my furniture or knocking
over any of my stuff.

"Yes, *you* would get one of those mid-priced sports
cars. But there are other people in the world who would
rather have a car that made them look older rather
than younger."

"There are?" he said generating a series of rapid-fire
kicks with both of his feet. Again the ball skittered off. He
clearly hadn't brought his A-game to his fidgeting tonight.

"Yes, there are."

"Do we know any of these people? I thought one of the keys to our success was that we only handled clients whose products we could imagine using."

"I *can* imagine using this product."

He shot the ball off the wall one more time and caught it with his hands before turning to look at me. "Really?"

"Yeah, really. I mean, sort of really, anyway. You know, if I hadn't been an overnight sensation and all."

There was never a point in my life when I'd had any meaningful concerns about money. My mother and father both had very successful careers and if they provided nothing else – and there were plenty of times when I believed exactly that – they made sure my sister and I were well supplied with creature comforts. I got my first credit card (on my parents' account, of course) when I was sixteen. After graduating, though, I refused to have them support me in any way – it was time for me to make it on my own and *definitely* time for me to stop taking handouts – and though I was hardly making big dollars, I never worried that I couldn't pay the rent or that I would eat nothing but beans for months. Now, in spite of the big mortgage on the co-op and the not-insignificant cost of my lifestyle, there was always plenty of cash around.

If I hadn't jumped the shark with Keane, there might have been a whole lot more. I still hadn't mentioned anything about the lunch to Daz. First it was because I didn't want him to think there was anything to be concerned about. Now it was because I didn't want him to know how much I screwed up – though since I screwed up with him in mind, he probably wouldn't have teased me mercilessly about it for more than a couple of days.

"Are you telling me that when you grow up you want to drive a Lincoln Town Car and wear double-knit polo shirts?"

My father drives a Lincoln. "No, jeez, why'd you say that?"

"Because that sounded like what *you* said."

"I didn't say anything like that."

"Sure sounded like it."

"Do you think we could focus back on the account?"

"If you say so." Daz started bouncing the ball off the wall with his head, though he stopped thirty seconds later and sat down for the first time since we'd entered the office. "All right, so let's assume there are a bunch of people just like young Mr. Rich Flaccid who want this car. How do we turn them on to it?"

"I think that's what this meeting is about."

"Yes, it is." He sprung up, though he didn't go back to heading the ball. "What does the car look like again?"

I held up a photograph.

"It looks like an Accord," Daz said.

I turned the picture around to look at it. "Yeah, it does look like an Accord. With more chrome, though. And remember the leather and the wood trim and the sound system."

"This isn't a luxury car."

"Daz, really try to concentrate for five seconds."

He headed the ball twice and sent it into his waste-basket. I refused to give him any indication that this impressed me. If I let Daz know every time he did something that impressed me, his ego would occupy the entire west side of Manhattan. He sat down across from me and fixed me with his most attentive gaze.

"When is the pizza coming?"

"When we order it."

"You didn't order it yet?"

"If I order it now, will you promise me one constructive thought in the next half hour?"

"Order it and I'll see what I can do."

We managed to talk about the car for several of the twenty minutes it took for the pizza to show up. Nothing really came of this discussion, but with me and Daz, it was all about the process. Some of our best ideas, including the very first BlisterSnax campaign line, came directly after hours of flat-out inanity. In fact, Daz was doing handstands and babbling nonsense words when watching him inspired me to come up with the phrase, "Get blistered." We didn't quite subscribe to the notion that there were no bad ideas, but we did believe that every bad idea we put out there increased the chances of our having a good idea sometime soon after that. It was all about the law of averages.

"How about if we do something with light glinting off the chrome," I said while eating my third slice.

"Gee, there's an original concept."

"Well it would be if the *art director* came up with a new way to do the lighting."

"Yeah, of course, put it all on me. Once again, hot images compensating for tepid ideas."

"Do you have any open wounds I can rub this cherry pepper into?"

"Psychic injuries only, please. Remember, the softball season is starting. Speaking of which, do you think Chess is serious about his acting lessons conflicting with our games?"

Chester Hampton, known amongst friends as Chess, was the star center fielder on The Shop's softball team. Like many of the transients at the agency, though, his back office gig was really just a way to stay solvent until Broadway or Hollywood called. He even tried to convince me to cast him in one of our commercials, but I explained that he'd have to quit his job before I could do that. That always got him to go away.

"Sure sounded like it."

"But he really can't act. Do you remember how awful he was in that off-off-off Broadway thing last year?"

"I guess that's why he's taking the lessons. And it's not like chasing down fly balls for our team will further his ambitions."

"Yeah, but it'll further our chances of winning games. Who's gonna bat cleanup if he doesn't play for us this year?"

"Looks like that falls to the man with sauce on his chin."

Daz wiped his face with a napkin. "Can't. You need me to set the table. If I don't do that, the cleanup batter won't have anyone to clean up."

I held out my hands in a gesture of surrender. "Well, don't look at me. I'm there for my keen strategic mind and the occasional bloop single."

Daz guffawed. "I think you'd better look up the word 'occasional' in the dictionary. I think something has to happen more than once a century to be deemed occasional."

I smirked at him and then slapped the table. "Hey, how about using 'occasional' in the car campaign. Something like, 'Because your life isn't an occasional thing.'"

"What does that even mean?"

"What does 'Just Do It' mean?"

"It means *just do it*. People can figure that out." He shook his head derisively, muttering the word "occasional." He took a couple of bites of pizza while mulling something. This might have been anything from his next jibe, to our center field crisis, to whether we should order the pizza with prosciutto next time.

"How about going back to that chrome thing," he said finally. "Let's say I come up with some world-class, never-before-seen lighting effects and then we tag it, 'Only your future is brighter?'"

I put down the pizza crust I was munching on. "That might actually be good."

He shrugged. "I just toss 'em off."

"I mean, it *probably* sucks. But it might be good. Could you make it work in a print campaign?"

"Color or black-and-white?"

"Both."

"Color definitely. Black-and-white might be more of a problem. It'll take me at least three hours to solve it."

"Take four and make it perfect." I sat back in Daz's desk chair.

He retrieved his soccer ball from the wastebasket. "Hey, what do they call this car again?"

"They want us to come up with the name."

"Wow, really? We get to name a car? That's like a little moment of immortality. Even if the car is kinda dorky."

"They knew it would make you happy. So what do we call it?"

"How about 'Lumina?'"

"Already taken."

"'Shimmer.'"

"Too pedestrian."

"'*Brilliante.*'"

"I think I feel my pizza coming back up."

Daz threw the soccer ball at me. "Hey, I came up with the campaign; you come up with the name."

"Technically, I came up with the campaign. You just refined it."

"Whatever. Listen, I'm burnt. Let's crash."

"You're burnt? It's 8:30."

"I don't know, I'm just really tired. We did enough tonight already, right?"

"Yeah, we probably did." I closed up the pizza box and handed Daz the last piece. I always had three slices and he always had five.

"I don't want it," he said, holding his hands up. "You eat it."

"You're full of pizza?" I picked up the phone. "Think we can still get this on the eleven o'clock news?"

"I won't make a habit of it."

I put down the phone. "You too tired for a few rounds of *Search and Destroy*?"

Daz smiled. "When have I ever been too tired for that?"

————

I'll admit right up front that I was only in it for the explosions. *Search and Destroy* is an XBox game that is short on plot (essentially two teams of aliens try to vaporize each other), challenge (anyone with a modest level of eye-hand coordination can blast a serious number of aliens) and social value. However, the explosions (and there are many of them) are spectacular – especially on my sixty-inch television. The music is pretty great, too, a sort of combination of speed metal and thrash that makes me feel sixteen again, and it sounds especially good coming out of my Bang and Olufsen.

Daz and I were Zen masters of *Search and Destroy* combat, sometimes staying at the game long into the night with little more than bathroom breaks. We have played the game over dinner, while brainstorming, while listening to sporting events, and even once on a double date that unsurprisingly didn't turn out very well.

We were back at my place by 9:00 and had the game fired up no more than ten minutes later. Daz chose to be Admiral Krus of the Flurg Republic. I was Blitar, the rogue Vanzian who could be trusted by no one.

"I can't believe you chose Blitar," Daz said derisively. "His resources suck."

"And you think Krus is such a great choice? What's the fat old thing gonna do, fart all over me?"

Daz leaned forward and started flicking his game controller, though nothing had started yet. "We'll see who's standing in the end."

I set the game in motion. "Don't worry, Daz. Blitar will be very respectful as he pisses on Krus' blasted body."

Daz sneered at me and turned to the screen. Within moments, we were fully engaged. Blitar set up camp on the desolate sands of Wizhn'h't and he and his army engaged the enemy from behind the desert-forged Walls of Defiance, electronically enhanced fortresses that gave Blitar a full view of the opposing forces while shielding him completely. I definitely had the best of the early action, with dozens of Krus' troops cut in half by pulse-rifle fire. I took down two of Krus' lightships in booming Technicolor displays – which never failed to inspire me to whoops of joy.

Then Daz caught me off guard when Krus authorized a particle-flanking maneuver. Hundreds of his soldiers atomized and rematerialized behind my lines. It was a dangerous move and one that I could have countered by making materialization impossible if I'd anticipated it. It took me by surprise, though, and suddenly we were in one of the bloodiest firefights we'd ever exchanged.

I was pinned down and in danger of a humiliatingly fast defeat when the phone rang. I thumbed the pause button on my controller.

"I can't believe you're gonna get that," Daz said in loud protest. "I was just about to vaporize you."

"That's exactly what I wanted you to believe," I said with manufactured bravado. "You might want to spend the next few minutes thinking about what could go wrong with your little plan." I of course had absolutely no countermeasure in mind and he was going to tear me to pieces when we put the game back on. Still, if I could make him think I had something up my sleeve, it was possible he'd make a mistake.

I couldn't figure out where my phone was right away, finally finding it in the bedroom.

"Rich, I hope this isn't a bad time to call." It was Noel Keane, recognizable immediately by his singular accent.

"No, no, not at all. I was just hanging out with –" it dawned on me that saying Daz's name to him wasn't the best idea – "a friend."

"I'm glad to hear I'm not disturbing you. Listen, I was very pleased with our lunch yesterday."

"You were?"

I heard a little chuckle on the other end. "You say that like you're surprised. Weren't you pleased with it?"

"Yeah, of course," I said, hoping I didn't sound like I was fumbling. "You just never know what someone else is thinking."

"You're a smart guy, Rich, and you asked a lot of the right questions. I talked to Curt Prince about our conversation and he asked if I could set up some time for the two of you to meet." Curt Prince was to creative admen what Eric Clapton was to guitarists. He was brilliant, powerful, admired by his peers, and absolutely ubiquitous in the trades.

"Yeah, of course," I said while trying to calculate how much I would have paid for a meeting like this. "I'd love to have a chance to get together with him."

"Well, let's make that happen, then. Next Tuesday lunch okay?"

It seemed a little strange to me that these super-powerful ad guys had so much free lunch time (I was booked almost every day in April), but I chose not to quibble. "I'll make it okay," I said without even looking at my calendar.

"That's good. I'll have my assistant call you with the details that morning."

We exchanged a couple of pleasantries and I hung up with Keane a few moments later. I stayed seated on my bed for several minutes after that. I needed a little time to digest this. How could I have misread Keane's expression at the end of that lunch – the one that told me, "Have a nice life"? When he said that I asked a lot of good questions, did those questions include the ones about bringing Daz in as part of the deal? I needed to think this over. I also needed to catch my breath before going back out to the living room. Once again, I felt that I couldn't mention this to Daz. This time it was because I hadn't mentioned it to him before. This was getting more than a little complicated – and I was starting to feel more and more like I was "cheating" on Daz. Finally, I picked myself up off the bed.

"I hope you've considered all of your options," I said to Daz as I walked into the room. "Not that it matters, because you have no idea what I have up my sleeve."

When I looked at Daz for a response, I saw that his head was tilted back and he was fast asleep. It was 9:45.

This was an absolute first. I thought about letting him just spend the night on the couch, but he didn't seem to be in a very comfortable position and he was too big for me to move. I tried a bit of repositioning but that didn't help at all. Finally, I just jostled him awake. He seemed completely disoriented when he opened his eyes. He saw my face, looked confused, and then closed his eyes again and shook his head. I got up to get him a glass of water.

"How long have I been sleeping?"

"Not very long but you look wasted. You'd better go home and crash."

"What about the game?"

"We'll play again tomorrow. I was kicking your ass anyway."

He stood up but he looked shaky. I thought for a second he might sit back down again. "That's not the way I remember it."

"You were probably winning in your dreams."

He ran his fingers through his hair and then reached for his jacket. He still seemed very much out of it.

"Do you want me to walk you home?"

He smirked, a bit of life returning to his face. "Thanks, Honey, but I think I can make it."

"You sure you're good?"

"I'm fine. I'll see you tomorrow."

Daz left and I walked over to the couch and sat down. The impression his head had made was still on one of the cushions. I really hadn't been on the phone with Keane that long. Daz must have knocked off right after I left the living room.

I took the XBox off pause and immediately half of my army was pierced by streamflash. I quickly exited the game.

I switched the television to cable and put on ESPN. I absently watched a basketball game while I continued to think about how weird it was that Daz had fallen asleep like that. Maybe he had been up really late the night before. Maybe with a woman he hadn't told me about.

That wouldn't be like him. Unless he had a compelling reason. Daz didn't keep secrets from me.

Then again, I didn't keep secrets from him, either.

The chapter about taking off

The next morning, I got to Daz's apartment and he was still fast asleep. After using my key, I shook him awake, though it took some doing. This wasn't the first time I'd ever done this. It wasn't even the twentieth. Still, I never expected it when it happened. After all, he was usually at least conscious when I came to get him, even if he wasn't moving particularly quickly.

"Are you okay?" I said as he very slowly rose up on the bed.

"Just really tired."

"You look like crap."

He grunted. "Sorry. You look quite stunning yourself."

I always dressed more formally than Daz, since I usually had lunch dates and the places I liked to go weren't keen on flannel. Today, I was a little more traditionally dressed than usual because we had a meeting with the Hanson family. "We're supposed to talk with the SparkleBean people at ten today. That's an hour and a half from now. Do you think you'll be in the shower by then?"

He held a hand to his head. If I didn't know better, I'd say he was hungover. "Yeah, I'll get in the shower now." He drew his covers back and unfolded himself at a glacial pace. When he stood, he took a deep breath and for a while I thought he would stay rooted to that one spot. Eventually, he shuffled forward into the bathroom.

The contrast between the fidgety Daz in his office last night and this Daz was striking. He didn't get sick often (though considering the way he ate and the way he took care of himself – ridiculous for someone who considered himself an athlete – I'm surprised it didn't happen all the time), but when he did, he tended to go down hard. I sometimes wondered if it was a ploy for sympathy. He knew that I would bring him things or that Michelle or Carnie would stop by with soup or cough drops or something. It was just about impossible not to react that way when this ebullient puppy had trouble getting out of his crate. I knew he wasn't putting me on here, though. He couldn't fake the pallid color of his skin.

Eventually, I heard the shower running and I went out to eat my bagel. Fifteen minutes later, he hadn't come out to ask for fashion advice or to show me which toothbrush he was using. I walked into the bedroom to retrieve him and heard that the shower was still on. I knocked on the bathroom door and then, when he didn't respond, I opened it. Daz was leaning against the wall of the shower, letting the water spray his face.

"I think this might be a sick day," he said when he saw me.

He dried off and got into bed naked, pulling the covers around him. He really looked terrible, like he had the flu or something. The sickest I'd ever seen him was when he got food poisoning after an ill-advised 3:00 a.m. foray into an all-night taqueria when we lived in Hell's Kitchen. He retched for most of two days and lay balled up in the fetal position when he wasn't throwing up. He didn't seem quite that terrible this time, but he was groaning an awful lot.

"Sorry about the SparkleBean thing," he said after one of these.

"I'll just have to blow them away by myself. You realize, of course, that this means I'll take all the credit for our new idea."

"That's what I love about you, Flash."

I patted him on the shoulder. "I'm pretty sure I can handle this one on my own."

"Yeah, of course you can. And I'd probably only screw things up by calling one of the Hanson boys a dinosaur."

"Most clients hate that." I took a careful look at him as I prepared to leave. His eyes seemed a little unfocused. "Do you need anything?"

"For it to be tomorrow."

"I'll see if I can make it happen."

I went into Daz's kitchen and filled a thermal mug with milk. Then I took his box of Cap'n Crunch out of the cupboard and placed both of them on his nightstand. I had no idea if he was going to get hungry at all, but I wanted him to have something within easy reach just in case he did.

"Thanks," he said. "You're a good mommy."

"That's what all the women tell me. Call me later if you need anything."

"I think I just need to sleep."

I got the TV remote, put it on the pillow next to him and then headed off. Even with all of this, I wound up getting to the office earlier than I had in weeks.

———

Michelle and I had our drinks date that night. Since she first mentioned it at the April Fool's party, I'd been trying to figure out what she wanted to talk to me about. Was she unhappy with her job or with having me for a supervisor? Was she going to confess an undeniable passion for Daz? Was she going to confess an undeniable passion for *me*? If the latter, would I immediately eschew my "no dating staff" policy?

I had to admit that I found her interesting in any number of ways. Of course I imagined going out with her. I even imagined what the two of us would be like in bed. As was the case with Carnie or any of the other half-dozen great looking women at The Shop, I always kept my desires under control. I just didn't think it appropriate to pursue people I worked with. If *she* came on to *me*, though, that would change the rules, wouldn't it?

Of course there was the other matter of Daz showing an interest in her – an interest he had expressed to me for more than half a year now. We never talked about this kind of thing, never really had any reason to, but I had to believe that if he hadn't done anything about this interest after six months, I had no obligation to hold back if she approached me now. I'd seen Daz talk himself out of pursuing any number of women over the course of our friendship, and in spite of any "eye thing" they might have had recently, it seemed he was in the process of doing exactly that here. All of which meant that if Michelle asked me for a drink to tell me that she couldn't live without me, I might just have to let nature take its course.

My dating life had been inconsistent at best since I'd returned to the New York area. I wasn't actively looking for anyone to get serious with and no one seemed particularly interested in convincing me to think otherwise. The amount of time I spent working made it difficult for me to meet women outside of the office, and I chose not to go out with the ones I worked with. This meant that most of the connections I made were either via fix-ups (which rarely went well) or people I met at bars or clubs (which were comically worse). Since this wasn't a critical agenda item at the moment, I didn't find this situation particularly vexing, though I wouldn't have minded having sex more often.

I had several female friends, so I got plenty of whatever it was that one got from the platonic side of those relationships, and I certainly never had to worry about keeping my social calendar full. But in the rare moments when I allowed myself to project this scenario forward and thought about being in the same place when I was forty, I found it rather depressing.

Other than the time when I called Daz to see how he was doing (he'd moved into the living room, and when I spoke to him, he was eating salt and vinegar potato chips and watching a *Duck Tales* marathon on one of the Disney channels) and report to him on the meeting with the SparkleBean people (which had gone fabulously and where I apologized for Daz's absence and told them the new pitch was all his idea without saying anything about dinosaurs), I thought about my impending encounter with Michelle the entire afternoon.

We went to Feel, a bar over on 10th Avenue. It wasn't elegant and it certainly wasn't romantic, but it was the closest thing to quiet in the immediate vicinity. Regardless of what she wanted to talk about, I figured quiet was useful.

We talked about things related to work on the walk over, and I updated her on Daz's condition after the waiter took our order. When the drinks arrived, Michelle tipped her glass in my direction and then looked down at the table.

"I'm thinking about going back to Indiana," she said.

She needed to take me out of the office to talk about a vacation? "So go. How much time do you want?"

"I'm thinking about forever," she said glancing up and catching my eyes. "Do I have that much time coming to me?"

Frankly, I had forgotten that Michelle came from Indiana. She seemed like such a New Yorker. "Why would you want to do something like that?"

She tilted her head and stirred her drink. "Doesn't the emptiness ever get to you?"

"What emptiness?"

She pulled herself up in her chair and moved forward. "The emptiness of *everything*. Hey, maybe I'm assuming too much here, but I'm kinda guessing that your life isn't that different from mine – except for the disposable income, of course. And for me it just seems like nothing is happening. Working and drinking, working and drinking. Sometimes you throw in a decent restaurant between the working and the drinking. Sometimes you see a good band while you're drinking. In the summer you do your drinking on Fire Island instead."

"Maybe you should stop drinking."

"Yeah, that's the answer." She shook her head. "Then what'll I do with the time when I'm not working?"

"And you think the solution to this is going back to Indiana? What's in Indiana?"

"The *world* is in Indiana. It could be Minnesota or Delaware or Oregon. I just happen to come from Indiana. My family is there. My unbelievably wonderful three-year-old niece who I never get to see is there."

I'd never heard her mention her family before. I just assumed they were part of her past. "You know, a lot of people think that New York is the world and everywhere else is just everywhere else."

Her eyes flared. "Well, they're wrong."

This really surprised me. Michelle was so sophisticated, so impossible to ruffle, that she was made for Manhattan. It never really registered on me before that moment that just because you were strong enough to handle the place didn't mean that you wanted to use your strength that way. "Are you telling me you're quitting?"

"I'm telling you that I want you to try to convince me to stay."

What exactly did that mean? Was she telling me to convince her to stay by expressing my attraction to her? If that was an opening, it wasn't the kind of opening I could walk through. "You have a great future in advertising," I said.

She smirked. "They have ad agencies in Indiana too."

"Not really."

There was disapproval in her expression. "Yeah, really. They're real enough for me, anyway."

"I think you might have a big time career here if you stick with it."

She shrugged. "Rich, that's not the beginning and end of things for me."

That was another surprise. I tried a different tack. "Your New York friends would miss you a lot."

"You'll get over it."

"Only after being miserable for a very long time."

She offered me a complicated smile. "What are we doing with our lives?"

"I think one of us is thinking about it too much."

She shook her head again. "Or not enough." She looked at me meaningfully, though I didn't know what the meaning was. "Maybe I just need to get back home for a little vacation. Or maybe you can lend me your parents for a while."

"Take 'em. They're yours," I said, holding my hands out to her in a gesture of offering.

She put a hand on my shoulder. "That's very generous of you."

"You haven't met them yet."

She looked off toward the front of the bar for a few moments. "I miss Tawny," she said.

"Your niece?"

"The family dog. She's twelve now. I don't know how much longer she has."

"I'm really glad your niece isn't named Tawny."

She smiled. A simple one this time. "We don't do things like that in my family."

I finally put the name together. "Wait a second. Your dog is named 'Tawny Dancer?'"

"I probably shouldn't have mentioned that, huh?"

"Who had the Elton John fixation?"

"I'll take that secret to the grave with me."

"*You* named the dog?"

She laughed out loud. "It seemed clever at the time."

"And this dog loves you in spite of what you did to it?"

"It's not like people go around referring to their dogs by their full names. Besides, the dog doesn't get the pun."

"I can just imagine your vet chuckling behind his hands every time he looks at your pet's paperwork."

She finished her drink and then tossed a droplet of what remained in the glass at me. I flinched back, which got a giggle out of her. She signaled to the waiter for another.

"So, the big birthday bash is in a couple of weeks, huh?"

"Construction is already underway. I don't think I can get the roller coaster past my co-op board, but I should be able to sneak in the monkeys without anyone noticing."

"Good music?"

"Two playlists already developed, four more in the planning stages. At this point, it's a question of how much reggae is too much and whether people can understand the subtle irony of juxtaposing Aretha Franklin with Jesse J."

"If you're going to go for irony, you'd better make it early in the party. Especially if Daz is planning to serve his Elixir of Life again."

"Yeah, I'll keep that in mind." Michelle's drink came and I ordered another, which got me a frown from the waiter, who probably wondered why I hadn't ordered it when Michelle ordered hers.

"Hey, you weren't really thinking about going back to Indiana, were you?" I really didn't want her to go, especially if she intended to stay there forever.

She shrugged. "Just a shameless ploy for attention."

"Consider it a success. I mean not to get maudlin here –"

"– God forbid."

"– but I really would miss you. I mean our little group might be bowing at the altar of emptiness, but it would be a lot emptier if you weren't around."

She took my hand and squeezed it. "That's incredibly sweet."

"I mean it."

"Thanks." She took another drink. "I really do think a lot about going. I don't know, I think I need to get back there at least for a visit at some point in the near future."

"Just don't be rash, okay? Who knows what's waiting around the corner. Maybe it's something really meaningful."

"Like a big sale at Sephora?"

"Exactly what I was thinking."

———

Michelle and I had a quick dinner together and then she went off to some club in Hoboken. She asked me to come along, but I had already been to New Jersey once this quarter and therefore going again would exceed my quota.

On the way home, I stopped off to see how Daz was doing. He answered the door in boxer shorts and there was a bag and a foil tray from Burgerville on his coffee table. Burgerville claimed to have the best burgers in town, but in my mind, they weren't even the best on the block. I think Daz loved them because they had the highest fat content of any burger in the neighborhood.

"Hey, I'm glad you showed up," Daz said when he opened the door. "I'm having a hell of a time doing this."

"Doing what?"

"I'm trying to play myself at air hockey and it just isn't working." To illustrate, Daz shot the puck from one side of the table and then reached across and tried to stop it.

"You thought this was going to work?"

He looked at me sheepishly. "I'm pretty bored."

"I assume this means you're feeling better?"

"Yeah, a lot," he said brightly. "I don't know what that was this morning. Come on, let's play a game."

I picked up the other pusher and reset the scoreboard, which had shown that Daz-right was beating Daz-left 12-9 when I arrived. I wondered if Daz felt incredibly competitive or especially triumphant with that result.

Probably a little of both. I had to chuckle imagining what he looked like doing this. It was certainly a more appealing image than the one I had of him leaning against the side of the shower this morning.

"So I think we need to have a party next weekend," he said as play started.

"We're having a *huge* party the weekend after that. Even for you that's a little over the top, isn't it?"

"I don't want to have a *huge* party this time. Just a warm-up. A test run."

"Why do we need a test run? We've been throwing parties together for ten years."

He sent a blistering shot in my direction and it caromed off the side board and into my goal. "Why are you giving me a hard time about having a party?" he said with unusual force. It caught my attention and I looked up at him, but he stayed focused on the air hockey table.

I didn't intend to upset him. "I'm not giving you a hard time. Three parties in April definitely fits my definition of the word 'excessive,' but if you want to have a warm-up, fine, we'll have one." We started volleying again. He showed no sign of that momentary flare-up. In fact, I wondered if I had imagined it.

"I'm still trying to think of a theme," he said as he pushed the puck back and forth on his side of the table, looking for an opening. I knew this trick and concentrated on his movements as we spoke.

"How about overkill?"

"No one would get that."

"No one ever gets any of your themes."

"Leave this to the professionals, okay." He faked one way and then shot in the other direction. I somehow managed to block it.

I gained control and moved forward cautiously, keeping my eye on Daz the entire time. He'd been known to leap across the table. I went to take a hard shot, but the pusher only caught the side of the puck. Daz sprung at the puck, but he mistimed it and it landed softly in his goal.

"My change-up," I said.

He seemed impressed. "Where'd you learn that?"

"I have only begun to reveal my vast array of talents."

"In other words it was an accident."

"Yeah, it was an accident."

It was after midnight when we stopped playing. Daz beat me four out of five games, but I took some consolation in the fact that I had extended him to tiebreakers in two of those. On some nights, he would shut me out entirely, so this was a big deal for me.

"Are you planning to wake up tomorrow?" I said as I got ready to leave.

"If you insist. I kinda liked hanging around the apartment all day. I could do this for a living."

"Nah, the pressure would get to you. Having to decide between Nickelodeon, E! and the Weather Channel would become too much of a burden after a while."

"Tell me about it. I missed three other shows I wanted to watch during the *Duck Tales* thing."

"What about your DVR?"

"I ran out of space."

"And you couldn't erase anything?"

He slapped the side of his head. "I didn't think of that."

I laughed. It was nice to see he was back in form.

"What's on the agenda tomorrow?" he said.

"Not a lot. Which is good because we have to get a production schedule going on SparkleBean and Carnie has some gonzo ideas about BlisterSnax Max that we need to sit down about."

"I'll be there."

"Only if I come here first to retrieve you."

"I only pretend to be that dependent because I like the attention."

"Yeah, I saw through that years ago."

Inexplicably, he punched me on the arm. "Hey, for the party, what if I had everyone dress as their favorite characters from *Duck Tales*?"

"I don't think most people *have* a favorite character from *Duck Tales*."

"How about if they dressed as my favorite characters then?"

"There are limits to what others will do for you out of affection."

"There are?"

I clapped him on the shoulder. "I'll see you in the morning."

The chapter about princes

Kander and Craft had managed to pique my curiosity. I still wasn't sure how I got through that first meeting with Keane without botching it, and I definitely wasn't sure that I was interested enough in making a move to have this little courtship thing become more than a bit of a dalliance, but I had to admit that I was totally intrigued by the notion of meeting Curt Prince.

I knew Prince only by reputation. He had a shelf full of Clios and was responsible for some of the hottest ad campaigns of the last couple of generations. He was the ultimate rainmaker and could have been a partner at any of the major agencies if not the head of his own, but he chose this sort of "Genius-at-Large" gig with K&C for some reason that I didn't entirely understand. I guess everyone makes decisions based on their own criteria, but this seemed strange to me. Regardless, meeting him was a little like having lunch with a rock star or a supermodel.

It took everything in my power to avoid telling Daz what I was doing. I really wanted to share this with him, but at this point, I was totally tangled up in the complications arising from my not telling him about the very first call from K&C, and I didn't know how to get into it now without a messy explanation of how it got this far without his knowledge. In the end, I convinced myself that this was going to be my last meeting with these people, after which I would tell Daz I'd had lunch with Curt Prince, he'd call me a liar, I'd pull out an autographed napkin or something and he'd kick a soccer ball at me. Then we'd go back to the car campaign and forget this whole recruitment thing ever happened.

It wouldn't be the first time since we were friends that Daz got all the details of something that happened to me in summary fashion. I once had an entire romantic relationship while he was away visiting his sister. He was gone for a week – Linda was the only person in his family he talked about and I assumed the only one he could tolerate; he called her on the phone regularly and sometimes spoke about her for an hour afterward – during which time I became obsessed, committed, frustrated and ultimately fairly pissy about a woman I'd met. This thing with Kander and Craft was different, of course, but I was relatively sure that Daz would respond to it in the same way. He'd ask a slew of questions, make a few jokes, and then relegate it to its place in our shared history.

Keane's assistant called in the morning to let me know that our lunch was at The Modern, the gorgeous restaurant inside The Museum of Modern Art. All glass and chrome, it reflected MOMA's elegant approach to contemporary beauty. It also had a sensational menu. I got there a little before Keane and Prince did and munched on a piece of bread while I stared absently out one of the floor-to-ceiling windows. It was nice to have some flat-out down time. After a few minutes, I was so zoned out that I didn't even notice that the two of them had approached until they were at the table.

"Meditating?" Prince said, snapping me back to attention.

I laughed and stood up, extending my hand. "Hi, I'm Rich Flaster."

"I guessed that," he said, shaking my hand. "In case you haven't guessed, I'm Curt Prince. You've already met Operations Man over here, right?"

I reached over and shook Keane's hand as well.

"What? No small-batch bourbon?" Prince said as he sat down. I was a little confused by this question until I remembered that I'd tweeted two days ago about a bourbon I'd had the night before. Curt Prince was one of my Twitter followers? More likely, he'd had someone on his staff pull up my feed just before he left to come to this meeting.

"No, I never drink at lunch."

"A shot of bourbon is not a drink – unless you have four of them in which case you're a drunk." He turned to the waiter and ordered three shots of a brand I'd never heard of before and then looked back to me. "Your parents will even think it's good for you," he said, quoting a bit of copy I wrote for a granola snack. "I loved that line."

I was flattered that it had even registered on him. Again, this could have been something an associate had suggested he say, but even that was impressive. "Thanks."

"No, thank you. Makes my whole day when I see a crisp bit of advertising."

I grinned. "I think you just made *my* whole day."

Prince smiled back. I knew he was in his mid-forties, but I would never have been able to tell you that if I hadn't read it in the trades. His eyes danced and his gestures and inflections were that of someone my age – maybe even younger. I realized no one was saying anything and I guessed that this was a cue.

"Oh, and you're very good too," I said broadly.

"Thanks," he said with a nod. "Glad to be of service."

Keane leaned forward. "Curt's ego needs to be fed hourly. We have several people within the organization whose sole job is to do this."

Prince tossed a wry glance in Keane's direction. "They handle me very well." He then looked back at me. "So Noel tells me that you have some doubts about the downtown operation."

"Did I say that?"

"I hope so, because he told me you had a good business head and if you *didn't* have doubts about the downtown operation, you couldn't possibly have a good business head."

"Well, I probably don't have a clue about what I'm saying, but the track record is a little spotty down there."

Prince grunted. "Yeah, another way to look at it would be that it absolutely sucks. We've been hemorrhaging money and losing clients to small-time agencies who we should be spreading on this piece of bread here."

Keane chuckled. "Gee, Curt, you're kicking into the hard sell so soon."

Prince pawed the air. "I'm just making it clear to Rich that his dubiousness is justified and that I appreciate his voicing such opinions." The bourbon came and Prince downed the shot faster than I'd ever seen anyone do so. I took a sip of mine. It was bracing and stimulated several taste buds at the same time, as great artisanal bourbon should. "Of course, you're not so dubious that you aren't interested in continuing this conversation."

I finished my shot. "To tell you the truth, I just wanted to be able to say I had lunch with you."

Prince laughed. "Very flattering. And total bullshit. There's something about K&C Downtown that fascinates you. This is something that a mega-agency should be able to pull off. And you know what? There's something about it that fascinates me as well. That's why I decided to oversee the rebuilding of that office."

If Prince had intended for me to be impressed by this, he'd succeeded. This spoke volumes about the agency's intentions for its ugly duckling. If they were getting ready to board the place up, they would never let someone like him get involved. And if he didn't think he could turn the shop around, he would never waste his time with it.

"And you know what's going to make the downtown office a huge success?" he said, eyeing his empty bourbon glass.

Keane leaned forward. "I've been telling him it's fiscal conservatism."

"Fiscal conservatism my ass. That's someone else's job. The thing that's going to make the office a huge success is creativity. Quick, Rich, name three ads that came from the downtown office in the last year."

I hadn't expected to be put on the spot like this. I'd done a fair amount of background reading on K&C over the past week (not to mention all of the reading I'd been doing about them over the past several years), but not this kind of homework. "The shoe campaign for Sprong was one of them, right?"

"Actually, that was the midtown office. We tried to make everyone think it came from downtown, so I'm glad you got that impression."

I felt like I'd pressed my buzzer accidentally on *Jeopardy*. Finally, I just shook my head. "Sorry, I can't come up with anything."

Prince nodded energetically. "My point exactly. We're Kander and Craft, for God's sakes, and you can't come up with a single campaign that our high-profile boutique satellite agency developed. Do you know why? Because all of it was forgettable. You don't want to get me started on Mind Bombs or shred.com or Freewheels."

"Gravity is your only limitation," I said, reciting the hook for the latter.

Prince pointed in my direction, as though I was a particularly astute student in his classroom. "Tell me something. What was the first thing that came to your mind when you heard that line?"

I decided to go with honesty, since that appeared to be working and since Prince seemed to demand it. "Truth? That it was pretty lame."

"Why?"

"Because you shouldn't be selling fourteen-year-olds limits."

He slapped the table. "Exactly. 'Gravity is your only limitation,'" he said derisively. "Shit. I could give you five lines right here that work better than that one."

"'Give gravity a run for its money,'" I said.

"A definite improvement. How about, 'Gravity? You are *so* over that.'"

I warmed to this. "'Gravity? We don't need no stinkin' gravity,'" I said with a laugh.

"Or forget the gravity thing entirely. Here's a novel idea: let's play off the name of the product. 'Free. Because you're supposed to be.'"

I moved to the edge of my chair. "'The best things in life are wheels'."

Prince leaned back. "Pretty good. Just imagine if you took ten minutes to think about it. The guys working on it had three weeks." He looked like he'd just eaten some bad sushi and then his expression shifted quickly. "What are you having for lunch?"

I hadn't even noticed the menus in front of us. I concentrated on mine for a few minutes and chose the chorizo-crusted cod with white Coco bean purée and harissa oil. Keane had the quail baked "en terre glaise," and Prince ordered the slow-poached farm egg with black truffles and squid in spaetzle. It was an appetizer, but Prince had them make it up as an entrée.

Over the course of our meal, we talked about great advertising campaigns the way a couple of old friends might exchange opinions about key sporting events or notable pop music moments. The greatest Super Bowl ads. The greatest soft drink ads. The sexiest ads of all time. The most laughable attempts to be sexy of all time. Keane contributed when he could, but I could tell that he wasn't nearly as interested in this kind of talk as Prince and I were. Either that or he simply couldn't get a word in edgewise.

From this we segued into comparing strategies. When social media was most appropriate. When you eschewed one demographic for another. When it was smart to aim over the heads of your audience. And my personal favorite: how to convince the client that he's getting what he wants when you're doing what *you* want instead. I'd rarely had the opportunity to engage in this kind of conversation for this long, and I'd *never* had one with someone like Curt Prince. This was like discussing making records with George Martin in the late sixties, or coaching basketball with Phil Jackson during the Bulls' or Lakers' championship runs, or making movies with Kathryn Bigelow while she was doing "The Hurt Locker" or "Zero Dark Thirty." I was exchanging points of view with a master at the absolute top of his game. It was far more intoxicating than four bourbons and had the opposite effect on my brain cells.

Things finally settled back a little as we waited for our coffee to come. Prince's attention was drawn to the windows, Keane's to a beautiful woman two tables over.

"Okay, so how *are* you going to turn the downtown office around?" I said a short while later as we drank double espressos.

"Well, the first thing I'm going to do is hire a top-notch Creative Director. Know anyone I should talk to?"

I looked down at my coffee. "I might."

Prince leaned forward. "Look, Rich, I'm not gonna screw around with you. I'm only discussing this with a few people. I like what I've seen in your work and I like talking to you. If you want to keep your hat in the ring, I want to keep the conversation going."

I nodded. "Believe me; this is very appealing. And I really appreciate that you want to keep the conversation going. It's just that The Shop has sort of become home for me over the last few years."

"You're meant to *leave* home."

"I understand that," I said, screwing up my face.

"Listen, I'm not asking you to make a decision right now, and I'm not offering you anything yet anyway."

I gestured to make it clear that I understood this as well.

"But how about this: come spend the weekend with me and my girlfriend in East Hampton. We'll kick back, we'll talk, I'll show you an outtake reel that will make you piss your pants and we'll just see where it goes."

The offer was a complete surprise to me. "This weekend?"

"If you're not busy. I'll send a car to bring you there Saturday morning and you can hang out with us until sometime on Sunday."

"Wow, that's very nice of you."

"He doesn't just do this for anyone," Keane said, sending Prince an expression of indignation. I couldn't tell whether it was real or playful. "It took him a year to get me out there."

Prince rolled his eyes, which made me laugh.

"Okay, that would be great," I said.

We finished our coffee talking about inconsequential things, which was just as well, as I'd lost nearly all of my objectivity at this point. As we stepped outside, Prince's cell phone rang. He said a quick goodbye, not even waiting for Keane before he headed down the block. Keane walked me to the corner before we peeled off in opposite directions.

I went back to the office as buzzed as I had been about anything in years. This job, which I'd convinced myself wasn't the right move for me to make, had begun to sound very appealing. The fact that the recruitment process included a weekend in the Hamptons with a living legend in my chosen profession was fairly attractive as well.

It wasn't until I got onto The Shop's block that I realized I hadn't mentioned Daz's name once during the entire lunch. That definitely wasn't the plan. Just before entering the restaurant, I'd decided that I was going to test those waters again. But the conversation had just taken off in an entirely different direction.

On top of this, it wasn't until I'd gotten off the elevator that I remembered that Daz was planning for us to have a party that weekend. A more honest person would have chosen this opportunity to come clean to him. I started making up stories instead.

The chapter about convenient excuses

Daz popped into my office a few minutes after I got back from lunch. He was holding a Snickers bar in one hand and a bottle of SparkleBean in the other.

"This is a *great* combination," he said, his mouth half full. "If you take a bite of the Snickers and then a swig of the soda and slosh them together," he did exactly this by way of demonstration, "you get this monster flavor rush. Think we should try to get these companies together for a joint campaign? Who makes Snickers anyway?"

He offered me a taste and I declined, still quite full of my chorizo-crusted cod.

"We gonna do some more work on the *Brilliante* this afternoon?" he said, wiping his mouth.

"We're not calling it the *Brilliante*."

"I don't know, I'm really starting to warm to it. I think we should throw it out there for the client."

"I think we might want to put a teensy bit more work into it first. That can't be the best we can come up with."

He shrugged, taking an unaccompanied drink of the soda. "If you insist. When do you want to come in?"

"Give me a little while. I got backed up with phone calls this morning because of the staff meeting." In reality, I only had one call to return, but I needed a little decompression time after my lunch, and I needed at least a few minutes away from Daz. The transition back to The Shop after my lunch with Prince was turning out to be a little tougher than I'd expected it to be.

"Whenever. I'm around." He started to walk away, doing another candy bar/soda shot as he did. Then he stopped and turned back into my office. "Hey, I came up with the theme for this weekend's event. What do you think about making it a pajama party? You never know what *some* of our guests will show up wearing."

"Sounds like a winner. One problem, though: I'm not gonna be there."

His expression was a blank, as though had I asked him to calculate the rate at which the universe was expanding right on the spot. "Wow, really? I don't think I've had a party without you since we came to New York. I'm gonna have to check our contract to make sure I can even do something like that. Why can't you make it?"

I had already decided which excuse I was going to use. That the lie came out so easily made me more than a little uncomfortable. "I got a call from my mother this morning. Some big family reunion thing is happening this weekend at my aunt's house and she insists I be there."

"That sounds better to you than a pajama party?"

"Command performance, Daz. I wasn't given the option of saying no. You know what it's like with my mother." I sneered while I said this to sell the lie. I really believed that I needed to put on this show. At this stage, Daz was certainly going to be very upset that the thing with K&C had progressed – and was still progressing – without my mentioning it to him, and doubly upset that I was foregoing his party to frolic in the Hamptons with the guy trying to break up our team.

"Hard to believe you're gonna pass this up. I mean, some of the women might show up in *lingerie*."

"You have a very vivid imagination," I said, unable to avoid chuckling. "Get out of here so I can return these calls. I'll come by in a half hour or so."

He toasted me with the nearly empty soda bottle and walked away. I immediately felt guilty. I hated blowing Daz off, and I really hated the fact that I didn't feel I could tell him what I was actually doing this weekend.

At the same time, though – as ridiculous as it seems – I was a little miffed at him for making this hard on me. I told myself I shouldn't have to report every detail of my life to him and that he needed to give me a little space every now and then. We were best friends, not life partners. It was only when I said out loud, "I wish he could be a little more understanding" that it finally occurred to me that he couldn't possibly understand something he was completely unaware of. This somehow managed to irritate me more.

I returned the phone call and then made a few more just to put a little distance between The Modern and the next order of business. When I went to Daz's office about forty-five minutes later, we worked for a very short while before he started complaining about feeling nauseous.

"So much for the SparkleBean/Snickers combo, huh?" I said.

"Yeah, maybe." He looked pale.

"Was that the only thing you had for lunch today?"

"No, I had a couple of jelly donuts, too. Listen, I'll be back in a couple of minutes. I need to get to the bathroom."

This still didn't mean anything to me.

———

That night, after an unproductive session on the car campaign and after Daz promised that his stomach was up to it, we went to a club called Mark with Michelle, Carnie, Chess, and a few other people from the office. Loud techno music rumbled through the room, which was crowded for a Tuesday night.

"I wonder if we'll get to meet Mark," Daz said, barely audible over the din.

"Who's Mark?" I said.

"The guy who owns this place."

"The guy who owns this place is named Mark?"

"Isn't that why the *place* is called Mark?" he said with a grin.

"This is a stupid conversation."

We found a table not far from the dance floor and immediately after ordering their drinks, Michelle and Carnie popped up from their seats to dance. Since my drinks date with Michelle, I'd found myself more and more drawn to her. When she told me she was thinking about going back to the Midwest, it changed her for me a little, made her seem a little more precious. Watching her wriggle to the music definitely did nothing to depreciate her value. She really was spectacular looking and I again thought about what it would be like to wriggle alone with her.

"Are they the most beautiful women in the room or is it just me?" Daz said.

Chess pointed his beer across the dance floor toward a gorgeous Asian woman with lustrous hair that went all the way down her back. "I think that one might give them a run for their money."

A woman in a shimmering halter top caught my eye. "Or that one."

Daz shrugged. "I don't know. Those women are fine, but I still think Michelle and Carnie are the most beautiful. Not that beauty is the most important thing."

"Beauty isn't the most important thing?" Chess said.

"*The* most important? No."

"What's more important?"

"What's more important to Daz," I said, "is their willingness to go out with him."

"Yeah, definitely that."

We all laughed. Daz was probably right that physical beauty wasn't the most important thing in a relationship, but in many ways it was a prerequisite. Certainly, it had been in my experience. If I wasn't physically attracted to a woman (and presumably she to me), the interchange would never get to the point where we could learn much more about each other. If I didn't find a woman particularly attractive, I never thought about her as a romantic partner no matter how interesting she might be otherwise. I realize there was a certain shallowness to this thinking (maybe quite a bit of shallowness), but I would guess that the overwhelming majority of people feel the same way.

The song shifted and Michelle and Carnie came over to our table, beckoning me and Daz to join them on the dance floor. Michelle reached out for Daz's hand and pulled him along. I followed with Carnie.

One of the contradictions in my no-inter-office-dating policy was that it made no provisions for going to bars with people from the office, having all-night parties with people from the office, or writhing suggestively on a dance floor with people from the office. The dancing

Carnie and I did could definitely be considered sexual – I considered it precisely that while we were doing it – but since it was in public and there were other people from the office around, it wasn't off-limits. It was an extension of our already-established relationship, our friendship. Daz, a better dancer than me, and Michelle, who was much better than any of us, did something rather sultry themselves, but it had a grace to it that made what Carnie and I did seem crude.

"They're good together, aren't they?" Carnie said when she noticed me looking at them.

"Yeah, they are."

"He has a real thing for her."

"Daz? Yeah, he has a rich fantasy life."

"It might not be as much of a fantasy as you think."

I looked at Carnie carefully and nearly stopped moving. "What do you mean?"

"I mean that Daz is an incredible guy. Who would argue with that? Certainly not Michelle."

"Michelle likes Daz?"

"Everyone likes Daz."

"But she likes him in a different way than most people like him?" I said this sharply, feeling an odd bit of jealousy.

"I can't tell you exactly what she's thinking," Carnie said plainly.

"She's your best friend and you can't tell what she's thinking?"

"Hey, Daz is *your* best friend. Can you always tell exactly what he's thinking?"

I looked over at them. They were practically having intercourse to the beat of the music. "Yeah, I think I can."

"Well, *anyone* can tell what he's thinking right now."

Daz was being ridiculously obvious. I was surprised he wasn't simply prostrating himself at her feet. At the same time, Michelle didn't seem entirely uninterested in his attention. Though nothing was going on between me and Michelle, that still irritated me.

The song ended a minute later and Carnie and I made our way back to the table. Daz and Michelle stayed out on the dance floor for several additional songs and then surprisingly came back in the middle of something from Beam. Daz gulped his drink and then quickly ordered another one. He was sweating profusely. Michelle, on the other hand, was shining like a beacon.

Not long after that, Chess and Carnie went out on the floor and the rest of us talked about little things that didn't require much concentration. It was a typical night out for us. Ebbs and flows, pairing off and gathering.

We were there less than an hour total when Daz leaned over to Michelle and whispered something in her ear. She got a very thoughtful expression on her face and then she nodded. The two of them stood up together.

"We're calling it a night," Daz said. He was still sweating and he dabbed at his brow. By this point, he'd stopped dancing more than twenty minutes ago.

"You're doing what?" I said with an edge.

"We're calling it. I'll see you in the morning."

I looked at my watch and then back up at Daz. It wasn't the early hour that stunned me. What did was that Daz was leaving with Michelle. After whispering in her ear.

"Okay, see you in the morning," I said carefully. The tone of voice I used was an easily recognizable indicator to Daz that I didn't understand what was happening and that I required further explanation. He couldn't have mistaken it, even in the loud bar. For whatever reason, though, he chose to ignore it.

The two of them left the table, and Michelle walked over to Carnie, who was still on the dance floor, and said something to her. Carnie seemed a little confused for a moment and had a strange smile on her face. Then she just waved. While they were having this exchange, Daz was looking off across the room, in my mind consciously avoiding making eye contact with me.

I had another drink, danced some more, and got into an animated conversation with Christine, one of The Shop's account execs, about potential Democratic candidates for President in 2016. But inside, I was pretty miffed. Daz had just cavalierly gone off with Michelle, giving no consideration to how I might feel about his doing this. I told him about the drinks date I'd had with her. Surely he had to notice that I thought of her as something more than a colleague – even though I couldn't particularly say what. Did he think he had some prior claim because of "the thing" he imagined passing between them at the Beam concert? Did he think my absolute refusal to date colleagues had no conceivable exceptions?

Suddenly I didn't feel guilty at all about going to the Hamptons with Curt Prince and blowing off Daz's party. If he could act the way he was acting, then I had every right to act the way I was acting.

Maybe this was just the kind of thing that happened in a friendship after a while. Maybe Prince was right; at some point you just had to move on.

———

I got home very late that night, having gone to another bar with Chess after everyone split up. I hadn't been this drunk in months. I flopped onto my bed without bothering to undress and quickly fell asleep, my last conscious thought being about Michelle lying in Daz's arms at that very moment.

As I slept, I had an extremely vivid dream, one that was still very clear to me in the morning, which was unusual for me. In it, Michelle walked into my office wearing a string bikini. She looked as stunning nearly naked as I'd always imagined. She closed the door behind her, sat across from me and crossed her long, supple, airbrush-smooth legs. She said something to me about hotel accommodations for our business trip to Indiana, and I slyly suggested we share a room. Michelle got a seductive grin on her face and leaned toward me, the top of her bikini barely containing her. I inched across my desk, preparing to sweep the papers off of it.

Then Daz opened the door without knocking and entered my office. I started to say something to him about interrupting, but he didn't even look at me. He simply put his arm on Michelle's shoulder, kissed her earlobe and whispered something to her. The two of them laughed, and Michelle rose and slinked out of the room with him, Daz cupping her ass as they left.

The dream left me feeling a level of sexual frustration I hadn't felt since I was a teenager.

Daz compounded this the next day by absolutely refusing to talk about what had happened with Michelle. "We just left; let it go," was his response to my various attempts to get him to offer me details. I even went so far as to suggest that I expected to find Michelle there when I came to pick him up in the morning. This got a

glare out of him but nothing else. Daz and I weren't kiss-
and-tell kinda guys and I don't ever remember one of us
going to the other with the description of a particularly
steamy night. We definitely kept each other apprised
when a new relationship started, though. It was one of
the unspoken rules.

———

That Thursday night, we held the first practice for our
softball team, which was part of the City Advertising
League. We were never great – we didn't have a big
enough pool of talent to draw on to compete with some
of the other agencies – but we were always good enough
to stay with the middle of the pack. Regardless, we
always prepared for the season as though we were going
to challenge for the league championship, even though
we knew this was unrealistic. Where would the fun be
in preparing to finish sixth? On this night, though, from
the time we stepped onto the field in Central Park, it was
obvious that Daz's heart wasn't in it.

Daz could not have picked a poorer time to show
his lackadaisical side. As co-captains, we were ostensibly
responsible for putting the team together, weighing the
strengths and weaknesses of our players and getting the
most out of everyone. While I could easily be accused
of taking this much more seriously than I should under
the circumstances, if it had to do with behavior around
our colleagues, to me that meant we acted as role models.
We could let our guards down when we were with close
friends from the agency, but there were people on the
team who only knew us as high-level staff. That required
a certain degree of comportment and I would continue

to take this seriously regardless of what we were doing and, for that matter, regardless of whether I was currently being wooed by another agency.

Daz, on the other hand, seemed to think that the best way to lead the team was to sit out the wind sprints, fail to get in position to take cutoff throws, and let easy ground balls pass him with little more than a wave of his glove. I'm not sure how much attention our teammates were paying to this, but I was already pissed at him, so my tolerance for his actions was especially low. As the practice wore on, I found myself getting increasingly frustrated. Yes, he had been sick a couple of days earlier, but it never took him a long time to recover. The only reasonable explanation for his actions was that he was slacking.

Afterward, I let him have it. "Was that too much trouble for you tonight?"

"Huh?" he said, as though he had no idea what I meant.

We walked out onto Central Park West and headed uptown. "You sucked out there. You were ridiculous."

"It was the first practice. Give me a break."

"This wasn't the Tour de France; it was freaking softball. You hardly need to be in optimum condition to give a little effort."

He smirked. "I did what I needed to do."

The more casual his responses, the more my ire rose. "You didn't do shit. You looked like you wanted a recliner out there. Were you expecting someone to bring you a glass of lemonade and your comfy slippers? You're a captain, Daz. You're supposed to take charge."

"Gee, Rich, do you think you could be a little more over-the-top here? What do you want me to do, treat this like it's a matter of life or death?"

I couldn't understand where this attitude was coming from. "You always used to really get into the softball team. What the hell is going on here?"

He stopped and turned to me. It was only during rare times like these that I noticed that Daz was eight inches taller than me. "Back off, okay?"

"What's the matter? Are you too busy thinking about your next date with Michelle to play with the rest of your friends?"

Daz looked down the street, and for a moment I thought he would pivot and come back at me with both barrels blasting. Then he stuck out his hand and a cab pulled up next to us.

"I'm done with this conversation," he said, pulling the cab door closed.

I couldn't believe he'd cut me off that way. Daz never bailed in the middle of an argument. Stunned and furious, I watched the car drive away, and my first thought, absurdly, was to complain to someone about it. I figured that any one of the dozens of strangers around me had to have been equally appalled by Daz's rudeness.

Deciding against that option, I continued my walk up Central Park West. I was still perturbed when I arrived home an hour later, having stopped for a burger (at the *better* burger place on Daz's block) that I couldn't even taste.

The next morning, I did something I had not done once before without telling Daz ahead of time – I decided not to pick him up on the way to work. I was simply too ticked off and too confused about everything. It was nearly 10:00 before he showed up. He stuck his head into my office, looked at me like he was profoundly disappointed, and then left without saying a word.

We didn't speak the entire day. At the time, I could only assume that he thought he was as right in his actions as I believed I was in mine.

It didn't register on me at the time, but I realize now that the past several days were all about making my upcoming indiscretion as easy for me as I could.

The chapter about
blissful ignorance

The car Prince sent for me was a yellow Range Rover. I felt very conspicuous as we made our way across town to the bridge, but it was a good kind of conspicuous. Like I couldn't avoid being noticed and so there was no point in trying to pretend that I didn't want to be.

When we hit the highway, I realized that in my rush to leave the apartment, I'd left my cell phone on the kitchen counter. This was an awful lot like leaving home without my pants, and I thought about asking the driver to turn around. Instead, I decided to live dangerously for one whole weekend. I had no pressing business with clients, and if any of my friends wanted to talk to me, they'd catch me Sunday night. It was a surprisingly liberating feeling.

As we went over the bridge, I thought again about the tussle I'd had with Daz. I tried to call him a few times the night before, just because I didn't want so much time to pass without our speaking, but he wasn't picking up. Finally, I left a message on his cell wishing him fun at the party and asking him to take lots of pictures – especially if certain people showed up in teddies. I didn't want this thing to turn into a rift. I think we both understood that at some point something was going to come between us to greatly reduce our time together – I think we both assumed this was going to be the women of our individual dreams – but I certainly didn't want it to be a job or a colleague I shouldn't have even been thinking about dating in the first place. If things continued to progress with K&C, Daz and I would figure out a way to keep it from getting in our way too much. If things happened with Daz and Michelle the way they seemed to be happening, then I'd be happy for him and even happier if their relationship made Michelle decide to stay on the East Coast.

The ride on the Long Island Expressway was predictably stop-and-go and 27 was a crawl, but I paid it little mind. The Range Rover was equipped with a DVD player hooked up to an active matrix screen, and the sound system was the best I'd ever heard in a car. Carl, the driver, seemed to be genuinely pleased with my music selections – first a little Coldplay, then some Bob Marley, then the new Atoms for Peace, the side project by Radiohead's legendary Thom Yorke – though I suppose he was professional enough to have appeared that way even if I'd asked for *The Powerpuff Girls' Greatest Hits*.

It was a little after noon when we pulled onto Prince's driveway. It was a hell of a driveway. It must have been a quarter of a mile long, wending through carefully manicured shrubbery on either side. It delivered us to a faux Tudor house that looked like it had been spit-shined that very morning. Early spring blossoms dotted the precision landscaping leading up to the ocean. Prince might like to keep things loose when the creative juices are flowing, but he obviously kept the people who maintained his property on a tight leash. The effect of the whole thing was breathtaking.

And this was his *weekend* home.

A woman with short brown hair and deep, intelligent eyes came out the front door. "Hi, I'm Andrea," she said, extending a slim hand with a surprisingly firm grip. "Curt decided ten minutes ago that he needed to get us lunch from Hampton Pantry. He should be back in a little while. Come on in."

I followed her into the house. Carl took my overnight bag from my grasp and delivered it up to the guest room before returning to finalize my pickup time tomorrow afternoon.

"Is there any new music or movies you want me to pick up for you for the ride?" he said.

I nearly laughed but held it in check. "Unless we hit *a lot* of traffic, I think you have plenty already, thanks."

Andrea led me through the entry hall into a den featuring a massive TV that made mine look like a laptop. From there we passed a living room studded with antiques and I noticed off to the side a dining room with furniture that looked entirely handmade. Big, intricately carved stuff. This led to the single biggest kitchen I'd ever seen in my life. Professional appliances were set into rosy granite, and pots and utensils hung decoratively from the ceiling. Hanging baskets held a variety of produce, and an entire corner of one counter was dedicated to glass canisters holding pastas of various shapes and hues.

"Wow," I said. "It looks like Hamptons Pantry should be doing their cooking here."

Andrea smiled. I guessed she was somewhere in her mid-thirties. "Curt and I both love to cook. I was a little surprised that he was going out to get lunch when we have so much to eat here."

All I knew about Andrea was that she was Prince's "girlfriend." Her comment about the kitchen and her bearing in the house suggested something more permanent than that, though. I wondered if Prince agreed with the assessment. I knew nothing about his personal life. The pieces I'd read about him made virtually no mention of it, and he kept an extremely low profile in social media. Was he the kind of guy who called his long-term, live-in lover his "girlfriend," or was she the kind of person who took her place in his life far more seriously than he did?

Andrea got me a glass of iced tea, and we sat out on the back deck waiting for Prince's return. The spring had warmed considerably in the past week and it was now temperate enough to sit outside comfortably, even with the breezes blowing off the water.

"You must love it out here," I said as we settled in.

"Every minute," she said with a dreamy smile directed at the Atlantic. "Not the whole Hamptons scene so much, though it's important to what I do, but this, right here. This deck, this beach, this ocean. It's really amazing how it affects me."

I watched Andrea watching her world. She obviously felt at home here, and feeling that way meant a great deal to her. Instantly, I hoped that Prince saw their relationship seriously. It was suddenly important to me that Andrea's illusions not be sullied. I have no idea why.

I learned that Andrea ran a women's advocacy group and that she met Prince out here a year ago when she "roped him in" during one of her fund-raising events. It turned out that he gave a considerable amount of his enormous earnings to charity every year, but that he always ran these organizations through the wringer first to guarantee that the money was going where he intended it to go. Their courtship essentially revolved around this process, and after two months, he gave her a big check and an invitation to move in with him. Andrea accepted the former about two weeks before she accepted the latter. I guess she wanted to run him through the wringer a little as well.

I found that I was hungry for details about Curt Prince. Before Tuesday, he was only an icon to me, and since then I had been a little starstruck. It was more than fascination and awe that drove this, though. I wanted to know what it was like to live the life he lived. Obviously, the trappings were spectacular, but how he dealt with the trappings was something that I wanted to understand. I was glad he was a charitable man and equally glad that he placed demands on the charities he benefited. For whatever reason, I was also glad that he put up with the two-week delay Andrea had imposed before accepting his offer.

I was there maybe fifteen minutes when Prince returned. He placed two huge bags on the counter in the kitchen and then walked out to greet us, kissing Andrea as he reached out to shake my hand.

"Did you have a good ride?" he said.

"Great. I watched *Argo* on the DVD player and got to listen to the new Atoms for Peace album."

"Yorke is so inconsistent," he said with a bit of a scowl. "I like what he's doing with this record, though."

"Yeah, there's some good stuff on it." It was interesting to me that he even listened to the band, although his calling the album a "record" gave away the difference in our ages.

"I hope you're hungry. I sort of bought out the store." He looked over to Andrea apologetically. "I know; it's the same story every time." He turned to me. "I'm hopeless when I go into that place. The people behind every counter know my name – and all of my weaknesses. Should we eat out here?"

While Andrea got plates, Prince laid out the containers of food: grilled tuna nicoise, tequila lime chicken, a salad of white beans with arugula, broccoli with lemon and garlic, sesame noodles, grilled shrimp with mango salsa, croissant bread pudding, and brownies. It was a ludicrous amount of food for the three of us, but Prince seemed to have delighted in buying all of it, and he certainly seemed intent on eating at least some of everything.

"How long have you had this place?" I said as we were eating.

"I bought it five years ago. It was my pacifier after a brutal divorce. My daughter loves this house."

"Oh, I didn't realize you had children."

"Just one. Callie. She's nine. After we split up, her mother relocated to Northern California. Some day when I know you better, I'll give you the blow-by-blow of that bout. The bottom line is that Callie spends the summers here and I get out there once a month. And I have a fetish room down the hall with all kinds of images of my ex."

He smiled to assure me he was kidding about that last thing. I twirled a sesame noodle, unsure how to respond to this.

"Anyway," he said, "I started coming out here on weekends. I never considered myself to be a Hamptons guy, but I needed something to do. I came to a party at this house, found out that the owner was planning to put it on the market, and I made him an offer he couldn't refuse. Definitely one of my top five impulsive acts."

There were four other things he'd done that were as impulsive as buying a palatial house on the spur of the moment?

"It was a great decision," Andrea said, smiling warmly at Prince. "And not a bad investment either."

"Yeah, you wouldn't believe how much this property has appreciated, even in this crappy economy. Not that I'm ever going to sell it. Did you try the bread pudding?"

"I'm still working my way through the entrees."

"Oh," he said, nodding, "you're one of those salad-entrée-dessert guys."

First screw-up of the day. "I didn't realize I was until just this moment."

"Here's the way I look at it: if the greatest bread pudding ever made on the planet is sitting in front of you, you have some of that first. The rest of the stuff will be there when you need it."

"I didn't know it was that good."

Prince leaned toward me in "trust me" fashion. "You truly haven't lived until you've tried it."

I spooned a bit onto my plate and tasted it. It was delicious. I smiled appreciatively. As it turned out, I wasn't as enamored with bread pudding as Prince, but I could see why he liked it so much. The tequila lime chicken, on the other hand, was spectacular. Running the risk of appearing way too conventional in Prince's eyes, I took another piece, though I grabbed half a brownie at the same time.

"You know what sold me on this place?" Prince said while I continued to eat.

"The kitchen? The driveway?" I laughed at the splendor of it all. "The ocean? The beach?"

"No, none of that stuff. And I made a massive renovation to the kitchen when I got here. The guy before me was totally wasting the space. No, it was this right here." He got up and directed me to a corner of the deck where someone, presumably a young child, had carved the name "Dani." "I was standing out here making small talk with some captain of industry when I saw that. Right in that moment I realized that some little girl had once played out here and that Callie would love to play out here too. You might say I was feeling a little vulnerable at the time. Worked out, though."

I looked up at Prince and he gave me a little shrug. The gesture completely warmed me. I suddenly understood how someone like him could do something like this on impulse. I glanced down at the carving again, wondered how Dani was doing, and hoped I'd someday get to meet Callie.

When we finished lunch, the three of us walked the beach, Prince with his arm around Andrea's shoulders. They were very affectionate with one another, kissing and touching casually. Watching people act this way sometimes made me uncomfortable, but not now. I liked that they enjoyed being together, that the relationship obviously meant something to both of them. Meanwhile, the magic of this place was working its way into me.

This really was quite a beautiful spot. The surf was roaring ten feet away and as we made our way across the sand, we came upon very few people. This was the best time of year to be out here, before the throngs descended in the summer. The Hamptons thrived year-round much more now than it had even when I was in high school, but it still moved at a much more relaxed pace during the three off seasons. Someone once told me that it was stunning at Christmastime. I wondered if Prince had a big holiday gathering every year for friends and colleagues.

"So what are you doing with your life, Rich?" Andrea said as we walked.

"Working most of the time and playing the rest."

"No woman?"

"Not if you mean that with a capital 'W.' I date, and I hang out with a bunch of women, but I don't have anyone I'm seeing seriously at the moment."

"Hammering down the career thing first," Prince said.

"Yeah, I guess. Certainly I feel like I have a better chance of hammering that thing down right now. The other thing? Who knows? Unlike a career, it's not like you can just decide to make it happen, right?"

"There are always mail-order brides," Prince said with a chuckle.

I flashed him a smile. "Yeah, I didn't think of that."

"Gee," Andrea said, "maybe you should advertise for your ideal woman. Curt tells me you're very good at pitching things."

I laughed. "I'm not sure I'm *that* good. And I kinda believe that you have to understand your product in order to pitch it properly. I don't think I understand myself yet as a partner in a serious relationship."

Had I really just said that? I suppose I'd thought it on various occasions, but I'd definitely never said anything like that out loud before, let alone to two people I barely knew. Must be the salt air.

As we walked, I found myself becoming increasingly accustomed to the pace, to the restorative properties of sand and surf. I never really understood why so many New Yorkers bailed on Manhattan during summer weekends. Why would you ever leave the most exciting place on the planet? Especially when so many other people left and it wasn't nearly as crowded. Now I started to understand in a way that I hadn't on any beach trip in the past. There was something to this notion of escape after all.

When we got back to the house, Prince needed to make some phone calls and Andrea had some work to do on a position paper. They showed me to the guest suite and left me with the run of the house for a while. The guest suite was bigger than my apartment and was considerably more elegantly furnished, though it had fewer toys. It did have a notable selection of books and periodicals, which seemed to be remarkably up to date. I was accustomed to seeing guest rooms dotted with two-year-old magazines and books published a decade or so earlier, but the shelves here included many titles that were on bestseller lists now and several books I'd read about in last week's *New York Times Book Review*. The magazines were in their own stand and were all current issues. The bedroom of the suite had a door leading out to a wraparound second-story deck and I took a *Time* and an *Entertainment Weekly* out there with me and sat back on a chaise lounge. As I relaxed, the thought came to mind that if I took the job with K&C, I might be invited here again during the summer, might even make party lists with some regularity. Just another fringe benefit.

About an hour and a half later, Prince came around the corner of the deck. "We're going to Nick & Toni's tonight if that's okay with you."

I laughed at the mention of the restaurant and their famously difficult-to-obtain tables. "Only if you guarantee that we get seated next to Tom Hanks."

"Yeah, I'll see what I can do about that." He sat down on the edge of a chaise across from me. "Are you comfortable?"

"It'll do," I said with a smile. "You know, if the deck were angled just a degree or so more to the west, I'd get the absolute perfect amount of sun at this very moment. And if this chair had been custom-designed for me, it might just be the tiniest bit more relaxing. And, you know, the valet hasn't been by to massage my feet in nearly a half-hour."

Prince chuckled. "Listen, I didn't ask you to come out here to amaze you with my worldly goods."

"I'm amazed anyway."

"Don't be. Worldly goods are bullshit. The nicest kind of bullshit, but bullshit nevertheless. You know what really matters? Juice."

"Fresh-squeezed from the Hamptons Pantry?"

Prince offered me a half-smile and shook his head. "You're not big on philosophical conversations, are you?"

I think I might have hurt his feelings a little by being so cavalier. I definitely needed to work on this. They say the first step in solving a problem is realizing you have it, right? I really didn't want to sound like a smart-ass to him. "Sorry, I wasn't trying to be a jerk, though it seems to come to me naturally. I think I get what you're saying. You need to be engaged."

"You need to be *emotionally* engaged. You need to feel like what you're doing is worth doing – all the time. Otherwise you're just passing the hours."

I still had a magazine open on my lap. I closed it and put it down on the deck. "I think I'm doing my version of that."

"I think you very well might be. That's why I had you out here, and that's why I want to keep talking about the Creative Director job. What are you thinking about K&C Downtown these days?"

I glanced at the sky for a second, then looked back at him. "I'm thinking that I want to keep thinking about it." That was a lie. The way I was feeling sitting back on this chair, taking in the spring breeze, surrounded by Prince's worldly goods, I would have signed on the bottom line that very minute if the man had handed me an offer sheet.

"That's good. Because I think I want to keep thinking about it as well." He looked off into the distance. There was a partial view of the ocean from this side of the deck. I'm sure his bedroom got the full view. "Andrea likes you, by the way, and she's not an easy person to win over. I guess before I got back you guys had a good talk about some of the stuff she's working on."

"She seems pretty great. And very impressive."

"You don't know the half of it. She's in weekend mode at the moment, which means she puts three-quarters of her brain on hibernate. She's one of the smartest and most aware people I've ever met."

"The two of you must make a formidable couple."

"Yeah, something like that. It's just good to have a reason to come home from the office. I haven't had that since Norma absconded with Callie. Otherwise I'd just be the mad man ad-man all the time."

"K&C would love that, I'm sure. You'd whip the downtown office into shape in record time."

"And probably kill several people doing so. At some point you realize that you can't go full-throttle indefinitely."

I was surprised to hear that from him. This was certainly not what I expected in a sales pitch. "When did *you* figure that out?"

"Truth? About a year ago."

I thought he'd say it happened with the birth of his daughter or maybe on his fortieth birthday. "What happened a year ago?"

He rolled his eyes and then shook his head in self-deprecating fashion. "I was in the middle of this insane pitch for a huge client – can never have enough of those, right? I have a presentation in something like two hours and Callie calls me just to talk. This is unusual, so I give her a few minutes, even though all I can think about are the five things I need to do in order to make the presentation perfect. We hang up and she calls again almost immediately. Instead of thinking that maybe there's something on her mind, I remind her rather unpleasantly that I'm a busy guy. Like she needed me to tell her that. She gets really quiet and then she tells me that her best friend is moving to L.A. My reaction? I blow her off. I didn't quite tell her that best friends were a dime a dozen, but you might have interpreted it that way.

"A couple of hours later, I learn that the client decided to go with another agency. I'm really pissed off about this and dump it all on my assistant. I even tell her about Callie 'interrupting' me earlier in the day. That's when the light bulb went on. My daughter, who never called me at work because she knew I was always ridiculously busy, called me because she was really upset, and I not only blew her off but made her feel like she did something wrong for bothering me. I flew out to Napa that night to apologize to her."

"Did she forgive you?"

"Yeah, she always does. I just don't want her to *need* to forgive me too often." He looked at me with an expression I wasn't accustomed to seeing, then slapped his leg. "Enough navel gazing. Andrea suggested we walk around town for a while before going to dinner. You up for that?"

Nick and Toni's was everything it was cracked up to be, including a big-time celebrity hangout, even in April. You had to wonder if they had people on call just in case it was eight o'clock and no other pop star had shown up. Maybe a Billy Joel look-alike. Or some guy with a supporting role on an HBO series who would have to do for a slow night. I think Prince could see that this was entertaining to me and I think that this pleased him, speeches about none of it really mattering to the contrary. I had to imagine that it was difficult to avoid becoming dependent on the trappings once you grew accustomed to them and I also had to imagine that it was nearly impossible to stay humble about them, though Prince did a better job of this than most of the rich people I'd met.

Afterward, we went to a bar in Amagansett to check out a local band Prince liked. He really knew his music, and it turned out that he sat in on drums at a club some weekends "just to stay involved." We wound up talking about concerts we attended for about an hour and for the first time, I saw Andrea tune out. Obviously, this was not a favorite subject area. I wondered if I could really live with a woman who didn't want to talk about music, but I figured anything was possible under the right circumstances, and Andrea certainly seemed to have her share of good points.

By the time we got back from the bar it was after one, and I was absolutely revved. It was obvious to me that Prince and Andrea were ready to call it a night, but I figured I would have a tough time settling down. It was too cool to go on the deck at this hour, so I sat in bed leafing through the new *Variety*. Around four in the morning, I realized that I'd fallen asleep with the tabloid beside me, and I tossed it onto the floor and pulled the covers up. I was out again in seconds.

I woke up Sunday morning around nine-thirty and found Prince working away in the kitchen. He was doing something with eggs and cheese and bread and sausage, though I wasn't sure how he planned to combine these things. All I knew was that he had impressive kitchen stuff. Back when I was at Tyler, Hope and Pitt, I did a campaign for a high-end small appliance company, so I had some idea about these things, though none of it came from actual hands-on experience. When I worked on the account, they gave me a great looking stainless steel stand mixer and it still sat prominently on my kitchen counter, even though I think I used it only one time to try to make frozen margaritas when my blender broke.

"Hey," Prince said when he saw me come in. "You sleep okay?"

"The lack of street noise was a little disorienting, but yeah."

"Andrea's still out. She likes to sleep in on Sundays. She's still too wound up on Saturday mornings to sleep then."

"Sounds like she takes her job pretty seriously."

"We all take our jobs seriously. She takes hers personally. Hard to argue with that, considering what she does. She did a battered women's shelter project recently and she came home in tears every night."

Andrea didn't strike me as the kind of person who ever came home in tears. For some reason, I glanced off toward their bedroom, as though this would give me some better sense of her.

"That's a tough gig."

"It's only tough if you aren't up to the task. I would've been a lot more worried about her if she *wasn't* coming home in tears."

I nodded and wandered around the kitchen while he worked away.

"I made reservations for brunch at East Hampton Point," he said, "but I woke up this morning feeling like cooking. I have a coffee cake in the oven and I'm throwing together a strata now. We'll eat when Andrea gets up, assuming she does. She slept until two on a Sunday a couple of months ago."

I walked over to the part of the counter where he was cooking and picked up a stick blender. "I worked on a campaign for these guys once."

"Really? I always thought their advertising sucked."

I put the appliance down. "I was a newbie."

"Hey, who among us hasn't done our share of shitty campaigns?"

"I know what you mean. What was your worst?"

He stopped what he was doing and stared up at the ceiling. "Absolute worst?" He laughed. "Probably Leg Dreams pantyhose."

"Oh my God, you didn't do the 'better than skin' campaign, did you?"

He offered me an exaggerated shudder. "Jeez, no. I've never in my life been that bad. But mine was the campaign they *left* to switch to 'better than skin.' And really, it was dreadful. All of these women showing off their legs in preposterous situations. The jingle was even worse. Sounded like third-rate Madonna. I must have suffered an undetected head injury before I did that one."

"Yeah, I've had a few head injuries myself. I once had an animated cat prancing around to 'Great Balls of Fire.'"

"Not for pantyhose, I hope."

"Flea and tick collars."

"Ouch."

We proceeded to put together a list of the absolute worst advertising we'd ever seen. Local cable ads were disqualified for obvious reasons, and Prince insisted that we each include at least one each of our own, though I had a feeling that neither of us had ever stooped low enough to truly qualify. Certainly he hadn't, anyway. I still hadn't seen the outtake reel that Prince promised when we had our first lunch, but he told me he'd show it to me later.

The strata eventually got into the oven and Andrea came downstairs about a quarter to eleven, fresh from the shower. She moved languorously about the kitchen, though she didn't seem groggy at all. We again decided to eat out on the deck.

"I can't believe the weather is even nicer today than it was yesterday," I said, sipping on a Bloody Mary. "Perfect for crawling along the L.I.E., I guess."

"What time is Carl picking you up?" Prince said.

"Three."

He went inside and retrieved his cell phone. "I'm gonna call and tell him to forget it. Stay here and you can drive back into the City with us in the morning. We'll take a ride out to Montauk. I don't know how often you've been out there, but it's very dramatic, especially this time of year. Unless, of course, you need to be back in town tonight."

"No, that would be great. I'd love to stay." It probably meant getting to the office later than I usually did, but they would forgive me. At this point, if they didn't forgive me, it might not matter much, anyway.

It would also mean that for the second workday in a row I wouldn't be picking Daz up. That was going to take some explaining. This weekend had been such a diversion, I hadn't really thought about his party or about how pissed off we had been with each other. Now that some time had passed, my own anger felt pretty trivial. The softball thing was just silly. And the Michelle thing? I'd have to deal with it. Hey, if I wasn't going to be working with her any longer, maybe I could finally get around to asking Carnie out instead.

I decided that I would come totally clean with Daz on Monday. I'd let this thing go too far without involving him. I also decided at that very moment to give it one more try to make him part of the package with K&C.

"Curt, do you know anything about Eric Dazman?"

He smiled. "Keane told me you might bring his name up at some point this weekend."

"He really is great."

"I'm sure he is. His visuals are certainly arresting enough. Just two problems. The first is that the art director in the downtown office might be the only valuable person there. The other is that I hear your friend Eric is a little on the lax side."

"Lax?" I said with absolute wonderment in my voice. "Where did you hear something like that?"

"That isn't really relevant."

It certainly seemed relevant to me, but the expression on Prince's face made it clear that I wasn't going to get an answer. "I just don't know how anyone who knew Daz could say that."

"Rich, maybe you're such a natural that you don't even realize it, but the big jobs have to go to people who are absolutely committed. Who think advertising in their sleep."

"What about not going full-throttle indefinitely?"

"There's a difference. When you and I dial it back, we can still get up to cruising speed in a matter of seconds. That's not what I hear about Mr. Dazman."

I really had no idea what he was talking about. There was no question that making it mattered less to Daz than it did to me, but he was sensational at what he did, and he *never* missed a deadline. How could Prince have even heard that Daz was anything but efficient? Who would have said something like that to him? We always went out of the way to leave the client happy.

I wanted to pursue this further, but something about the way Prince had dismissed him told me it was pointless to continue to pitch for Daz – and that doing so might diminish my own chances at K&C. I would have to work out my issues about splitting up the team on my own. If I wound up getting the job with Kander and Craft, I would make sure that Daz and I still got as much play time as we could. Meanwhile, once I was in the door, it would be easier to eventually get Daz on the team.

By the time we got into the car at six-thirty the next morning to make the long drive to Manhattan, I was utterly convinced that I was ready to split the professional side of Flash and Dazzle. Curt Prince didn't do a hard sell on me. He didn't dangle money or objects before my eyes (in fact, he didn't make an offer to me at all). What he did do was show me in the most persuasive possible way what K&C offered that neither The Creative Shop nor any other agency – including my own – could: Prince himself. If he was intimately related to the rebuilding of K&C Downtown, then I needed to consider very seriously any opportunity to be part of that process. The chance to learn – all kinds of things – from the master was too persuasive.

When he dropped me off in front of my office nearly three hours later, I leaned over and kissed Andrea on the cheek and then clasped Prince's hand with both of mine. I thanked him profusely for a great weekend and told him I looked forward to continuing our conversation.

I was buzzed. Truly, truly buzzed.

There were approximately seven minutes left before I fell off of this high-wire.

The chapter about our brief stay in the hospital

Carnie was standing in the doorway as I approached my office. Her expression was much more serious than it usually was, but I never could have guessed why.

"Rich, where have you been?" she said, sounding way more like a scolding parent than anyone her age should.

I looked at my watch. "I'm a little late. What's the big deal? There isn't anything going on this morning." I said this casually, but I was a little worried that I'd blown something. I didn't have my phone with me, so that meant I didn't have my calendar. Was it possible that I'd forgotten a meeting? Did blissing out on ocean breezes and the Hamptons Pantry make me so giddy that I'd lost track of my responsibilities? I was planning to take my work at The Shop very seriously until the moment I left.

"Have you been home yet?" Carnie said, which seemed like a truly ridiculous question since I was holding my overnight bag. I nodded toward it and didn't say anything.

"That means you don't know about Daz."

I stopped walking. People don't say something like that the way Carnie had just said it before they told you about the great party the guy threw Saturday night, or some goofy practical joke he pulled off, or about how he spent the entire time making out with Michelle in the corner. In that moment, I knew there was trouble, though I hadn't begun to understand how much.

"What's wrong?" I said, still rooted to my spot in the hallway.

"Rich, you didn't answer your cell phone all weekend," Carnie said mournfully.

This was unnerving me. "What's wrong with Daz?" I said, my concern growing by the millisecond.

Carnie leaned against the wall. "He's in the hospital."

For some reason, hearing he was in the hospital temporarily eased my mind. I imagined his breaking his ankle while dancing on a table or some such ridiculous thing. This was something Daz was more than a little capable of doing to himself. In fact, it was amazing that he hadn't suffered some kind of injury in all the time I'd known him, considering how reckless he was with his body.

"What did he do?" I said, my posture relaxing, taking a few more steps toward Carnie, assuming we could have the rest of the conversation in my office.

"It was like two in the morning on Saturday night," she said, her back now pressed against the door. "The party started to wind down, but not *that* much, you know? Daz went to get some more tequila in the kitchen and he just collapsed."

This stopped me again. I was probably a foot-and-a-half away from her. "He collapsed?"

"He just landed on the floor. Really, really hard. He was completely unconscious when we got to him. It was incredibly scary. We got an ambulance and Michelle and Chess and I spent the whole night and most of yesterday at the hospital." She looked down at the floor and held a hand to her face. I finally noticed that her eyes were sunken and rimmed with red.

"Do they know what it is?"

She looked up at me again. Then she started to cry, which made me very, very upset. I was forcing her to relive this and I wished I didn't have to make her go through it, but it was essential that I have this information. "The doctors won't talk to us. They put him through all of these tests yesterday and the results are due today."

I finally made it into my office. I put my overnight bag down, and then quickly headed back out again. "I'm going to the hospital. St. Luke's, I assume."

"Yeah. Listen, Rich; Daz is pretty out of it and I don't think the doctors will tell you anything more than they told us. They say we're not family."

I shook my head in mild recrimination. "I *am* family. I'll let you know as soon as I find out what's going on."

———

I got a cab going uptown the moment I hit the street. During the ten minutes it took to get to the area near Columbia University where the hospital was, I tried to process what Carnie had told me. Daz passed out and the hospital was running a battery of tests. That could mean anything. For the first time, his falling asleep while we played *Search and Destroy* and his running off to vomit at work and his lax performance on the softball field started to make a little more sense. Maybe he had Epstein-Barr Syndrome or something that required a few lifestyle changes but was otherwise easily treatable. Maybe he was anemic and just needed to take iron

supplements and eat spinach for the first time in his life.
Maybe it could all be solved if he just gave up Cap'n
Crunch. The solution was simple. This wasn't anything
to panic over. I began to sell myself on this line of thinking. This wasn't a big deal, just something that required
a course correction.

When I got into the hospital, though, I began to feel
apprehensive. I'd spent virtually no time in hospitals in
my life. One of the only times I could recall was when
I got stitches in my left leg after a really nasty bike-rid-
ing spill when I was thirteen. That wasn't a particularly
pleasant experience, though I kind of assumed the scars
it left behind were plainly visible to the naked eye. I
also went to the hospital to see my grandmother when
she was dying, but I only stayed about fifteen minutes
before my sister and I were excused, so I don't think that
had much of an impact on me either. Still, entering the
lobby made me uneasy. I couldn't think of many positive things that happened in hospitals. People had babies
there, but I never went to visit someone who'd just had
a baby. If Daz was here, it was not a good thing. This
wouldn't be simple, and it wasn't just going to go away.

I got up to his floor, but they didn't let me into his
room right away. A nurse told me that his doctors were
talking to him at that very moment. I wanted to hear
this conversation, thinking totally irrationally that my
being present could somehow change the diagnosis. Bad
things didn't happen to us when we were together.

I sat in a chair a couple of doors down and waited
intently. I couldn't believe that I had been luxuriating
in East Hampton – even extending my stay to go to a
movie and drink margaritas with Prince and Andrea last
night – while my best friend was lying in a hospital bed.

I should have been the one to call for an ambulance. I should have been there with him all day yesterday, and now that I was there with him, the fact that I had to wait longer to see him was physically painful.

I sat/fidgeted/paced for maybe twenty minutes when two doctors stepped out of his room. I tried to read something in their expressions but got nothing. I'm sure medical schools offer entire courses on maintaining poker faces when those close to the afflicted might be nearby. When they left, I got up. I didn't want to spend another second without seeing Daz.

As I entered, Daz was staring up at the ceiling. He didn't look down at me right away. His arm was hooked up to an IV, and he had one of those air tubes in his nose that I only recently learned didn't go all the way down your throat. He finally glanced over at me, a wan expression on his face. He looked absolutely wasted.

"I guess they finally got word to you," he said weakly. "How was your reunion?"

"Who gives a shit how my reunion was?" I said, walking toward his bedside. "What's going on here?"

He smiled, though it seemed like an effort to do so. "This is what happens when you don't come to pick me up in the morning. I wind up in the hospital."

I feigned contrition, though the thought crossed my mind that part of this was my fault. I'd messed with our karma. I patted the edge of the bed, a little concerned about touching him. "Come on, let's get out of here. We have stuff to do." If I could use that trick to roust him out of his own bed, it should work here too, right?

"Yeah, you might have to do that stuff yourself. Looks like I'm a little laid up."

I pulled a chair next to his bed and sat down. I felt very nervous, incredibly jittery. I wanted him to tell me that everything was okay. I wanted us to be back at my place watching *The Amazing Spider-Man* on the Blu-ray player or back at his place playing air hockey. "Did they tell you anything?"

He chuckled, though it was more like an expulsion of air from his body. "Yeah, they told me something."

I felt my mouth go dry. "Do I get to know?"

He grimaced. "It's better if you don't know. Trust me on this one."

I leaned into the bed. "Daz, tell me."

He made real eye contact with me for the first time, and in this moment he seemed absolutely foreign. He was weak and miserable and beaten down. The vision made me unbelievably sad.

"I have brain cancer," he said thinly.

You know, it really doesn't matter how many horrible things you imagine before hearing news like this. While I was in the cab and then outside his room trying to convince myself that this had something to do with his diet, I'd had the other side of the argument at the same time. I'd already considered the possibility that there was something terribly wrong with him. I even allowed the thought to creep into my head that he might be dead before I got to see him. None of that prepared me, though, for hearing that he was seriously sick. What was the point of preparing for the worst if it hit you like an uppercut from a heavyweight champion anyway?

"How is that possible?" I said.

"I don't think I know how to answer that question."

"I mean, shouldn't you have symptoms? You've been tired and stuff, but there should have been something more than that, no? People don't *come down* with brain cancer the way someone comes down with the flu."

Daz regarded me for a moment before speaking. "The tumor is in my temporal lobe. There aren't a lot of symptoms. Though I have some great shit to look forward to in the near future."

"Jesus," I said, marveling at the ways nature had of stabbing you in the back. "What are you going to do about it?"

He offered another expulsion of air. "I was thinking about getting really drunk."

"I mean about treatment."

He looked up at the ceiling again and didn't say anything for several minutes. I thought about prodding him, but realized he couldn't move from this place until he was ready. This might have been the longest single break in a conversation between us that didn't involve video games or loud music. He was still looking at the ceiling when he said, "It's really far along, Rich. There isn't a whole lot of point to treatment."

I recoiled in my chair. It was almost as though he'd blown me back in my seat. I looked up at the ceiling myself, though doing so certainly hadn't seemed to offer any reasonable answers to Daz. "How can it be really far along? Wouldn't there be some kind of indication of this in your blood tests or something? Are you telling me that this disease comes with absolutely *no* clues?"

He looked back over in my direction, but not really at me. "Pretty much, yeah. And when you're my age, these things grow very quickly. Not to mention the fact that I haven't had a blood test since my last physical for the Michigan soccer team."

"What are you talking about?"

He seemed mystified by this question. "What part of that don't you understand?"

Now that I thought about it, I never remembered Daz going to see a doctor. This wasn't the kind of thing you gave a huge amount of thought to when you were our age, but still I'd been getting yearly checkups my entire life.

"I'm having a difficult time comprehending all of this," I said. I was having a difficult time doing most things at that point. My skin prickled and I felt a little lightheaded.

He smiled. It was the closest thing to his real smile I'd seen since I got here. "Gee, maybe you should get your head examined."

I smirked, and I could see that this pleased him. I wanted to hug him, make some kind of real physical contact, but I was afraid that if I did we'd both turn into blubbering idiots. Instead, I pounded the mattress. "Shit," I said, "do you know what this means?"

"Sorta."

"It means I'm gonna have to come up with a name for that damn car completely on my own."

That got a real laugh from him. "*Brilliante*," he said dreamily.

I shook my head vigorously. "Daz, you know, you may be sick and all and I guess that means I'm supposed to be nice to you, but *Brilliante* still really sucks as a name for a car."

He quickly raised and lowered his left arm (the one without the IV) on the bed, which caused the sheet covering him to ripple. "I can't help you, then."

"Yeah, thanks for nothing," I said broadly, making sure he understood that I was joking with him. My mind cast around for something else to talk about. Did he want to discuss how he was feeling? Did he want me to make it go away for him for a couple of minutes? Again there was a pause in our conversation.

Daz tilted his head back and covered it with a forearm. "Figures that this would happen just as I'd started streaming every episode of *Cheers* in order. I'll probably kick off before I get to the Kirstie Alley shows."

I found this statement to be so totally absurd that I laughed out loud. This made Daz laugh, and then we suddenly both laughed without stopping for a long time. We'd done this so many times before, goading each other with laughter. While it lasted this time, things almost seemed a little normal. If anything could possibly seem normal when your best friend was in a white hospital gown and he'd just told you he was terminally ill. As we wound down from this, a doctor came into the room and asked me to step out.

I left the room feeling hugely unsettled. I wanted us to keep laughing. I wanted this to be an elaborate practical joke. I wanted to go back into his room to learn that Daz was just putting me on as revenge for not picking him up on Friday. I knew there was absolutely no chance to get what I wanted.

Daz was dying. This was utterly, undeniably, real.

I couldn't sit while I was outside, even though my legs felt wobbly. I thought about calling Carnie to let her and everyone at The Shop know what was going on, but I didn't want to be busy doing something else when Daz became available again. This reminded me that I still didn't have my cell phone – a cell phone with probably a dozen messages trying to let me know what was happening while I was busy doing the Hamptons thing. Needing to do something, I walked down to the nurses' station and back; three times in all before the door opened.

Daz had a very different expression on his face when I got back into the room. I couldn't imagine that there was anything the doctor could have told him that was more sobering than what he already knew, but he looked at me differently now. If possible, he seemed even sadder.

"We talked about options," he said.

This gave me a tiny bit of hope. "You mean experimental treatments, that sort of thing?"

"I mean options regarding where I want to finish things out." He made eye contact with me, and I really thought in that second that I was going to start crying. The words "finish things out" clutched at me. "I don't want to stay here. I don't want to go to a hospice. I want to go back to my place."

"Let's go," I said, moving toward the bed, trying to drive away the hurt with action. "How do you take this IV thing out?" I pretended to make a grab for it.

Daz held his hand up. "I wish it was that simple. I need to make a bunch of arrangements first."

"I'll make them for you."

"Thanks, but even if I wanted you to, I don't think they'll let you. I have to take care of it myself."

I sat down in the chair heavily. "Hospitals suck. I mean just about every single thing to do with hospitals sucks."

Daz shrugged. "This one beats the crap out of any of the ones I saw back in Manhattan."

He was talking about Manhattan, Kansas. He always thought it was hilarious that he started out in one Manhattan and wound up in the other. I always thought it was hilarious that he thought Manhattan,

Kansas even deserved mention in the same sentence as New York City, let alone that he referred to the latter as "the other." The thought momentarily distracted me from the true message in what he just said.

"How many hospitals did you see in Manhattan?" I said.

"All of them. And a few in the neighboring areas." He looked over at me and I'm sure he saw how totally confused I was by this. "This sort of thing kinda runs in my family. I had uncles on both sides – three altogether – who were taken out by brain cancer by the time they were in their early thirties. And while it isn't related, my mother was really sick a lot and then had a really bad bout with lung cancer."

I found this information almost impossible to grasp. "So you've known that this was a possibility."

"More like a probability."

How could I not have known this? "And you still decided that you should ignore doctors?"

He shook his head. "I just didn't want to hear it."

I couldn't decide what was more mind-boggling to me: that Daz chose to ignore a huge hereditary risk, that he had been running from a death sentence his entire life, or that he had completely avoided mentioning any of it to me. "If the doctors had intervened early –"

"– Flash, it's done."

I looked at him, stunned. I don't think Daz had ever said anything so abrupt to me before. Was his personality changing in front of my eyes? Could fate possibly be that cruel?

"I grew up with doctors being the equivalent to Darth Vader, okay?" he said. "I mean every time I saw one of these guys, he was telling someone else he was going to die. You tend to shy away from people who do things like that to you."

I nodded, feeling unequipped to contribute to this conversation.

His voice softened. I couldn't tell if he was having trouble getting the words out because of his condition or because of what those words were. "The thing with my mom was a freaking nightmare. I mean, at that point, I was at least a little used to the idea of my relatives going down in their prime, but when it hit that close to home, the message was a little jarring, as I'm sure you can imagine. She was convinced she was gonna die just like her two brothers had and she wasn't shy about sharing that opinion with everyone she knew and making sure they shared her anguish."

"How old were you?"

"I was thirteen. That was a knockout combo for you: full-blown puberty and your mother's potentially terminal illness. I didn't exactly personify 'grace under pressure.'"

I chuckled softly. "Daz, you've never personified grace under pressure."

His expression darkened a little, if that was possible. "Good to see you're not going to coddle me through this."

I felt chastised. "Sorry."

"No, really," he said with a little smile, "it's good to see. Anyway, everyone in the family sort of freaked out in their own custom-designed way. I'm sure it was fascinating to outsiders."

"But she turned out okay, right?"

"She didn't die, though they had to take out most of a lung to save her. She nearly killed the rest of us, but she didn't die."

I wondered how I would have handled something like that as a kid. Given how weird things were for so long with my mother, I wasn't at all sure. Then I thought about how I would handle what Daz was going through now, and I found that I couldn't begin to imagine it. In spite of what I'd just said to him about grace under pressure, he really seemed to be dealing with this news about as well as you could expect anyone to. I don't think I would have done that. I think I would have done a great deal of cursing and railing at the gods, and gotten very angry and probably demanded that every marginally conceivable treatment option be explored. I would have made the doctors miserable and my friends miserable and probably said half a dozen regrettable things every hour.

"You gonna be okay?" I said.

"Sure, I'm gonna be fine. I should be ready for the start of the softball season, though you might want to drop me down in the batting order."

"I meant are you gonna be *okay*. I'm here for you, whenever and however you need me. You know that. But do you, you know, need something to help you deal with this?"

Daz cocked an eyebrow. "You mean like hallucinogens?"

"If that's what you want."

He tipped his head forward and gave me a true, Daz-sized grin. "Are you volunteering to score drugs for me? Man, I wish I knew you were willing to do this kind of thing a long time ago."

"I'm not volunteering to score drugs for you," I said, a little irritated. I quickly got that under control. "Unless you want me to, I mean. I'd figure something out if you did. We have to know *somebody,* right? I could always go back to Alphabet City."

He set his head back softly on his pillow. "Thanks, but I think I can probably get by without the Ecstasy. I figure I have some pretty serious pharmaceuticals coming my way in the near future anyway." He leaned forward in the bed again, and I got up to try to help him move into a more comfortable position. He waved me away.

"You know, I've expected this day to come for a long time, but as it turns out, I really wasn't as ready for it as I thought I was."

"How can you possibly be ready for something like this? I mean how is that even conceivable?"

"You hear about it all the time. You know, people whose fathers and grandfathers and great-grandfathers all died of heart attacks who wake up every morning after they're thirty-five surprised to see the sun come up again. I figured I was one of those guys."

"You're not thirty-five."

"Yeah, that must be it. But you know what else? I think I also kinda convinced myself that I *wasn't* one of them. I mean this kind of thing is pretty regularly on your mind when you have the family history I have, but at the same time, I think I sold myself on the idea that I was going to be different. So much for the power of positive thinking, huh?"

"Heredity's an unforgiving master," I said morosely.

"Gee, that's a good line. Just come up with it?"

I looked up at him and nodded my head. He was wearing such a Daz-like expression in that very moment. "Yeah, I think I'll use it in the next SparkleBean campaign."

"I'm sure the Bean Brains will love it." He laughed, but that seemed to tap him out. He drew back into himself. "Listen, I could really use a hand with all the arrangements I have to make. Do you think you could help me out for a while?"

"As long as you need me."

"Sure, that's easy for you to say *now*."

I smiled at him. "Yeah, I can do anything in the short term."

"You're a hell of a friend, Flash."

We got to work, and for the next couple of hours, I served as Daz's able assistant while he arranged to spend whatever time he had left in the relative comfort of his apartment. I wanted to talk to him more about his family and how he felt and what was going on in his head, but we were caught up in the details now. All of those conversations would have to wait. But we would have them. I promised myself – both of us, really – that we would have them.

We eventually finished taking care of things. Daz would only have to spend one more night in the hospital before going home.

"I'm pretty exhausted," he said weakly. "I think I'm gonna get some sleep."

"Go ahead. I'll just hang out here, and I'll be around when you wake up."

He looked at me and I thought I saw appreciation in his eyes. Then I read something else.

"What?" I said.

"You're gonna watch me sleep?"

"I might look at a magazine or something, if that's okay with you."

"It's a little creepy."

"You don't want me to stay here while you sleep?"

"Not that I don't appreciate the thought, Flash, but no."

I felt a little hurt by this, but I hopefully didn't let it show. I stood up. "Okay, that's cool." I reached over and squeezed his arm that didn't have the IV. "I'll be back tonight."

"That'd be great."

I patted him on the shoulder and headed toward the door.

"Rich?"

"Yeah?" I said, turning back.

"Sorry about this."

I looked out the window quickly, then to the floor and then finally at Daz. "Me too."

I managed to get out of the room before I started crying. I sat in a chair in the hall for several minutes before I felt composed enough to keep going. This was so difficult to believe and impossible to accept. I felt more helpless than I'd ever felt in my life, more helpless than I ever thought I would feel.

As I walked through the hospital on my way out, I was thankful that at least we wouldn't play out our last few weeks together against this backdrop. That would have been too morbid, too much of a perversion of all the time we'd had before then. Nothing would make this better, but bringing Daz back to his apartment was at least a tiny improvement.

Even in this boggled state, I knew I hadn't fully faced the notion that I was losing Daz. I was still in shock and in more than a little bit of denial. At least when it finally hit me full force, we wouldn't be in a starched white, sterilized setting.

Daz would be home and I would be there with him.

The chapter about
taking care of business

I went back to work because I couldn't think of anyplace else to go. Being productive at work, however, was out of the question. All I could think about was Daz; what it was like for him to go through this, how frightened he must be feeling, how this wasn't anywhere near close to fair. A constant flow of people came into my office to talk about him. People from accounting and the mailroom asked about him, and it was clear from the way they did that he had some level of connection with every one of them. He was like the mayor of The Creative Shop. The thought of that provided me with one of the few smiles of the day.

People wanted details, and I found the recitation of them (at least those details that I offered) easier to deal with than the details themselves. Even when I told Michelle and Carnie and the others in our group, watching faces fall and hands raised to mouths, I found that the words gave me a little distance from reality. Talking about it was like talking about a book or some show I'd seen on television, and after I explained it to the fifth person, the words began to take on less meaning. I wished there was some way I could make Daz's tumor dissipate by simply sitting in a room with him and talking about it repeatedly until the disease became unreal.

I wondered if this would be one of those things that achieved legendary status in these hallways, if people would talk years from now about what they were doing when they learned that the great Eric Dazman had been stricken. I wanted that to be the case. I wanted to be one of the people who perpetuated it. If I was seen as nothing more than a living memorial to Daz, that would be okay with me.

Toward the end of the day, I got a call from Noel Keane. It was like getting a call from Mars. Two worlds could not have been more completely different than the one I had been in with Keane and Prince and the one I'd stepped into this morning. Keane told me he'd spoken with Prince about our weekend and that he was under the impression that things had gone very well. He wanted to get together again to have one more conversation before he could "put something on the table," and he hoped that we could do this very soon.

I didn't want to have this discussion. Not right now anyway. Maybe not ever. However, Noel Keane was a difficult guy to say no to. I told him I was in the middle of something and that it would be tough to get away, but he somehow managed to convince me to have a drink with him on Thursday. I felt a little cornered, like I was totally subject to the demands of someone else's agenda. Before we hung up, I almost told Keane that I really couldn't get together at all for a while, but I couldn't quite make myself say it. I knew that using my personal life as an excuse was unacceptable to the people at K&C, and for some reason, I wasn't ready for their pursuit to disappear on me as well at this point. This had already been such a miserable day.

After Keane's call, I got absolutely nothing accomplished. Whatever little I had been able to do before, like respond to my e-mail or fill out expense reports, became too daunting. At the same time, though, I'd already told Rupert that I was taking tomorrow off to help Daz get settled at home. Though I knew I had every excuse in the world to take a pass on the next several days, I felt like I owed The Shop more than that. To say I was a little conflicted at this point is an understatement. Rupert had been so crestfallen when I came back with the news about Daz. I couldn't just blow him off and leave him in the lurch. I needed to get something going on the car campaign. I needed to tap into the reserves, find that place I discovered on occasion that allowed me to push everything else aside and get something accomplished.

That night, several of us spent a few hours with Daz at the hospital, though Michelle couldn't make it. Daz seemed a little looser and seemed to be making an effort to keep Carnie's and Chess' spirits up. I found myself picking up on this and saying all kinds of nonsensi-cal things to keep things light. Most of the others in the room seemed baffled by my behavior, but I knew Daz understood why I was doing what I was doing. Eventually he made us leave, telling us he greatly pre-ferred sleep-over company. I think the effort to keep everyone else from breaking down had worn him out.

I went home with the intention of forcing myself to be creative, to put this night to some use, to push away the fear and the anger and the anxiety. I put on some music – one of the playlists we now wouldn't be using at the birthday party we now wouldn't be having – and settled on the couch with a yellow legal pad. The first thing I wrote on the page was the line Daz had come up with: "Only your future is brighter." I refused to get hung up on the all-too-obvious irony of that phrase and proceeded to work on variations of the line. However, nothing seemed better than what we already had. This happened sometimes. Every now and then, we hit on something in our very first session that we built the entire campaign around. It was rare when we had this level of clarity, but it did happen. I tried to think about how to set the line up in thirty-second TV and radio spots. Should I tag the ads with it? Should I use it multiple times throughout? I scribbled a number of things, but all of them were either rambling, stilted, or else just plain awkward. After about an hour, I had dozens of sentences on the pad, but none were an effective match for the line Daz had simply tossed off over pizza.

Maybe I couldn't do this without him. I'd certainly come up with my share of really good ideas over the years, but maybe that was because I had Daz to bounce things off of. Maybe I needed his creative energy to fuel my own. Wasn't that true of other great teams in the past? After all, Lennon and McCartney paled dramatically as solo artists compared to what they'd accomplished together. Was I destined to a lifetime of mediocrity – of ad campaigns the equivalent of "My Love" or "Whatever Gets You through the Night" because our duo was being torn apart? Was this some kind of karmic punishment for considering going off on my own with K&C?

I turned my attention to naming the car. I knew I could do better than *Brilliante*. Almost anything would be better than that. I thought of words that suggested light: corona, flare, beacon, blaze, sparkle, coruscation, glimmer, radiance, ray.

Dazzle? No, I didn't think so, even now.

I tried words that suggested potential: cunning, efficiency, promise.

Okay, that wasn't going anywhere.

I tried inventing words – gleamlighter, streamrider, flarefire – all of which sounded ridiculous, like something we might have found in one of our video games. I tried running words through an online translation program to see if anything looked better in another language, and then resorted to a favorite trick: searching for words on random objects. There was nothing to be discovered on the front page of the Metro section of the *New York Times*, the cheat codebook that sat on my coffee table, the bag of pretzels that sat next to that, or the DVD cover for the twenty-fifth anniversary edition of *Who Framed Roger Rabbit?* Nothing.

The word "spike" came into my head from that place from which these things come, and I gave that a little thought. A spike could indicate a sudden upsurge in a person's career or the quick acceleration generated by flooring your car's gas pedal. It could indicate the tent pole upon which you built your burgeoning profession, and it could indicate what you would do with the football after you scored that metaphoric touchdown in life's game. It had an edge to it that skewed young, but it wouldn't turn off all the forty-somethings who might be inclined to buy the car if they thought it made them seem youthful. It really wasn't bad.

I rejected it. It was up there with *Brilliante*.

I looked down at the yellow pages that held my scribbling and a few lame attempts at drawing the car in a shimmer of light. I was such a dreadful artist and you couldn't make something that looked like an automobile out of stick figures. In all, I didn't have much to show for a couple of hours. I tore the pages from the pad, crumpled them and threw them one by one into the garbage. Often a seemingly endless path of bad ideas led me to a good one, that notion again that the odds improved as you got the awful stuff out there, but I was certain I'd just gone in circles tonight.

I decided to turn on the XBox and work off the day's frustration with a little *Search and Destroy*. I set the computer to oppose me at a level of "Prepare to Get Bloody," not feeling quite up to being challenged at a "Resistance is Futile" level tonight. As I did the last time Daz and I played, I chose Blitar and set about blowing things up. This engaged me for a few minutes, and when I took down General Krus' shimmerscreen fortress, there was a massive Technicolor explosion and I actually cheered and shouted something inane. Unlike Daz, though, the XBox console didn't mutter obscenities back at me or promise retribution or try to distract me with offers of beer. After a while it became clear that the computer-operated Krus couldn't put up much of a fight at all.

I restarted the game, switching the console's skill level to the highest available, but while I lost a few allies in this new fight, the competition wasn't that much tougher. Through all the hours Daz and I had logged playing this, we'd surpassed the core programming of the game itself. That suggested all kinds of things to me, and none of them made me happy.

I took the disc for *Search and Destroy* out of the XBox, put it back in its case, and returned it to the shelf. I looked at the cheat codebook and wondered if there was any code I could input that would make the machine a more difficult foe. Of course, that wasn't what the book was for, and I'm sure there weren't many people who required that service.

It was a little after eleven, and I didn't know what to do with myself. I probably could have called some people to see what they were doing, maybe get a drink and try to commiserate and decompress for a little while. Company might be useful. After all, the only time I'd even approximated normal all day was when I was talking to others. I really wasn't in the mood, though. I almost certainly could have gone to sleep and I probably would have drifted off fairly quickly. I had awakened very early this morning. I wasn't really up for that, either. I thought about calling Daz at the hospital to see what he was doing and maybe taking a little abuse over the lame copy lines I'd come up with that night, but he'd said he was tired when we left him, and he was probably sleeping now.

I guess this was one of the reasons why they made home theatre systems with high-definition screens and surround sound. If you turned the lights off and cranked the volume up high enough to be absorbing but not so high that you got complaints from the neighbors, you could lose yourself in another world entirely.

That sounded good enough to me. I perused my shelves for a while and then put my copy of *The Matrix* on the Blu-ray player. I grabbed myself a beer and just watched. I didn't get lost. I didn't even get diverted. However, the time passed.

The chapter about best friends

I brought Daz back home the next day. Checking him out of the hospital required a ridiculous amount of paperwork, none of which I could take off his hands because I wasn't "family." The entire thing took hours, and I'm sure Daz was wondering how much of the rest of his life he would be spending trying to *get on* with the rest of his life. After that, we had trouble getting a cab, which frustrated the hell out of me because the orderly who'd taken Daz downstairs in a wheelchair wouldn't leave until I "secured transportation." I felt a very strong sense of urgency here, thinking, perhaps irrationally, that if I could get Daz away from this hospital his situation would improve. As long as he was anywhere near St. Luke's, he was still *hospitalized*, and while I didn't kid myself about something miraculous happening, I knew there was a profound difference between being hospitalized and being home.

Eventually, we were back at his building, exchanging niceties with his doorman as though this was just another day. I don't know how you break the news to the apartment staff that you have a terminal illness, and Daz didn't seem particularly interested in addressing that issue just then. I guess it wasn't terribly important for these people to know that Daz was sick, but it seemed to me they might want to. I knew they were paid to be pleasant and helpful, but, like the guy who drove me out to the Hamptons, the people in Daz's lobby always seemed to be nice to him out of something more genuine. I had to believe they would be touched to learn that he was sick and that the information should be conveyed to them gently.

When we got into the apartment, I saw that it was still messy from the party on Saturday, and while Daz sat in the massage chair, I cleaned up a little. This wasn't a strength of mine, but we couldn't just leave the stuff – including some old guacamole – lying around until his cleaning person came in a couple of days.

"No chips ground into the carpet and only one stain on the coffee table," I said as I gathered up a couple of glasses. "Was this a *tea* party?"

"Must be that you're the messy one, Flash. The rest of my friends seem to know how to handle themselves."

Daz seemed sharper and more alert today. I'd done some reading about his condition on the Web and knew that while the disease ran its course quickly, it ebbed and flowed like this. There would be stretches – at least for a little while – when he didn't seem sick at all. These would be juxtaposed against less frequent periods where he seemed weighed down and listless. Eventually, the situation would reverse and his lucid periods would become less common. All of this would be influenced by his reaction to the drugs he was taking.

The day nurse, Ana, showed up about twenty minutes after we arrived and made some changes to his bedding and gave him some pills. Other than that, I didn't know what she was going to do here. The doctors strongly recommended that he have a nurse, and Daz wasn't exactly concerned about money anymore, so he hired one. Still, all she did was give him medication, make him lunch, and watch whatever he watched on the television in the living room. I suppose she would turn out to be more valuable in the coming weeks, but she seemed extraneous at this point.

I could have sat with Daz all day, but Ana made me uncomfortable. I'm sure she wasn't particularly crazy about my being there either. She tossed me a few glances to suggest that I was in the way. Maybe she thought she couldn't put her feet up and relax, maybe take a little nap, if someone was monitoring her activities.

In the middle of the afternoon, Daz settled in with the daytime strip on the Cartoon Network, laughing and occasionally saying something to the TV. During a commercial break, he turned to me.

"Okay, one of us has an excuse for goofing off like this. What's yours?"

I was a little baffled to hear him say this and didn't answer right away. "I'm hanging out with you," I finally said softly.

"You're not sitting there trying to figure out how to catch up on all the work you've missed the last couple of days?"

"I wasn't, actually."

He looked at me skeptically, but I truly hadn't been thinking about work. Admittedly, I would normally have been thinking about what was piling up if I missed big chunks of time in the office two days in a row, but that wasn't the case now.

"Why don't you go down to The Shop for a while?" he said.

"Are you kicking me out?"

His eyes narrowed. "Did you have a plan here?"

"I'm not following you."

"Were you going to take a leave of absence so you could watch television with me every day?"

"I'm going to work a little tomorrow."

"You're going to work *a lot* tomorrow. Go to work a little today. Somebody has to maintain the legacy."

"The legacy?"

He reached over and touched me on the arm. "Rich, you need to be Flash *and* Dazzle now."

I felt tears spring to my eyes when he said this. This was obviously something I needed to get used to. I blinked quickly and looked off in the other direction, as though I was trying to find something.

"You're really gonna be all right?" I said after taking a moment to gather myself.

"I have Ana," Daz said, nodding toward the woman who hadn't seemed to notice this conversation. Then he nodded toward the TV. "And I have Scooby. I'm okay. Go do something spectacular. Or at least profitable."

So I went down to the office. It felt very strange leaving Daz's apartment, though. I really hadn't thought about how I would juggle work and his care, but obviously Daz had. He was going to send me off to the office every day with a very clear directive: *be as brilliant on your own as we have been as a team.* No pressure or anything.

I got to The Shop and tried my best to make some headway. I wasn't as terrible as I thought I was going to be. It was around six-thirty and I had already phoned Daz's apartment a couple of times during the day when he called me.

"You gotta bring me some Doritos or something when you come back. I just tried to eat maybe the single worst meal of my life."

"Really?"

He made a mock retching sound on the other end. "Is it possible for something to be tasteless and disgusting at the same time? I mean it. No flavor and yet awful. This woman is a sinister genius. Cool Ranch would be great. When are you coming over?"

"Carnie and I were just gonna talk for a few minutes about BlisterSnax Max. I'll be there in an hour if that's okay with you."

"Sounds good. Remember, Cool Ranch Doritos. The big bag. They have them in that size at the Gristedes on 86th."

"I'll bring you two."

"You're big time, Flash."

Carnie and I finished our conversation quickly, and I decided to try to offset Daz's dreadful dinner by stopping at the Carnegie Deli and buying us each one of their outsized pastrami sandwiches. Definitely not tasteless, and disgusting only in the best sense. Though I was sure he'd love the sandwich, I didn't want to disappoint him by showing up without the chips. I had the cab drop me at 86th and Broadway so I could make a quick run into Gristedes.

Ana's shift was over by the time I got there, which was a good thing since I figured she'd despise me more than she already did if she saw me bringing him another meal. I pulled out the bed tray I'd gotten for Daz earlier in the day, and his eyes widened when I produced the sandwiches. I placed a can of Dr. Brown's cream soda next to both.

"No SparkleBean?" he said.

I shrugged. "They don't carry SparkleBean at the Carnegie Deli."

"They will once our campaign gets going."

"Yeah," I said, smiling. "They probably will."

He took a bite of his pastrami and seemed supremely satisfied. I was glad he was hungry, even though it surprised me a little. I don't think I would ever eat again if I faced what he was facing now, but then again, maybe it made him savor a sandwich like this that much more.

"Get me one of these every day, okay?" he said.

I ate a stray piece of pastrami off of my wrapper. As though there wasn't already enough on my sandwich. Certain third world countries could develop obesity problems on one of these. "You'd get bored."

"Trust me, I wouldn't get bored." He took another bite and savored it. "We never went to the Carnegie often enough."

"There are always a million people there."

"No excuse. This is a singular experience. How many singular experiences do you get in your life?"

I bowed my head to acknowledge his point. I loved going to the Carnegie, but it was a huge hassle dealing with the crowds. Still, while other delis claimed they made sandwiches as good as this, I'd never had one elsewhere. Daz was right. We should have gone more often. Inconvenience shouldn't have been an issue.

We concentrated on eating for a while. I got to eat Daz's pickle. The new Beam album supplied our soundtrack. Daz got it the day it went on sale – three days before the concert we attended – because he didn't want to be unfamiliar with anything they played that night. He "studied" it repeatedly at work the next several days.

We had Doritos for dessert. Daz held up one and examined it as someone else might a fine cognac.

"Bill Franks and I would go through a bag of these a night when I was a teenager."

"Bill Franks?"

He ate the chip and washed it down with the rest of his cream soda. This really was haute cuisine for him. It made me wonder just how terrible the food Ana cooked must have been for him to reject it. "My best friend in high school."

"The guy with the Harley?"

"No, that was Frank Simmons."

"At least I got one of the names right."

"Totally different guys. Frank and I didn't hang out that much. Just when he took us for rides on his bike."

"Okay, so who's Bill Franks?"

Daz fished a few more chips out of the bag, not feeling any compunction about eating them and speaking at the same time. "I've told you about him, haven't I?"

"Yeah, you probably have, but I swear I've never heard his name before."

"Hmm," Daz said, settling back in his bed. He held the Doritos bag up to offer some to me, and when I demurred, he drew it closer to his body. "Bill and I spent almost all of high school together. I even stayed at his house for a few weeks one year. We were both on the soccer team and we used to do stuff after practice. Then once he got a car, we went out after games, eating Doritos – usually Cool Ranch, but sometimes Nacho Cheese – and drinking beer and riding all over Manhattan making a lot of noise. Sometimes we didn't come home until one or two in the morning. Every now and then we even had *company*, if you know what I mean."

"Soccer groupies."

He nodded broadly. "Don't you know it."

I reached over and grabbed a chip. "How come there aren't any advertising groupies?"

"I think that question pretty much answers itself."

I wasn't sure that it did, but it wasn't worth exploring further at the moment. "So you and Bill Franks drove around town in his convertible with adoring ladies draped all over you waiting to fulfill your every fantasy?"

"It was an '91 Taurus and I think the thing with the girls happened one time."

"That story doesn't sound as good."

"Well, you're the word man. Anyway, that was one of the things that Bill and I used to do together. We were constantly practicing, of course. I mean, even when we were in his room, we were heading a ball back and forth to one another. But he was the first guy I could really talk to, you know?"

"It must've sounded funny with the ball bouncing off your heads all the time."

Daz flashed me his patented look of disappointment, but this time I got the impression that he genuinely was disappointed. I decided to dial back the smart-ass attitude a little, the second time I'd told myself to do this in a week. Clearly I had some work to do in this area. Even acknowledging this, though, I still wasn't sure how to talk to Daz. If I softened up, would he appreciate it, or would he be upset that I was changing on him?

"No, you know, we talked about stuff. Bill wasn't the brightest guy on the planet, but he had a way of seeing things that made sense. At least they made sense to me back then. So we just had these long talks about whatever was on our minds."

It was odd to hear that this was appealing to Daz. I'd never known him to be particularly interested in any kind of long conversation unless it was about greatest guitarists or top wide receivers. I got this image of him bouncing around the room with Bill Franks like the Daz I knew but talking about hopes and dreams and fears and insecurities. It just didn't fit.

"So when was the last time you talked to Bill Franks?" I half-expected him to tell me that he'd been on the phone with him last week or that Bill Franks lived down the hall.

"Yeah, that's a story in itself," he said, settling himself down into his propped-up pillows a bit more. "I went off to Michigan on a scholarship as you well know. Bill was a pretty good player himself, but as I said, he wasn't particularly sharp. His grades weren't good enough to get him anywhere but Cloud County Community. I don't know why he even went to college. I think he thought that he'd do a good job on the soccer team, maybe pass all of his classes, and transfer someplace way the hell out of Manhattan."

"Didn't happen?"

"Not exactly. He got into drugs in a major way about ten seconds after he hit campus. It was kind of amazing to see him when I came back during winter break. He'd stopped playing soccer and got into moshing and *all* he wanted to talk about was getting high. All of this had happened in three months." Daz seemed as confused by this now as he must have been when he'd gone home that Christmas. He even seemed a little hurt.

"So you guys stopped hanging out?"

"Not right away. Actually, we spent a fair amount of time together during that vacation. You know, I got looser during my first semester at Michigan and I just figured that he got even a little looser than me. But what was weird was that he didn't want to talk about anything other than drugs. And there really isn't that much to *say* about drugs. Other than that, it was just a lot of loud music. He seemed to think he was the first person on the planet to discover The Ramones. One day, I tried to get him to kick a ball around with me and he looked at me like I was from another planet. He was done with soccer. Not enough drugs and headbanging in it for him, I guess.

"But it didn't get really bad until the summer. Even though that winter break was really strange, I looked him up when I got back. I mean, we were friends for so long, right? Anyway, he had this girlfriend now; I can't remember her name. The three of us went to a party at another friend's house and Bill was okay for a little while – borderline normal, even. But he'd gotten pretty high before he picked me up, and then he and the girl went off to get high again right after we got there. Sometime during the night, he must have taken some more stuff because he got very weird and then he and the girl started fighting. I mean physically fighting. Bill was probably close to a foot taller than her, and I was really worried about what was gonna happen. Everybody else at the party just stood around watching them, and I stepped up to him and grabbed him on the shoulder. He wheeled around to me and got right into my face. He said, 'I love you, man, but if you touch me again, I'll kill you.' Then the girl started screaming at me too. And then, because things weren't weird enough already, they started pushing each other again while they were still both screaming at me. Bill just kept saying the same thing over and over and over: 'I love you, man, but if you touch me, I'll kill you.' It was surreal."

"Did you get the hell out of there?"

"I couldn't. I really thought he was going to hurt her. So I stepped in between them. He went to take a swing at me and I just slugged him right in the jaw. He went straight down. I wasn't exactly used to punching people out, but I really connected. His girlfriend bent over him and started cursing at me. I mean it was okay for her to try to beat on him, but if anyone else touched him it was an abomination. It was unbelievably pathetic. I told her to go to hell and left the party." Daz paused to contemplate this.

"That was the last time you saw him?"

He looked at me and nodded. "That was the last time I saw him. I heard I actually broke his jaw, and I half expected him to come after me but he never did. At some point, he just moved away. I have no idea what happened to him after that."

"That's some story."

"Yeah. Heck of a way to break up a friendship." He looked over at me and I wondered what he was thinking. Certainly he couldn't think that anything like that ever would have happened between us. The one thing that was absolutely safe to assume about our friendship was that it never would have turned violent. If one of us ever even considered getting physical, the other would have laughed and defused the entire episode.

"I can't say I had any friendship end that badly. My best friend for the longest time was Toby Macklin. We met in preschool and hung together for a long time after that. He was a good guy and a huge baseball fan, and we used to talk sports twenty-four seven. We once stayed on the phone for an entire World Series game analyzing the action as it happened. When I was fourteen, his family moved to Northern California. We wrote for a while and then just got on with our lives. We probably would have stayed in touch with e-mail and Facebook if that was around back then, but writing letters turned out to be too much for both of us. I heard he got an MBA from Stanford. I always meant to send him a card or something, but I kept forgetting to do it.

"Then when I was in high school, Zach Farley became my best friend. We'd known each other since elementary school and were pretty good friends for a while, but then we sort of lost touch. He was much cooler in high school than he was when he was younger. He learned to play the drums and was in this really hot band with a bunch of older kids. I liked going to their practices and I wound up becoming their unofficial sound man. In my senior year, I traveled with them to a lot of their gigs, which was great because I got to hang out in bars I wasn't old enough to get into. Turns out there are no sound-man groupies, either, by the way.

"When it was time for us to make decisions about college, I chose Michigan and Zach – who had been accepted to places like Boston College and Virginia – decided to skip out altogether so he could stay in the band. Things got really ugly with his parents, and one night he just packed up what he had and moved into the bassist's apartment. We didn't see much of each other after that."

"Did he wind up making it?"

"No, of course not. I heard he's in dental school now. He really could play the drums, though. He'll probably wind up playing weddings on the weekend when he's fifty."

Daz laughed and shook his head. "How many times did we figure out the solutions to all the world's problems with these guys?"

"Yeah, I definitely did some of that. Zach was big on trying to solve puzzles. He considered the crisis in the Middle East and the plight of the spotted eagle to be puzzles."

"Maybe he has a future as a politician."

"Not if you heard his solutions. Zach was big on *profound*. Only thing was that 'profound' turned out to be synonymous with 'utterly ridiculous.'"

"Bill wasn't much for profundity. I mean, we talked about a lot of stuff, but it was more of the how-to-get-through-the-day variety. That and how to get laid more often."

"The subject that all good friends are required to explore at length."

"No kidding. We talked – in great detail – about nearly every girl in school. Bill liked to speculate on what each of them was like in bed, even though most of them hadn't actually been to bed with a guy yet. He had a vivid imagination and a surprising understanding of human anatomy." He shook his head and drifted off someplace for a while. "He really was a good guy, though. I wish he hadn't freaked out the way he did." It fell silent in the room. "The album is over; we need to queue something else up."

Daz had a wireless system with speakers in the living room and his bedroom that streamed music from his phone. I'd tried for years to get him to set up playlists, but he'd always resisted, arguing that he never knew in advance what he wanted to listen to.

While he decided on new music, I balled up the sandwich wrappers and took the food tray into the kitchen. I saw that Ana had cleaned up the party dishes I put in the sink, which I appreciated, since I wasn't looking forward to washing them. She might not be able to cook, but at least she didn't spend the entire afternoon watching cartoons with her patient.

"You know what I think about most when I think back on high school?" Daz said when I returned to the room. He'd switched the music to Mumford and Sons and settled back under his blankets. "The way I used the think about how my life would turn out."

"You mean because of all the stuff with cancer in your family?" I still hadn't gotten over this revelation from the day before. It was the second part of the combination punch that hit me every time I thought about Daz being seriously ill.

"That definitely. But not just that. More like what I would wind up doing with my life. How things were going to be for me."

"Did you ever think you'd wind up in the *other* Manhattan being a genius art director?"

He shook his head briskly. "Not once. To tell you the truth, I didn't even know what art directors did until I met you. When I applied to Michigan, I knew I could draw, and I knew I could make money doing it if I learned how to do it well. I figured if it was something I could make a living at someone would point me in the right direction."

"So what *were* you going to be?"

"Well, it went without saying that I was going to be the first big-time American soccer star. This would happen after my victorious performance in the Olympics and the World Cup, and I would be really famous. I even had this whole Lou Gehrig bowing out thing played out in my head."

"That's like saying you wanted to be an astronaut when you grew up."

"Yeah, something like that. But what was the point of thinking I would be a commercial artist? I mean it might be hotter than being a bean counter or something, but it hardly qualifies as stardom."

"I didn't realize you were so interested in being a star."

"A shooting star. There was a time when I was obsessed with it. I don't know, maybe it had something to do with wanting to leave a mark or something. You know, if more people know who you are, there's a better chance that someone will remember you."

This statement caught me up short. I truly didn't know how to respond to this. I suppose I should have told Daz that there would be tons of people who remembered him, but I was completely taken aback that this kind of thing was important to him. He never seemed particularly worried about anything like this. I'd always admired the fact that he could appear so laid back without ever giving anyone the impression he didn't care.

"You didn't really grow up thinking you were going to be an ad exec, did you?" he said.

"No, of course not."

"What, then?"

"Well, there were the sports fantasies of course, but they went away pretty quickly when I couldn't even crack the starting lineup on my Little League team. Then I decided I wanted to be a writer."

"You are a writer."

"A real writer. A playwright, actually."

Daz gave me one of his patented looks of disbelief. "At twelve years old you wanted to be a playwright?"

"Yeah, that probably sounds a little dorky, but we lived close to the City and we went to the theatre all the time. When I was in my early teens, my mother took me to see a production of *Six Degrees of Separation* and I decided I was going to write a play like that some day."

Daz seemed confused. "You have never even *gone* to a play since I've known you."

I shrugged. "The novelty wore off. And by the time I was a freshman at Michigan, I sort of discovered that I didn't have much to say as a playwright. I guess that's when advertising started to sound appealing."

Saying these things about myself was nearly as startling as hearing some of the things Daz had said. It had been a very long time since I thought about writing plays or using the written word in that way at all. It was almost as though I was talking about someone else. Daz and I hadn't been very good friends when my drama writing professor told me my dialogue seemed forced and my situations lacked conviction. By the time we were, I'd mothballed the whole dream.

"How'd we do?" Daz said after another pause.

"At what?"

"At becoming what we became."

"You mean aside from your not being a soccer superstar and my not winning a Pulitzer Prize?"

"Yeah, that."

I sat back and thought for a moment. "I think we did okay."

"Do you?"

I wanted to say that it wasn't time to talk about "how we did," that people in their late-twenties didn't need to consider this sort of thing, but of course I couldn't. Not with Daz.

"Yeah. We did, didn't we? I mean we have a lot of fun, we make a lot of money, we get a lot of compliments, and we have a lot of friends. That says something, doesn't it?"

"It says something." Daz looked off in the middle distance briefly. "I'm glad you think we did okay." He looked at me with an expression that I expected to show sadness or at least a little regret, but which actually seemed somewhat satisfied.

The conversation wound down after that. I told him a little bit about the minimal amount of work I'd gotten done at the office, and he gave me instructions for handling the softball team in his absence (I suggested that we turn the team over to someone else, but he wouldn't allow me to resign my captaincy). When the Mumford songs ended, Daz turned the television on, and we settled back to watch a simple-minded movie on HBO.

For the second time in two days, though, I'd come out of a conversation with Daz feeling a little disoriented, a little surprised, and a little melancholy. I couldn't remember ever before feeling that way after we talked.

It wasn't an unpleasant feeling. Surprising, but not unpleasant. Not at all.

The chapter about broken hearts

We referred to ourselves as S.U.L.K. – the Stiff Upper Lip Klub. The group of us at The Shop who were Daz's closest friends gathered informally but regularly to commiserate about his condition and about our feelings about his condition. I suppose it was a necessary exercise, one that kept all of us on a more even keel. Given how much we cared about Daz, it would have been a mistake to keep everything we thought to ourselves.

There were a couple of fundamental requirements to membership in S.U.L.K. – no crying and no maudlin sentiments. The absolute last thing any of us needed at this point was to bring each other down more than we already were. This was about support, not wallowing. We were probably all doing more than enough of the latter on our own.

Michelle called an impromptu S.U.L.K. meeting the next morning. We were the only two members present.

"He's all settled in?" she said, sitting in a chair opposite my desk and putting down her cup of coffee.

"He is. I stopped by this morning to make sure the day nurse showed up, and she was right on time. Daz says she's an awful cook, but she seems okay otherwise, even though I'm not entirely sure why she needs to be there all day. She brings him some pills and fluffs up his pillows and sits around a lot. I think he probably could have gone a little while longer without hiring her."

"He's in bed?"

"He doesn't *have* to be in bed. He can move around if he wants. He spent some time hanging out in the massage chair yesterday and then some more time on the couch. But I get the feeling that he's gonna spend most of his time in bed. He just seems more comfortable there."

I'd obviously painted a disturbing image for Michelle. She glanced away from me for a long moment. When she looked back, she seemed dangerously close to disqualifying herself from membership in our *Klub*.

"Wouldn't it be better if he moved around more?" she said with a little catch in her throat.

"Better in what way?"

"I don't know, it would seem less … resigned, I guess."

I leaned forward and touched her hand. I never would have done something like this with her under any other circumstance. That I had recently harbored lustful yearnings toward her seemed like an entirely separate stage in my life, swept away in the maelstrom of the last few days. "Daz *is* resigned, Michelle. He's been resigned for a long time without telling any of us about it."

"So he's just settling in to die?"

"I don't know if he's looking at it exactly that way, but I think he knows he isn't going to beat this disease."

She nodded and looked away again. "That's so incredibly sad." She took a deep breath and made a visible effort to try to pull herself together. She tapped her fingernails on her leg and she looked down to watch them. "I know this is terrible, but I'm having trouble getting myself over there. I'm afraid to see him this way."

"He looks like Daz."

"But he's different. I don't think I could be with him without seeing that."

I didn't want to trivialize her feelings, but at the same time, it seemed important for both of them that she get over this. "I think he'd really appreciate a visit. Especially from you."

She stopped her tapping and tilted her head. "What do you mean by that?"

I realized that I still had no idea what had gone on between them that night last week or in the days after. "I just think you're important to him and that it's especially meaningful for him to see the people who are important to him right now."

She closed her eyes and opened them very slowly. She reached for her coffee. "I'll get over there. Maybe I can get Carnie or Brad to come along with me after work."

"I'll be with him tonight. Why don't you guys try to see him this afternoon? I'm sure he'll appreciate the company, and he's forbidden me from coming to see him during business hours – thinks I'm supposed to *work* or something."

"All right, we'll try." She took another sip of her coffee. I wasn't sure if we were done with the conversation or not. This wouldn't have been the first time in the last couple of days that I'd sat silently in this office with another friend of Daz's.

"Listen," she said after a long pause, "remember what we talked about when we had that drink? I've decided that I'm gonna go pay my family a little visit."

"Okay."

"Maybe a little more than a little, actually. I'm thinking about spending a month out there."

"A month?" This didn't sound like a vacation. It sounded like relocation scouting.

"I need to figure some stuff out. I think you had me **sold** on sticking with New York when we talked, but then I started to lean in the other direction again. I need to wrap my mind around what I'm going to do with the rest of my life. I'm feeling pretty off these days. I realize The Shop won't pay me for a month, but I have a couple of weeks of vacation and I hope you can just spare me for the rest of the time."

This was one of the things about being a boss I still hadn't mastered. Was I supposed to tell Michelle that there was a reason employees got a specified amount of vacation time and that she couldn't have more than that, or was I supposed to do what I really wanted to do and just let her have as much room as she needed? If we hadn't been friends the past few years, would I have had a different reaction entirely? I wanted to believe that wouldn't have been the case.

"I'll talk to Steve about it. I'm sure we can work something out." I looked at her carefully. "Are you okay?"

"No, not really," she said softly. "I'm even a little less okay now after the thing with Daz. I think I'm having what John Mayer would call a 'quarter-life crisis.'"

Again, I reached out for her hand. I wasn't typically a toucher, but it seemed like Michelle needed to be touched. "Do what you have to do. Just try not to leave us forever."

She smiled sadly and got up to leave. "I'll gather some people up for a field trip to see Daz this afternoon."

"He'll really like that."

She hesitated at the doorway. "Do you think it's awful that I haven't been there yet and that I feel a little weird about going to see him?"

"You're about to make up for it, right?"

She nodded.

I didn't know what she was going through, couldn't comprehend it, really, but one of the unspoken by-laws of S.U.L.K. was that we didn't judge how we were each dealing with this crisis – as long as everyone kept a stiff upper lip. So far, Michelle had teetered on the edge of that requirement, but didn't go over – at least not in my presence.

"He really looks just like the regular Daz?" she said.

"Almost a hundred percent like the real thing."

"Guess I'll see for myself this afternoon."

———

Just before noon, Steve Rupert called me down to his office. It was obvious he'd been having an awful day. Even the especially terrible tie he wore seemed to suggest as much.

"I just came back from seeing Daz," he said.

"Everything all right?"

"He seems fine. I mean, as fine as you can be under these circumstances. He was listening to all of the Allman Brothers Band's albums in order. This seemed to keep him entertained."

"Great, that means he'll be up to the lame ones by the time I get there tonight."

Rupert perused his cluttered desk, as though trying to put his hands on something. "I don't think the nurse likes his taste in music."

I leaned against the door frame. "That should be the hardest thing she ever has to deal with."

He looked up from his casting about and motioned me to sit down. That was something he almost never did. Our conversations in his office tended to be brisk and were either too quick or too provocative for sitting down. I moved over to his sofa.

"I'm sure you don't want to talk about this," he said in the same tone of voice he used to tell me a client had rejected a concept, "and I *know* I don't want to talk about this. But we have to. The Koreans will be here in ten days."

I threw up a hand. "I'm on it. Don't worry about it. We have some decent ideas."

He got up from behind his desk and sat in a chair near me. "Rich, how are you planning to *execute* the ideas?"

"They're not ready to be executed yet. We're still refining the pitch."

Rupert pulled his lips together tightly and then said, "We have to talk about hooking you up with another art director."

I swear until that moment, I hadn't even thought about it. I was fully cognizant that Daz wasn't coming back to work, and I was equally cognizant that I couldn't do the whole thing by myself since most ad campaigns consisted of something other than stick figures. For whatever reason, though – and I can think of several – it hadn't registered that not only would Daz and I not be a team anymore, but that someone else would need to come in to take his place.

"Who'd you have in mind?" I said tentatively.

Rupert seemed relieved that the conversation was underway. He put his hands on his knees. "I'm thinking about Vance Beals."

Vance had been with The Shop a couple of years and had done some very good work. He was definitely the hottest emerging art guy at the agency, and I knew that several of the writers had collaborated well with him. "Vance is good."

"Do you think the two of you can work together?"

I shrugged. "I'm sure we can work together." I gazed at Steve carefully. "On this project, right?"

"Yeah, to start."

"On this project. Maybe someone else can work with me on BlisterSnax and someone else on SparkleBean and we can just keep going that way for a while. This way no one needs to deal with too much of my insanity."

He leaned back. "Do you really think that's the best way to approach it?"

I stood up without even realizing that I was doing so. "I'm not just gonna partner up with another art director, Steve. I'm *not* doing that." The words came out of me forcefully and I think they threw Rupert for a loop.

He calmly motioned me to sit back down. "I'm not sure having my top guy flitting around from art director to art director is a great idea. That can't be the best way to work, and it probably isn't the best thing for you either. As much as both of us hate the idea, we need to think about the future, Rich."

It angered me that he'd brought this up, though the small part of me that was being rational at the moment understood that it was his job to do so. A tiny voice in the back of my mind suggested that I shouldn't be getting worked up about this, that in addition to being too emotional about Daz right now to think clearly, I also had a drink date with Noel Keane on Thursday. The latter really wasn't the point, though. I currently worked at The Creative Shop. There was an excellent chance that I would continue to work at The Creative Shop for some time. Regardless, I was a staff member of The Creative Shop until that was no longer the case.

"Steve, trust me when I say that I understand all the things we need to do, but you have to understand that it's going to take me a little time to get used to the new state of things. You want me to work with Vance on the car campaign, I'll do that. But if you're telling me that Vance is my new partner, I'm gonna have to refuse. No reflection on Vance, but I'm not doing new partners right now."

Rupert looked out his window for a while. If anything, he was looking more miserable now than he'd looked when I walked into his office. After a lengthy pause, he turned back to me.

"I realize this is hard for you. I'm not trying to force anyone down your throat and I'm not trying to make you *move on*, but I have to keep things running here, even when I don't want to. Work with Vance on the car campaign. We'll deal with the other stuff as the needs arise."

I stood up again, this time without excess propulsion. "Thanks, Steve. I don't mean to be difficult here. I'm sure I can work with Vance, and I'm sure we'll get some good stuff on the table."

"I know you will."

"It's been a while since I've done anything like this."

"I know it has."

"It might take me some time."

"It might. We'll play it out."

Before I left, I talked to him about Michelle's request for extended time off. We got through this conversation easily, with Rupert agreeing to give Michelle one of the two extra weeks as comp time for all the late nights she'd put in. I was glad we'd come to a solution without any hassles. It was so much simpler speaking about someone else's issues than speaking about my own.

———

For dinner, I got us Asian food from Ruby Foo's. Lobster and Shrimp Spring Rolls, Tamarind-glazed Baby Back Ribs, Seven-flavor Beef and Thai Chile Garlic Chicken. All very intense – Daz's palate was not a delicate one – and all very delicious.

"Ana somehow made a hamburger seem tasteless today. I think I'll tell her to stop trying. We'll stick to delivery from now on. I hope it won't hurt her feelings."

"She'll get over it."

He looked at the collection of foil containers I'd laid out on his bed tray. "You know, you didn't have to go to Ruby Foo's. The Hunan Wok around the corner is perfectly fine."

"We aren't doing *perfectly fine* right now. We're doing state-of-the-art."

He looked at me appreciatively. "Thanks. This is great."

I was glad to see that Daz had an appetite again. I knew that wouldn't always be the case. I was a little short on specifics regarding the progress of this illness. You could only get so much of this from the Web and, while there were people I could call for details and hundreds of books on the subject, I couldn't get myself to do that. I knew at some point soon, he would get a lot less mobile and that his faculties would diminish rapidly from there. To me, that meant we had to make the most out of every remaining moment. That's really all I needed to understand.

"Listen," I said. "I had a conversation with Steve today about the car campaign. He wants Vance to hook up with me on it."

Daz put down his chopsticks and looked skyward. Then he looked down at his bed and uttered an obscenity. I felt awful. I hadn't handled that nearly as delicately as I should have and I castigated myself for not finding a more sensitive way to convey this information.

"Daz, I don't know what to say," I said, feeling chastened.

He shook his head, laughed, and filled his face with beef. "Asshole," he said, still chewing. "Steve talked to me about it this morning. What did you think I expected you to do, retire?"

"You're all right with it?"

"The Vance part or the tossing me on the trash heap part?"

I recovered quickly. "The Vance part. I don't care what you think about the other thing."

Daz flicked some rice at me with his chopsticks. "He has some skills. Sucks at motion. Always goes for the same angle. But he's really good at a lot of stuff and he'll get better."

"This isn't a long-term thing. I'm just working with him on this project."

He nodded. I wondered if he thought I'd said that just to make him feel better. "Got a name yet?"

I grimaced. "Watch this space."

He laughed. "You're useless without me."

"Did I ever argue that point? In this specific case, however, I was also useless *with* you."

"Only one of us believes that."

"Oh, come on; you're not still trying to sell me on that *Brilliante* thing, are you?"

"Hey, it's your account *with Vance* now."

We ate quietly for a few minutes. Dickie Betts of the Allman Brothers was in the midst of one of his long, looping guitar solos. I tried to get Daz to explain to me why he was listening to all of this band's albums in order, but he didn't really have an explanation. As much as I admired their music and their musicianship, the first thing that always came into my mind when I thought about the Allman Brothers was how two band members had died in motorcycle accidents within a year of one another – including the irreplaceable Duane Allman, one of the great rock guitarists of all time.

"Did Michelle come to see you this afternoon?" I said.

"Yeah, for a little while. She had Chess and Brad with her. We watched *Johnny Test* together."

"I can't think of a more exciting way to spend the afternoon. Did she tell you she's going back to Indiana for a while?"

I could tell from Daz's expression that she hadn't. A look of hurt and confusion crossed his face. Again, I felt as though I'd approached a topic the wrong way, and this time Daz wasn't just playing me with his reaction.

"When is she going?" he said quietly.

"We didn't work that out yet. Sometime next week, probably."

I could see that Daz was replaying the afternoon's conversation in his head. He probably wasn't thinking about whether he'd somehow missed this announcement, but rather what they'd talked about instead. "No, she didn't say anything."

I took a drink of my club soda and watched Daz carefully. "What happened with the two of you, anyway?"

"What do you mean?" he said blankly.

"At the bar last week. You know, the thing I asked you about a half-dozen different ways the next day? You whispered something in her ear and then the two of you left together. That usually means only one thing."

His face opened up and he laughed loudly. "You really thought we went off to sleep together?"

"Kinda appeared that way," I said, a little unsteady.

"In my wildest dreams, maybe. Actually, in my wild-est dreams, *definitely*. But no, we didn't sleep together."

"Then what was that thing in the bar about?"

"I thought I was going to pass out."

"Huh?"

"I felt really awful and I thought I was going to pass out, and it seemed like a bad idea to do it in the bar. The crowds, the potential for getting stomped on, the possibility of someone screaming and all. I asked her to get me into a cab and she wound up taking me home."

I found this news disorienting. "Why didn't you ask me to do it?"

"Two reasons. One: she's a lot better looking than you are. If a woman like Michelle is willing to take you home – and I was fairly sure she would be – you don't look for alternatives. I also didn't want you to worry."

"So you worried Michelle instead?"

"It's different," he said, throwing me an expression that suggested I should have been bright enough to fig-ure that one out myself.

"And as it turns out, I would have had a genuine reason to worry."

He looked at me soberly. "I know that. I was already worrying enough for the two of us. This didn't feel like a stuffy nose, if you know what I mean."

I shook my head in frustration and bewilderment. I couldn't decide whether I should be offended or touched that he'd tried to spare me. Then I thought about the scene between him and Michelle again and chuckled. "I really thought you two were getting it on."

"Trust me, you would have heard."

"You do sort of have a thing for her, though, right?"

"Not really relevant any longer."

"It's always relevant. Even if you don't do anything about it, it's relevant."

"In that case, I've had numerous relevant relationships in my life."

Neither Daz nor I had been particularly successful daters since we'd gotten to New York. I sort of understood why that was from my perspective but I really didn't get it from Daz's. He was an incredibly nice, open-hearted guy, he was decent looking, and he had plenty of extra cash. From my perspective, that made him a prime candidate for a serious relationship or even a series of them. For whatever reason, though, he never really sustained – or even really tried to sustain – a romance.

"You know which woman I always thought you would get somewhere with?" I said. "Veronica Bishop."

"Really?" He smiled, perhaps at the memory of her. "Why do you say that?"

"You guys just seemed really into each other. You know, more than just for sex."

Veronica and Daz had dated throughout the latter part of the spring two years ago. It was the closest he'd come to getting seriously involved with a woman, and for a while it seemed like something significant was happening between them. Then suddenly they split up and he wouldn't talk about it.

"Veronica was great. I think she kinda got me, too. But we had this intense period where it seemed like it was going to go one way or the other and I just double-clutched. I don't know why we broke up. It was loud, if I remember correctly."

I'm sure he remembered correctly. I'm sure he remembered everything about it. "It really seemed to me that she was crazy about you."

"Yeah, what the hell do you know?"

"Were you upset about it?" I never would have asked that question two days ago, because I would have assumed that I always knew when he was upset. His reaction to it at the time seemed rather subdued, and I even wondered if I'd mistaken the level of his affection for her.

"It got to me. Not like head-under-the-pillow got to me, but definitely something. I stopped eating Warheads for a week."

"Translation, please."

He looked at me crossly, as though he was perturbed that he had to explain. "I love that candy and I was *denying* myself. It was a form of self-flagellation."

"Right, that makes sense," I said, though I didn't really think it did. I tried to retrofit this latest bit of insight into Daz's character to other situations in our past. Had there been times when he'd avoided strawberry toothpaste or Dave Matthews songs or new episodes of *Survivor* to punish himself for failing at something? Was this a signal I should have picked up on in the past?

"You know, I felt the same way about you and Liz," he said.

"That you needed to flagellate yourself?"

"That you were going to be together for a long time, you idiot."

Liz Painter was an amazing woman. Smart, clever, incredibly physical, and exciting enough to keep me on my toes without leaving me completely turned around on a daily basis. Since I'd known Daz, she was the woman I dated the longest – nearly three months in the summer and fall of '09. I was intrigued by how things were developing – until she disappeared for a long weekend, came back, and dumped me.

"Nah, Liz was another Alicia."

"Who?"

"You know, Alicia Bingham. The girl who ripped my heart out when I was a junior in high school."

"Alicia?"

"I'm sure I mentioned her to you. I know I was still thinking about her all the time when I went off to college. Alicia Bingham was my very first personification of my dream woman."

"Blonde?"

I scowled at him. "Dark, dark black hair. Jewel-like green eyes. Really amazing looking. When she asked me to go with her to the homecoming dance, I had to pick my chin up off the floor. She was the first girl I ever said, 'I love you' to, the first girl I ever got to third base with, and the first girl I ever took to a family function. I was totally, over-the-top crazy about her. We spent hours kissing. I mean just kissing. Not grappling over each other – which was saying something because I was in serious grappling mode at that point – but just kissing and looking into each other's eyes. It was the definition of romance for me. I was gone big time."

"This ends badly, doesn't it?"

"Of course it ends badly. Did you think I was secretly married or something?"

Daz shrugged and took the last piece of chicken.

"Before it ended badly, it got really, really good, though. We stayed together the entire school year and had this amazing summer that we spent mostly at the beach and mostly touching. We even got to spend a night together when her parents went away for the weekend. I really thought I was going to marry her. We even sorta talked about it in the way that people do when they're trying it on for size. Then we got back to school and two weeks later it was completely over."

"A guy on the yearbook committee."

"Someone on the swim team, actually. How'd you know?"

"Been there."

"Well, I *hadn't* been there when this happened. To say the least, I was a little blown away. I had trouble speaking for a couple of days."

"So let me guess, Alicia and her lane buddy wound up being the class couple and you wound up giving yourself a thousand little paper cuts."

"That would have been preferable. What really happened was that Alicia and – what was his name? – Spence, that's it – only had something like four dates and then he dumped her."

"How badly did you rub it in?"

"I asked her to get back together with me."

Daz threw his hands up in the air. "You didn't! That is unbelievably pathetic."

"Thanks for the empathy. And yeah, it was pathetic. But I still felt miserable about losing her, and I let that cloud my judgment. I also happened to be seventeen."

"Since, as we've already established, this ends badly, I'm guessing the reunion wasn't a happy one."

"We went out one time. I took her to a French restaurant in Chappaqua to show her how serious I was about her. She spent the entire time talking about Spence."

"Please tell me that you dumped her this time."

"I'd really like to do that. And trust me, as I've relived it over the years, I have dumped her in the most heartless ways imaginable."

"But in real life …"

"She told me at the end of the night that she just couldn't be *that way* with me anymore."

Daz guffawed. "That might be one of the most humiliating stories I've ever heard."

"I really love sharing with you, Daz."

He laughed a little more and then said, "No, look, who among us hasn't done equally idiotic things in the pursuit of women? I once 'helped out' a girl I had a major crush on by taking her awful best friend to the senior prom. The girl was certifiably crazy. Talked about her fascination with mass murderers for something like half the night. I mean, we're on the dance floor and she's telling me about Ted Bundy. Then I drive her home and she exposes her breasts to me. Right there on Rte. 18. She wouldn't get out of the car until I touched them, and when I did she started moaning ecstatically and really, really loudly. I thought her father was going to come out of the house and beat the crap out of me. It was a little terrifying if you want to know the truth."

"I don't suppose you ever got to go out with the girl you had the crush on."

"Nah, it never works out that way. But I saw her at a couple of parties the next summer and she was insanely drunk at both of them, so maybe it was all for the best."

"My prom date was my mother's best friend's daughter."

"How'd that happen?"

"It's a long story but it had something to do with the fallout over Alicia and my mother's insistence that I needed to 'get back up on the horse.'"

"Interesting image."

"I always thought so. Anyway, my mother hounded me into getting tickets to the prom even though I didn't have a date, and then when I still didn't have a date two weeks before, she just made these arrangements for me. It was pretty freaking humiliating, but I went ahead with it anyway."

"And of course the best friend's daughter had a growth on her nose that looked like Vladimir Putin, right?"

"No, actually she was great looking. She was a junior and she was gorgeous. She was also an immovable object. Literally didn't want to do anything the entire time we were there. She wouldn't dance, she wouldn't get up from the table with me to talk with my friends, she wouldn't go outside for a walk with me. She just sat and listened to the band and made it obvious that hot pokers in her eyes would have been preferable."

"Did she have sex with you afterward?"

"Yeah, the kind of sex that involves her getting out of the car while it's still coming to a stop."

Daz laughed and picked up one of the bones on his plate looking for any extra meat. "I think we'll need a judge's ruling to determine which of us has had the sadder romantic life."

"Let's just call it a tie. The judge will just say really demeaning things to us. Do you want this last piece of spring roll?"

"No, go right ahead."

"You know what the weird thing is? I really want to have a great romantic life. Not something over-the-top, waves crashing on the sand or anything like that. Just something passionate and meaningful and satisfying."

Daz seemed surprised to hear this from me. "White picket fence?"

"Or chain link. I can deal with either."

"Kids?"

I hesitated for a second. This had always been one of those grey areas for me. "Yeah, I think so."

"You gonna name one after me?"

"Please, that's such a cliché. I'm gonna name one after the crazy Ted Bundy girl instead. What was her name?"

He rolled his eyes. "Stacy."

"Stacy Flaster. Yeah, it works."

"So you really want all of that stuff?"

"I really think I do."

"How come you aren't doing anything about it, then?"

I tossed him my what-planet-did-you-come-from look. "What do you *do* about it? Personals ads? Gym memberships? Bar-hopping?"

"How the hell do I know? It just seems to me that you never really tried to keep things going with any of the women you dated."

This stopped me for a second. I wasn't sure if he was wrong or not. "You really think that's true?"

"It's totally true. You usually bail at the first opportunity. I always figured it was a love-'em-and-leave-'em thing with you."

I had to think about that. I'd always believed that I would respond to the right woman and that I would do the best to make the most out of the relationship. Meanwhile, he always assumed that I was in it for as many one-night-stands as I could accumulate. It appeared that we were going to have to get the judges involved after all.

As happened the night before, the conversation ultimately slowed and we settled back into the rest of the night. The Allman Brothers' *Where it All Begins* album was playing in the background while we watched a Premier League soccer match on the TV. Daz fell asleep while I cleaned up the dishes. He never fell asleep while watching soccer.

I turned off the TV, turned off the music (assuming he hadn't intended to program The Allman Brothers into his dreams) and locked up behind me.

I wasn't quite ready to go home. I wound up going to our usual coffee bar on Columbus Avenue, drinking espresso by myself and watching people interact with one another.

I gave some more thought to the things Daz and I had talked about the past couple of nights. As I did, I imagined him sitting with me with the two of us throwing observations and memories back and forth at one another. He reminded me about how he talked me down from the ledge when I thought I might get fired from my job at Tyler, Hope and Pitt, and then told me about how it almost happened to him as well. I told him about the run-in I had with a couple of University of Wisconsin students during one of his road games after he scored a goal. He told me about why he looked so out of it after coming back from visiting his sister Linda a couple of years ago when he usually came back glowing with stories about her, and I finally gave him the details about the stiff New Year's Day brunch I had with my parents this year that I was too angry to tell him about when I got home.

Eventually I made it back to my apartment, exhausted from all of this conversation.

The chapter about
facing more reality
than I was prepared for

Thursday night, Keane and I met at the bar in the Millennium Hotel for a drink. This would be an exercise in restraint for me. Since the last time I'd seen him, enormous things had happened. However, only some of it – the part he already knew – was open for discussion tonight. Keane had made it abundantly clear during our first lunch that he believed that whatever went on in one's personal life was not a factor in one's professional life and that letting the former impinge on the latter – even if only to the degree of mentioning it to a potential colleague – was a sign of weakness. Therefore, nothing that had gone on since Monday morning was an available topic. Not if I had any interest in remaining in the running for the job with K&C.

"Prince has a hell of a house, doesn't he?" Keane said as he sat down and ordered a Skyy vodka on the rocks.

"It's amazing," I said, glad that we had leapt into the safest of all topics. He didn't even bother with such inane preliminaries as asking me how I was doing.

"He loves that thing like it's another child. I swear he has separation problems on Monday mornings." He looked across the room. It wasn't the first time he'd done it in the couple of minutes we'd been together. It seemed as though he was trying to spot someone he knew or to perhaps be noticed himself. He looked back in my direction. "So Curt said he thought your weekend went well."

"I'm glad to hear that. I thought it went very well."

"It's good that the two of you enjoyed yourselves. If you can't get along with Prince, there really wouldn't be any point in continuing this conversation."

I nodded, unsure how to respond to that, and got a break when our drinks came. I'd ordered a cranberry juice and seltzer, even though I wasn't going back to the office.

"I'm not going to lie to you, Rich. You've emerged as somewhat of a frontrunner here. We've had a number of excellent conversations with other candidates, but Curt has sort of latched onto you. He tends to do that kind of thing, which means it's incumbent on me to not only retain the clearer head but also to make sure we aren't kidding ourselves."

I took a sip of my drink. "So you're the bad cop."

"Let's say I'm the rational cop."

"I can appreciate that," I said, though I wasn't entirely sure that I could. I mean, in a field like advertising, what was really so wrong with the idea of going with your gut? However, my opinions were irrelevant – at least if I wanted to keep my hat in the ring with K&C. It was clear to me that, while the job might involve daily contact with Curt Prince, Noel Keane was the gatekeeper. The entire firm was his operation, and one didn't become part of that operation without his approval.

Over the course of the next half-hour, Keane and I engaged in an exchange that was much more like a job interview than any conversation I'd had with either of them before. He wanted to know about my management style, about issues that had come up with staff and how I dealt with them. He quizzed me on situations and briefed me on the policies and practices of the agency. He told me about the corporate seminars they held in Los Angeles twice a year and about the annual gathering they held in London that people at my level weren't invited to.

I couldn't determine whether this was a formality that someone like Keane felt required to perform or whether it was just the opposite – that only after I passed the compatibility tests was I now worth engaging in a real interview. When Keane said I was the frontrunner, did he mean that I was the frontrunner in his eyes as well as Prince's, or was he just saying that because Prince was hounding him to hire me? Regardless, like all interviews in my life, I felt perfectly comfortable with this one. Encapsulating strategies and philosophies into soundbites had never been a problem for me, and I think as a result I'd always interviewed well. I was the kind of guy who tended to make a good first impression, though technically, I was making my *third* impression on Keane.

I found myself automatically reacting to this test with zeal. I was like a dog with his favorite chew toy – when I saw it, I always responded the same way, regardless of the circumstances. For the first several minutes of this interview, I was absolutely "on." The more Keane challenged me with follow-up questions or tossed me a situation he felt defined some kind of acuity, the more aggressive I became in my answers. It was a bit like Olympic table tennis to me, and I was determined to score as many points as possible.

Through it all, though, I kept going back to the question that had nagged me since the very first call from Keane: do I really want this job? While I felt no doubts when I was out in the Hamptons and had even imagined going into Rupert's office to resign, the decision seemed harder to make when it was just Keane and me talking. Moving to K&C meant leaving The Creative Shop behind and that was tough to consider. It wasn't a matter of whether I could find people at K&C who I liked and enjoyed working with. It was a matter of no longer seeing the specific people I worked with now on a daily basis. I didn't expect this to be a huge issue – after all, how many of those people were wedded to The Shop indefinitely? – but it had become one.

Which inevitably brought me around to thinking about Daz – and the return to my conscious of the biggest thing that had changed since the last time I'd seen Keane: it no longer mattered that they weren't interested in bringing Daz along with me.

I don't know why this hit me as hard as it did. Certainly, I had already had an emotional and intellectual reaction to the consequences of Daz's illness. Still, there was something about this conversation with Keane and the context in which our previous conversations had occurred that threw it into new relief. Until this moment, the K&C courtship had happened at a time when the biggest personal issue on my plate was whether or not my best friend was having sex with a woman I'd had romantic fantasies about. Back then, I could be pissed at Daz but still consider us very much a team, could ultimately decide to blow Keane and Prince off if I wanted to because they didn't understand how important it was for us to work together. Now, it wasn't a matter of K&C

breaking up the team. The team was splitting permanently, and there was nothing I, or Noel Keane, or Curt
Prince, or anyone else on the planet could do about it.

This version of the realization I'd already come to
in any number of different ways made me incredibly
sad. The kind of sad I knew I wouldn't be able to mask.
The kind of sad that Keane would find irrelevant – and
which he also had no right to be privy to. He was in
mid-sentence, talking about something I'd lost track of,
when I interrupted him.

"I'm sorry, Noel, but I need to cut this short."

He seemed shocked by this, though I couldn't be
certain if it was because of what I said or because I said
it while he was speaking. "Did something happen?"

I looked at my watch. "I'm an idiot. I just remembered that I'm late for something I totally can't get out
of. I'll be headless if I don't go now, and you probably
aren't in the market for a headless Creative Director."

He seemed a little bit baffled and more than a little
bit miffed. He also seemed, surprisingly, a little embarrassed. "Well, if you need to leave, you need to leave," he
said, gesturing to our waiter for the check.

I stood up. I thought exchanging a few sentences
might help calm me down, but that didn't happen. I
really needed to get out of there. "I do and I'm very sorry."

"I assume we can pick this up some other time," he
said, not hiding the fact that he felt inconvenienced.

"Yes, definitely," I said, though I wasn't entirely sure
how I felt about it at that moment. I looked at my watch
and blinked my eyes again. "I really have to run."

I was out on 43rd Street less than a minute later,
walking quickly east. I wanted to get away from the
Millennium fast, because I didn't want Keane to come

out and find me losing my composure. I turned the corner at Fifth Avenue and crouched down against the side of a building, covering my face with my hands. As ridiculous as it seemed even at that moment, I felt as though I had just then learned how sick Daz was. Would this keep happening to me? Would I break down every time something made me think of Daz in a different way?

I took several deep breaths to try to calm myself. I tried listening to the sounds of the pedestrians and motorists passing me as a form of distraction. I tried telling myself that I was overreacting, that I was already fully aware of everything that was now getting me so upset.

I wasn't overreacting, though. I was just fully reacting for the first time.

———

I did something then that I never thought I would do. I walked the few short blocks to Grand Central Station and took the next train up to my parents' house in Scarsdale. It was an impulsive act, and they tended not to respond well to impulsive acts, but still I bought a ticket and boarded the train.

During the entire half-hour trip, I asked myself why I was doing this. Certainly, it wasn't so I could benefit from their advice. It most assuredly wasn't because I sought comfort from them. There was nothing rational about this, but something told me it might be useful to take this journey, if for no other reason than that the train ride itself might calm me down a little.

As I had found on many previous occasions, the rocking motion of the car and the passage of the landscape lulled me, at least a tiny bit. By this time, it was toward the back end of rush hour. Commuters still filled much of the train, briefcases and laptops open, cell phones beaming signals all over the country. Not everyone there was headed home after a long day at work, though. A little girl a few seats up talked excitedly with her mother about their adventures in the City and about how much she loved riding on trains. A casually dressed couple across the aisle from me whispered to each other and kissed tenderly. Then there was the raggedy guy in the back of the car who looked like he'd been riding up and down the line all day who was doing nothing other than staring at the wall upon which he leaned his head.

As we passed the Crestwood station, which meant we were just a few minutes from my stop, I got an uncomfortable feeling in the pit of my stomach. My parents would be completely confused by my simply turning up. There would be awkward questions, the most embarrassing of which would be, "What are you doing here?" By the time I got off at the Scarsdale station, I had nearly convinced myself to simply wait for the next train back to the City. In spite of this trepidation, I felt a strong compulsion to complete the trip. There had to be some reason why I had taken it, some reason why I did something this impulsive, even if my subconscious offered me few clues.

It was a ten-minute cab ride to their house. When the taxi dropped me off, I pictured how weird this little moment would be for me. My mother would immediately jump to the conclusion that I'd done something wrong. My father would probably just regard the entire thing as an interruption, giving me a couple of minutes at the kitchen table before returning to the television.

Would I cry in front of them? If I did, would they think I was having a nervous breakdown? Did I want any of this? Still, I made it to the door and rang the bell.

It turns out that I needn't have bothered being concerned about what they thought. They weren't home. For all I knew, they weren't even in the country. I had a key, which I'd kept on various key chains since I was in high school, but I was sure I didn't have the correct alarm code anymore. That spoke volumes. Now that I was standing on the doorstep, now that I'd gone on this journey waiting for a reason to come to me, I couldn't think of a single purpose in doing it. My parents didn't know Daz. They'd met him a couple of times, but they had no idea who he was or what he was about. They wouldn't by any stretch of the imagination know what I was going through or why.

I went down the steps and made my way around the house. My parents had done a huge amount of landscaping since the fall, and spring flowers were in bloom everywhere. So much color on the outside. The backyard was almost unrecognizable from the one I'd grown up with. There was no screened-in porch then, no brick path leading out to a gazebo. The shrubbery was thick and seamless, and like everything else it was perfectly manicured. The house was truly a showpiece, something I knew was terribly important to them.

I walked toward the back of the yard and noticed a baseball lying on the ground soaked and dirty. I picked it up and hefted it in my hand. Toby Macklin and I had spent endless hours on this grass playing catch, pretending we knew how to throw curveballs when we really didn't have a clue. Was it possible that this ball had been sitting here since I was a teenager? Of course it wasn't.

My father would have reamed the gardeners out if they'd left it lying around for even a week. This ball was here only since the last time the lawn had been cut. I looked across the fence and noticed a swing set, a volleyball net, and a trampoline in the back yard that abutted my parents'. Obviously, there were kids there and obviously the ball had come from that direction. I flipped it up in the air one more time and then tossed it back toward the children who would make much more use of it than either my parents or the gardeners.

I sat in the gazebo for a few minutes, something I'd done only once before – last summer when my parents threw a dinner party for a cousin who'd graduated medical school. It was getting chilly and I was starting to feel a little uncomfortable. It was cooler up here than it was in the City, and I wasn't dressed for the drop in temperature. I hunched up my shoulders and drew my arms across my chest, but I didn't get up to leave just yet.

I tried to place myself in this house. We'd moved here when I was two. I spent sixteen full years here and then parts of four others. Even after all of that time, though, none of this seemed like mine. While there were boxes of my things in the attic, I hadn't left any of myself here. I took everything that mattered to me to Ann Arbor and then to the City. My life wasn't defined by the years I'd spent growing up in this home. It was defined by the years I'd spent growing outward after that.

Daz was with me for every one of those years. Maybe that's why, in the face of the strongest grief I'd felt yet over the inevitability of losing him, I'd made the snap decision to come up here tonight. To confirm that what I was losing was more meaningful than what I had already lost. If so, then mission accomplished. I even managed to do my good deed for the day, getting that kid his ball back. He was probably terrified of climbing the fence and running into my parents.

For one more minute, I watched the house from this perspective. Then I pulled out my cell phone and called a cab, waiting on the front porch until it arrived.

The chapter about trying new things

It was time for me to come clean with Daz. That I'd managed to let the job thing with K&C go this long without mentioning it to him was a stinging indictment of my character, and I couldn't allow it to continue any longer. I went to his apartment on my way to the office the next morning.

"Rich, I'm telling you, you really need to get yourself to a head doctor," he said when I got there. "Remember? You don't need to pick me up on the way to work anymore. I'm on *really* extended leave."

"Gee, I forgot," I said with a smirk. "Listen, I came to talk to you about something."

He looked at me apprehensively, and I could tell that he thought more bad news was coming. I couldn't imagine what he would define as bad news at this point in his life, but I didn't want to cause him any discomfort.

"It's not a big deal," I said, sitting down next to the bed. As I did, I heard the door open and close, which meant that Ana had arrived. "It's just that I didn't have a client dinner last night."

His eyes opened wide. "You have a new girlfriend?"

It was funny that he'd leapt so quickly to that conclusion. "Something like that. For the past couple of weeks, some people at Kander and Craft have been after me because they have an opening for Creative Director in their downtown office."

Daz thought about this for a moment and then said, "I thought they were shutting that office down."

"Yeah, a lot of people think that, but Curt Prince decided to make it a pet project and he's determined to turn the place around."

Ana came in, said good morning to Daz, handed him a pill and a glass of water, and then busied herself in the room while Daz took it. He needed to get her attention to give her the glass back.

"Wow, Curt Prince, huh? You think you'll get a chance to meet him?"

I hadn't been looking forward to any of this conversation, but this was the part I'd dreaded the most. "I've already met Prince, Daz."

"Really? Is he as cool as he seems in his interviews?"

I'm ashamed to say that I considered telling Daz only half of the truth here. Even now. Some part of me even tried the argument that it would be "best for him" if I lied. Fortunately, I didn't listen to that voice. "Daz, I spent the weekend with Prince at his house in the Hamptons."

I could see Daz trying to do the math. I was with him the previous weekend, so I had to have been talking about some other weekend. "When did you do that?"

"The weekend when I told you I had that reunion thing with my mother's family."

Daz tilted his head back toward his pillow. "Which was why you couldn't come to my party."

"Yeah. Or go with you when you went to the hospital."

Daz closed his eyes so tightly that his brow wrinkled. I'd never noticed him doing that before. "Why'd you lie to me about that?"

He seemed so hurt. I didn't know what to say to avoid hurting him more. "The whole K&C thing started as a goof. They called and said they wanted to talk to me, so I agreed to have lunch with the COO. I mean, why not, right? I should've said something to you at that point, but I didn't. I think I even had a reason for it that made sense to me at the time. After that, it got complicated." Ana came over to the bed to do something, and I looked up at her. She made eye contact with me, made it clear that I was getting in the way, and then she left the room.

"They were coming for *me*, Daz. Not *you* and me."

Daz absorbed this and didn't say anything for several long beats. Ana put the living room television on. "So you didn't tell me because you didn't want me to know that you were thinking about breaking up Flash and Dazzle."

"I *wasn't* thinking about breaking up Flash and Dazzle," I said defensively. "I tried pitching us as a team."

He considered this new information and then suddenly laughed, saying, "You are such an asshole."

"I know I am."

"You tried pitching us as a team when they were coming for *you*? For a Creative Director's job? You're a total asshole."

This definitely wasn't how I'd expected him to react. "What do you mean? What would you have done?"

"If they came to me with a job like that? I would have dropped your ass in thirty seconds flat."

This stunned me, and I felt more than a little offended. Until I realized that he was putting me on. "No you wouldn't have," I said broadly.

Daz laughed again and then leaned toward me. "No, I wouldn't have," he said softly. "But I definitely would have listened to what they were saying to me *very* seriously. Come on, Rich, this is K&C we're talking about, and it's a big freaking gig. I mean, I appreciate your mentioning my name and all, but how often do you think shots like this come along?"

"I should have told you right away."

"Yes, you should have told me right away. What the hell were you thinking?"

"I was thinking this was going to be difficult."

"What was difficult about it? Did you think I was going to cry and hold onto your leg and beg you to stay with me at The Shop?"

"I didn't know how you would react."

"Asshole," he said, shaking his head. "So are you taking it?"

"They haven't offered me anything yet."

"What do you think about it?"

"I think I'm glad they haven't offered me anything yet."

"Creative Director at K&C – even K&C downtown – would be a pretty nice job. So what did they say when you talked to them about me, anyway?"

I had no trouble with giving him a half-truth here. "They have an art director there they really like."

"Carleen Laster. She's great."

It was a relief that he knew her, and even more of one that he knew her reputation. "They seem to think so. My guess is that she couldn't even shine your shoes."

"Not really an issue any more, is it?"

He'd said this so matter-of-factly that my eyes immediately flashed to his for a reaction. I couldn't read what I saw there. He was starting to go places where I couldn't follow.

"I'm sorry I lied to you, Daz."

He held me with his eyes for a long moment. "Yeah, you should be."

"I won't do it again."

He nodded. "No, you won't."

That was it. A wrist-slap. I'd been an awful friend, and when I finally admitted to Daz how awful I'd been, he didn't punish me for it. I really shouldn't have been surprised by this, and I suppose I really wasn't.

———

That night, I stopped at Dawat to take out Indian food for our dinner: Vegetable Samosas and Mulligatawny Soup, Shrimp Bhuna and Chicken Tikka Masala, Lemon Rice and Garlic Naan and their remarkable Onion and Black Pepper Kulcha. Indian food was the absolute outside edge of dining acceptability for Daz, and it literally took me years to convince him to try it. Once he acquired the taste, though, he welcomed it, if on his own schedule ("Once every couple of months is fine. More than that is really unnecessary, don't you think?").

I was glad I'd finally had the conversation about K&C with Daz that morning and I looked forward to an evening with one less thing standing between us, though it was almost fanciful to think back on that time a couple of weeks earlier when concern about breaking this news to Daz would have qualified as significant.

When I got to the apartment, Daz was not alone. With him was a woman who was a slightly younger, considerably smoother version of him. If I met her without him in the same room, I might have thought she was Daz in drag.

This was Linda, the sister who'd stayed behind. She and I had spoken a few times on the phone, but we'd never met in person before because she never came to New York. She'd attained an almost mythical place in my mind: the other significant person in his life, the one from the parallel universe some called Kansas. Daz spoke to her nearly daily, and he often told me about what was going on in her life, but Linda had always seemed a little unreal to me. It was therefore fascinating to come face to face with her for the first time.

Linda was holding Daz's hand when I arrived, and she continued to do so as I walked into the bedroom. When Daz introduced us, I extended my hand to her, and she offered me the free one, not wanting to break the connection with her brother. There was something about her posture and about the way Daz leaned close to her that told me their reunion had been a painful one for both of them. Not that it really could be anything other than that.

Badly Drawn Boy's *The Hour of Bewilderbeast* album was playing in the background, Daz deciding sometime the previous day that he would listen to his entire music collection in alphabetical order by artist. Maybe it was the moody nature of the music that lent an air of melancholy to the room. Or maybe I felt that way because Linda was here. Daz had always told me that the thought of coming to the City intimidated her. The only reason she was here now was because her brother wouldn't be making any more trips to Kansas.

For the first time in a long time, I wondered where Daz's parents were. We'd so completely edited talk of family from our conversations that it hadn't registered on me to think about this until now. Why hadn't they come along with their daughter? Would they show up in a few days? When they did, would I be as welcome as I had always been in this apartment? The thought of maybe being replaced by "real" family sent a little ache through my system.

"I stopped at Dawat on the way up," I said to Daz. He reacted appreciatively.

I turned to Linda. "I didn't realize you were going to be here, but I probably got enough for five people anyway. Do you like Indian food?"

"I haven't had a lot of it," she said a little tentatively.

I assumed that meant that she'd never tried it. "Well, if you don't like this, you just won't like Indian at all. It doesn't come any better than it does from Dawat – at least not in this country."

Daz laughed. "There's a totally decent Indian place a couple of blocks away, but Rich of course had to get this stuff from Midtown. He's decided that all of our dinners need to come from the most expensive places in the city."

It was good to see that there weren't any residual effects from our conversation that morning. I'd been half-wondering if he would be angrier at me once he'd had time to think about what I told him. "What's the point in settling for second best?" I said.

"I think that's very thoughtful, Rich." Linda's eyes glittered a little when she said this. This instantly charmed me. Someone being that unguarded wasn't the kind of thing I saw very often. I smiled at her, and the smile she returned seemed to be a heartfelt one. I felt as though I knew her a little better in that very moment.

I went into the kitchen to bring in our dinner. As I did this, I wondered what Linda was thinking about the evening routine Daz and I had settled into. Maybe it didn't seem so unusual to her. Maybe back in her hometown friends tended to friends-in-need all the time. I always got the impression that this was the way most of the world worked, though probably without the pastrami and the samosas. Still, it was not standard practice in the world I'd grown up in.

There seemed to be less of a cloud over the room when I got back. Maybe my arrival had allowed Daz and Linda to step back a little, to acknowledge that he was still alive and that there was still time to enjoy each other's company. Given the way I'd felt last night, I was surprised to think that I could have that effect on anyone. In all likelihood, it had nothing to do with me at all.

Now that there were three of us eating in the bedroom, we were almost certainly better off sitting at the dining table, but Daz was becoming less and less inclined to get up. I don't think it was a physical thing, at least not yet. He'd settled into the room, surrounded himself with creature comforts, and seemed pent on staying this way. As I told Michelle, he had resigned himself to his fate. If this was how he wanted to play it out, then this was how he should.

Linda took a careful bite of the chicken. Obviously, she would have preferred just about anything else to Indian food, but when she tasted it, her eyes opened wide and she took another bite quickly, obviously concentrating on the flavor.

"This is excellent," she said. "Indian food doesn't taste like this back home."

So she had at least tried it before. "It doesn't taste like this a couple of blocks away, either," I said, glancing toward her brother. He shrugged and continued eating.

She took a bite of the Kulcha and smiled. "My first surprise in New York City."

Daz stopped long enough to hold up a piece of Naan and say, "Maybe we should eat our dinners in alphabetical order based on country of origin. How come we never did that, Flash?"

"Because it's a stupid idea."

"No, really. We could start with Albanian food."

"Right, of course, because you love Albanian food so much. They're not famous for their french fries, you know."

"I'm stunned that Eric is eating Indian," Linda said. "He didn't do this kind of thing at home. Lots of meat. And anything that involved Oreos."

"Not that much has changed, really," I said plainly.

"After Albanian, we would do ... American, I guess. So we could have steak and Oreos. And then Australian. And after that Austrian. I'm starting to like this idea."

"Linda, talk to him, please."

Linda put a hand on her brother's arm. "Eric, I don't want Albanian food tomorrow night."

"We'll skip Albanian."

"And I don't want Australian food a couple of nights from now."

Daz appeared to search for a persuasive argument. Then he settled back against his pillow. "Yeah, it's probably a bad idea." His expression brightened. "How about we do desserts in alphabetical order? We start with Apple Crisp, then we move on to Apple Pie –"

"– You forgot Apple Pan Dowdy."

"You're right, I did. I need a piece of paper."

"Let's do this later."

Daz nodded and picked up his fork. "Great Shrimp Bhuna, by the way."

"You know," Linda said, "back when we were growing up, the idea that I'd ever visit my brother in New York City was almost inconceivable."

"I was kind of a small-town boy," Daz said while shoveling more bread into his mouth. His appetite seemed especially large tonight, and his motions especially animated.

"Really? I never would have guessed."

"Eric even used to talk about becoming a farmer."

This made me guffaw. "They have farms in your Manhattan?"

Daz gestured with his fork. "Way outside of Manhattan. Out on the plains. Cornfields and cattle."

"You know, farmers have to get up really early."

"One of the main reasons I decided to go to college."

Linda ate some Lemon Rice and nodded approvingly. "I think the farmer thing was just a passing phase, but I can assure you he never once talked about settling down in a big city."

"And yet here we are in the center of the world."

Linda looked over at her brother and some sadness crept back into her eyes. "The center of the world."

I moved quickly to lighten the mood. "So tell me, Linda, was Daz as much of a chick magnet and man about town when he was younger as he claims to have been?"

Daz began to protest, but Linda smiled at him and said, "All of my friends thought he was very handsome."

"They did?" he said.

"Very. And when he became a soccer star, it made him even more attractive. He wasn't a *football* star, but still he could have had his pick of just about any one of my friends."

"This is the kind of thing you might have wanted to tell me back then."

Linda waved a hand at him. "Oh, you wouldn't have listened." She turned to me. "He never listened to me when it came to girls."

Daz sat up straight. "When I was eleven, she tried to convince me that Melanie Reston liked me. I finally got the courage to ask Melanie if she wanted to do something together – and she laughed right in my face."

"That was Melanie's sister's fault," Linda said, punching him lightly on the arm. She offered me an explanation. "Annie Reston was one of my friends, and she told me that Melanie really liked Eric. I didn't realize back then that I couldn't trust her."

Daz nudged me. "Over the years, Linda has enjoyed gaining experience through my failures."

Linda hit him with a piece of Naan. Her eyes sparkled when she did it and she grinned broadly. "That is *so* unfair. Besides, it's your responsibility as the older sibling. Comes with the territory."

It was absorbing watching the two of them spar this way. The affectionate way in which they jibed one another was a revelation.

I wished Linda could have been here under different circumstances, maybe cajoled after all these years into taking her first halting steps into Metropolis for a wild week on the town with her brother and his erstwhile sidekick. Given how open and bright her expression could be when she was engaged with her brother, I could only imagine what she would have been like if the specter of Daz's illness wasn't shadowing her.

"It was Linda's job," Daz said to me, "to make me look as bad in retrospect as possible to authority figures all over town. I can't tell you how many times teachers or even, like, people at the local YMCA came up to me and said, 'Your sister is such a pleasure to be with; why aren't you more like that?'"

"He's exaggerating."

"It's supposed to be the other way around. You know, big brother establishes an impossible legacy and little sister struggles valiantly but ultimately in vain to live up to it."

"The gym teachers always gave me a hard time."

Daz smirked at her. "Here's a great example. In my freshman year in high school, Linda is starting her first year of junior high. One day in October or something like that, I need to pick her up, which means standing outside the building while classes let out. Linda takes an especially long time getting out the door –"

"– Eileen Stark was my best friend that year and she was very slow."

"– during which time I just stand around. My old art teacher comes by. You know, art, a class I was pretty good at. She sees me and I smile at her. And you know what she does? She starts shaking her head. She walks up to me and tells me that she didn't realize how much I was wasting my talent until she met Linda."

I looked at Linda. "I didn't know you were an artist too."

"I have absolutely no talent for it."

"That's right; she has absolutely no talent for it. But my junior high art teacher still thought I was a disappointment after she met Linda."

"I don't get it."

Daz threw up his hands. "Yes, exactly."

Linda took one of Daz's extended hands and patted it gently. "We just got along. She liked that I tried hard even though I wasn't any good. You know, some people *squander* talent when they have a huge amount of it, while others make the most of what they have."

I found this fascinating. "Did you ever go back to the school to tell her that you're a big-time art director now?"

Daz shrugged. "Nah, I should've done that."

"She's retired, anyway," Linda said.

Daz shook his head. "Another missed opportunity. Rich, you're keeping a record of all of these, right?"

"Eric isn't exactly telling you both sides of the story," Linda said. "When I was a little kid, he was this enormous presence among my friends."

"That's because I didn't have any friends of my own."

"That's *not* the reason. It was because he was bigger than the rest of them. Not only physically bigger, but bigger as a person."

"Yeah, I could always mesmerize the six-year-olds."

"No, I mean it. This was the thing that Eric never understood." She leaned into him. "That he *forgot* over the years. He was someone people wanted to be with, wanted to be like. Do you know Andy Kresher still talks about that thing with the bike?"

Daz laughed and studied his plate. Linda looked back at me. "When Eric was eight years old, Andy was out riding his bike when a bunch of older bullies started chasing him. Andy wound up going down this path where he crashed his bike and got the spokes tangled in a bush. Andy's knee was bleeding and he was terrified." Linda sat up in her chair, rising to the energy of the story she was telling. "The bullies descended on him. Then, from out of nowhere, Eric showed up on his bike and scared the bullies away – from what I heard he used some language eight-year-olds weren't supposed to use. Then he straightened the bent spokes on Andy's bike and helped him make his way back home."

"Jeez, Daz," I said admiringly, "you were like freaking Spider-Man."

Daz rolled his eyes. "I happened to be there."

"You happened to be there," Linda said, clearly appalled at her brother's humility. "Andy says you heard the kids threatening him and you came dashing down the path."

"I think the story has grown over the years."

"Hey, it doesn't matter," I said. "I am seriously impressed. You know, Linda, Daz did a similar thing with me once. These two clients ganged up on me, absolutely eviscerating the campaign we put together for them, and Daz asked them if they *wanted coffee*."

"Hey, it defused the situation."

I nodded. "It did. Ultimately we lost the clients anyway, but not because they weren't adequately refreshed."

"See what I mean?" Linda said. "Eric, you've always been a hero."

"Always been *my* hero," I said.

"And mine," Linda said.

Daz guffawed. "Please. All this adulation is going to make me vomit. And since I just had Chicken Tikka Masala, that wouldn't be pretty."

The audio system switched to Erykah Badu, and this felt like a signal for me to get up to clear the dishes. Linda rose to help me but I gestured her back. I rinsed the dishes and threw them into the dishwasher. I think this and the refrigerator were the only appliances Daz had ever used in this kitchen. I was surprised that Ana could even light the stove when she cooked for him.

I took the garbage bag down the hall. The trash chute was all the way on the other side of the building, a fact I suggested Daz use to negotiate down the price of his apartment. It literally took a couple of minutes to go back and forth. This seemed like a lot of effort to throw out the trash. Not that Daz ever had much trash to throw out until recently.

When I came back, I heard strained voices from the bedroom.

"It doesn't matter," Daz said.

"It'll *always* matter. No matter what has happened, it will always matter."

"Linda, let it go."

I closed the door and they must have heard me do so, because the conversation stopped at the same time.

"Hey," I said brightly, sitting back down. "I'm ready for some more trips down Memory Lane with that wacky Dazman clan."

Daz offered me a half-smile. "I think I'm kind of up for a little television," he said abruptly. With two clicks, he silenced Erykah Badu and brought a rerun of *The Cosby Show* to life. Something had definitely happened while I was away. Linda didn't seem to be happy about the television going on and about the conversation coming to a halt, but neither of us were voting members of this organization. I clapped Daz on the leg, which got me a brief glance I didn't fully understand, and then I turned to watch the show.

Watching television is a different experience amongst different people. With Daz and me, it was a communal thing. We talked – you know, about the commercials or about a line that caught our attention or about the desire for more pretzels or more beer – and we definitely watched whatever we watched *together*. It wasn't a matter of parallel play. With Linda in the room, though, and after the exchange I'd overheard when I came back into the apartment, I could only think of the TV as an avoidance mechanism. Even when I had no idea what we were avoiding.

We watched *Cosby* and then another sitcom and then a cop show that came on after that. In the middle of the latter, I volunteered to make a run to the ice cream shop a couple of blocks away. Daz thanked me, but didn't take his eyes off of the screen. Linda initially politely declined and then changed her mind. When I came back into the apartment this time, I was relatively certain there had been no further conversation in my absence. There was also little upon my return.

I thought about saying something to get things rolling again, but nothing came to mind that wasn't an obvious attempt to break the silence. I thought I got a break when a dreadful ad for an online dating service came on the TV. It was a client we'd pitched and lost to a bigger agency. However, my snide comment about the company's slogan got little more than a snicker from Daz.

After the first segment of *SportsCenter*, I went back to my place.

The chapter about taking time off

The next night, I decided we would forego Albanian food
for hot dogs from Gray's Papaya. They were state-of-the-art
in their own way – I believe their slogan was something
like "the filet mignon of hot dogs" – and I thought Linda
might enjoy this distinctive New York experience. Daz, who
bowed at the altar of Gray's Papaya, was more than satisfied. Fortunately, he didn't suggest that we work our way
through all the City's hot dog joints in alphabetical order.

They'd made at least a little bit of peace with whatever
had come up between them last night, and there was far
less tension in the room now. I got a little more brother/
sister banter from them, and Daz and I spent some time
detailing for Linda each other's foibles in the workplace.
However, Daz wasn't as on tonight as he had been previous nights and things settled down early. By eight o'clock,
the TV was on, and around ten, Daz said he was wasted
and really just wanted to go to sleep, asking us to leave
him alone. We went out and spent a couple of minutes
taking care of things in the kitchen, though hot dogs
didn't require much cleanup. After that, Linda returned
to Daz's room to report that he was snoring softly.

"Do you think he's out for the night?" Linda said.

"It's been my experience that when Daz crashes he
completely crashes."

"I don't know if experience means anything anymore."

She was right, of course. Given the nature of Daz's illness, it was entirely possible that he would awaken an hour from now disoriented and frightened. Of course, there was always the possibility that he wouldn't awaken at all. I found myself thinking increasingly about the fact that one of these dinners would be our last, and that I wouldn't have nearly enough advance notice – probably none – about which it would be. I kept trying to convince myself that there was at least a tiny bit of time left, but I knew this disease worked on its own schedule and that how much Daz would be conscious near the end was impossible to gauge.

Linda was standing in the doorway of Daz's room with her hand on the frame, watching her brother's sleeping form. I wondered if this was what she'd done all last night or if maybe she spent the entire time in the chair next to him. The airbed in the living room was still propped up against the wall, though she or even Ana could have straightened everything up at some point during the day. I just had this feeling that she hadn't slept there. I thought about going home. Certainly Daz was in good hands, and Linda might have felt more comfortable being alone with him. At the same time, though, I didn't feel like leaving.

"Hey, do you want a drink or something?" I said.

"No thanks," she said, shaking her head. "The two beers with dinner were right around my limit."

"There's a great coffee place down the block. How about I go and get us a couple of cups?"

Her eyes widened. "I would love a decaf cappuccino. Ana can't even make good coffee. What she made today was the worst I've had in years."

I stood up. "We can definitely do better than that. I'll be back in a few minutes with a decaf cappuccino."

"With an extra shot, please."

"An extra shot of *decaf*?"

"It's about flavor, not function."

I smiled. "I like that line. Mind if I steal it? Your brother lets me steal his best lines all the time."

"Be my guest."

I headed out of the apartment and down the street to Java Nirvana. The place had opened a little more than a year ago, making the gutsy and seemingly ill-advised decision to locate less than a block from a Starbucks. Daz and I figured they'd be around for all of a week and a half and stopped in on their third night to offer some patronage before they folded. I started to have second thoughts about their chances, though, when I walked through the door. This was a coffee lover's coffee shop. They roasted their own beans right behind the front counter, filling the entire store with the musky scent of developing flavor. The shop was a small space, maybe seven hundred and fifty square feet or so, and it had only three tables, but it was a veritable coffee museum. Old fashioned roasters, burlap coffee bags, and photographs and tasting notes from the owner's various trips to the major coffee growing regions of the world were on display everywhere. None of this would have mattered if the brew wasn't any good – Upper West Siders can be impressed by earnestness, but they demand performance. Fortunately, the coffee was excellent. Even the drip coffee, often a shortcoming of even the most dedicated coffee establishment, was rich and intense. I stopped there most mornings on my way to pick up Daz and often went there before going home at the end of the night as well.

"It's Mr. Flash," Koren, the owner, said when he saw me. "You're early tonight. What happened, struck out with a girl?"

"The night's young, Koren."

"That it is. Hey where's Daz? I haven't seen him around lately. He isn't double-timing me with another barista, is he?"

I hadn't mentioned Daz's illness to Koren. It was hard enough discussing it with Daz's best friends. I was utterly baffled about how to bring it up to casual acquaintances, even ones we saw on a regular basis. "Nah, he's just got some other stuff going on."

Koren didn't blink when I ordered Linda's decaf cappuccino with an extra shot. Obviously, this was something people did. I decided it was a café con leche night for me.

Koren made our coffees himself, sidestepping the guy who worked the espresso machine to do so. This was something he'd started doing a couple of months ago, regardless of how crowded the shop was. Clearly, it was his way of showing us that we were elite customers, and I appreciated it, even though I was sure that anyone he chose to employ was capable of making coffee the right way.

"Tell Daz I want his ass in here in the next couple of nights or I'm scratching his name off the list of my favorite patrons," Koren said as he handed me the drinks.

"I'll pass along the message. He's been really preoccupied."

Koren regarded me carefully for a second. "The two of you are still hanging out together, right?"

"Jeez, yeah," I said broadly. "I'll try to get *his ass* down here. I promise."

"That's good. You two are much more fun together than you are by yourself."

"Thanks for the compliment."

Linda was back at Daz's bedside when I got back. I gestured to her to come out to the living room and she reluctantly agreed.

"You can have the comfy chair," I said, motioning toward the massage recliner and sitting on the couch. Linda settled in and looked at the control pad on the arm as though it was the console on a spaceship. I suggested she press "knead" and she did, her eyes sparkling as the chair began to work its magic on her. She leaned her head back and gave in to the sensation for a short while. Then she turned the chair off and shook her head in wonder.

"I think Eric is the very last person I would expect to have something this extravagant."

"I goaded him into it."

She patted the leather. "Back home if anyone had ever told Eric that he would be living in an elegant New York City apartment with one of *these* things, he would have laughed in their faces."

"The trappings of success. Your boy's a pop star."

"I guess. He would have laughed even harder if anyone had told him that." She sipped her coffee and nodded approvingly. "*Much* better than Ana's work. You seem to have good taste, Rich."

"I cultivate it." I took a sip of my café con leche. "You know, I'm sure Daz is thrilled you came to see him."

This seemed to sadden her. I wished I hadn't brought it up or that I thought of some other way to say it.

"I should have been here sooner," she said mournfully. "Can you believe my boss actually gave me a hard time about getting away?"

I frowned. "Sounds like someone who shouldn't be your boss for very long. What do you do?"

"I work for a greeting card company," she said with a hint of shyness in her voice.

"Please don't tell me that you write them."

She laughed out loud. "No, nothing like that. *You're* the wordsmith, Rich. I do premium sales."

"You mean cross-merchandising and that kind of thing?"

"Yes, that kind of thing."

"Need a good ad agency?"

She smirked. "Don't think my brother hasn't tried that pitch before. I should have guessed you would do the same."

I signaled resignation with my free hand. "How long do you think you can stay?"

"I don't know. As long as possible. Maybe even, you know, all the way. I kinda quit my job."

"Kinda?"

She rolled her eyes. "It was the most impulsive thing I've ever done, but my boss really got me angry. I'm pretty sure he understood that I wasn't coming back, and I don't really care if he misunderstood."

"Their loss, our gain. Does Daz know?"

"That I quit?"

"That you can stay here indefinitely."

"There's nothing really 'indefinite' about it, now, is there?"

The sense of defeat in Linda's tone surprised me. "I guess that was a bad choice of words."

"There's no *good* choice of words." Her eyes flickered and for a second I thought she might start crying. "I don't know why, but I'm so unprepared for this."

I wanted to take her hand or maybe put an arm around her, to show her that I understood what she was going through and that she could count on me for support. Instead, I just took another sip of coffee. I wasn't sure I was supposed to cross that line, even though Linda and I were in some sense "related." Linda watched her cup for a long moment, and I thought I might lose her there, that she'd decided that talking to me was too hard under the circumstances. Then she made a visible effort to pull herself back together.

"So your nickname is 'Flash,' huh?"

"On good days. There are other less complimentary variations."

Linda nodded. "And Eric is 'Dazzle?'"

"'Daz,' really. It used to be 'Dazzle,' but two syllables is more than most of us can handle."

"Flash and Dazzle," she said, trying the name on.

"Low self-esteem really isn't an issue."

She smiled at me. "So I've heard." She seemed amused saying this, though I wasn't sure why. "Do you have a girlfriend? A wife? An ex-wife?"

"None of the above. I have a great office, though."

"One of those corner things with a wraparound view of the city?"

"Not that great."

She gestured with her chin as though suggesting that I muddle through. "You have time."

"Yeah."

"So what does one do for fun around here?"

"You mean after the cows settle down for the night? Nothing much: tell stories around the campfire, read the *Farmer's Almanac*, go dancing until three in the morning."

"Ah, just like home."

I appreciated that she was trying to rally a little here. "We have our usual haunts. And I'm kind of a restaurant junkie. Things just seem to come up. We're big on impromptu. I can show you around a little sometime if you'd like."

"I don't know if I have the constitution to go out on the town with a guy named 'Flash.'"

"You'd be surprised by how deceptive names can be."

Linda seemed to enjoy this conversation, at least a little. Her face was so like Daz's in so many ways, but her eyes were uniquely her own. I don't think I'd ever seen anyone's eyes show this much expression, and they could toggle from amusement to gloom remarkably quickly. They did so just then. It was as though she'd remembered at that very moment that she wasn't here for a pleasure trip. She stood up.

"I'm going to check on Eric."

She was gone for several minutes. Again, I had this urge to join her, to stand next to her while she watched her brother, to put my arm around her shoulders and show her that we were doing this together and that I could be leaned upon. Something kept holding me back, though. The two of them needed time alone together, even if Daz was asleep during it. I finished my coffee and leafed through a copy of *Extreme,* the sports magazine that was sitting on Daz's windowsill. Daz and I once promised ourselves that we would learn snowboarding. Another thing I wouldn't ever wind up doing without him. Not that I had any capacity to think about the future. All time, since I first heard Daz was sick, had become compressed into the now. Later was just something I didn't want to contemplate.

More time passed. I was about to get up to tell Linda that I was heading home when she returned to the living room.

"He's so serene," she said. "It's a little scary."

I recalled the numerous times I'd come to pick up Daz and found him sprawled across the bed. My guess was that he was rarely a serene sleeper. "It could be the medication."

"That might be it." She sat back down, but this time on the edge of the chair. She seemed so vulnerable. I knew what she felt like.

If I was too self-conscious to touch her, I figured the least I could do was try to distract her a tiny bit. I waited until she looked at me before I spoke. "So how about you? Any boyfriends? Husbands? Ex-husbands?"

She smiled sadly. "It's been a while."

"For all three?"

"No, just for the boyfriends. Thank God neither of the other two. Not many of the first one, either. Sometimes the town seems pretty small, you know?"

"Maybe you should move."

Her eyes glistened again. "The thought has crossed my mind."

I wondered what was keeping her in Kansas. Family? Friends? The belief that what she was looking for was somehow waiting for her there? It seemed to me that if someone like Linda was dissatisfied with what life was offering – and she hadn't technically said that – she owed it to herself to do something about it. Certainly sitting around Kansas waiting for life to happen made little sense.

"What do *you* do for fun?"

"Other than explore the endless array of wanton thrills that Topeka has to offer?"

"Yeah, besides that."

"I read a lot. And I volunteer at the neighborhood community center. And I like to drive."

"Just drive?"

"Well, not aimlessly for hours on end," she said a little shyly. "But I like to go for long drives and visit different places and stop in at the shops and just get a sense of what is going on there."

"Exploring different cultures."

"Nothing quite that exotic, though I've been to some Native American reservations."

"Wow, that really is exotic. I mean, half of the New York area is named after some Native American tribe or another but there isn't a trace of them anywhere other than the casinos in Connecticut."

"The trace isn't all that strong near us, either." Linda looked out the window and concentrated for a while, as though she just remembered that she was in the City. "Mostly, I just like to get out."

I felt an overwhelming sense of sympathy for her in that moment. I knew what she was going through, at least part of it. I wondered how much her expression mirrored my own. Could people tell what was happening to us just by looking at us?

We talked a short while longer, but I could see that Linda was tired. Regardless of whether she was planning to crash on the airbed or fall asleep in the chair next to Daz, I was in the way. I stood up to leave and impulsively kissed her on the cheek as I said goodbye. She held her cheek against mine for a moment before pulling back.

"I'll see you tomorrow night?" she said.

"I'll be here."

She smiled, her eyes brightening. It really was incredible to me that she could do that. "What's on the menu?" she said.

I had no idea. "Let's let that be a surprise."

———

It was after midnight when I got home. My phone started ringing as soon as I put my briefcase down. My first thought was that Linda was calling to say something happened to Daz.

"Rich, Prince. Listen, I have a couple of things on my mind. First, and I would have called you about this earlier but things have been insane around here, is that Keane told me you needed to cut short your drinks date the other night and that you've been a little elusive about rescheduling. Everything okay over there?"

I gave a moment's thought to telling Prince about Daz. Something told me he would understand, might even sympathize. I decided against it. "Just a bit of a personal crisis. I didn't mean for Noel to misunderstand."

"He can be good at that. So you're not having second thoughts on us, right?"

Frankly, I hadn't had *any* thoughts about them lately, but that wasn't the politic thing to say. "No, really. It's just that I have some stuff going on in my personal life and it's taking a huge amount of my attention."

"Anything to do with the law?"

I laughed a little. "No, I'm not a felon if that's what you're asking."

"So we're still on track?"

"Curt, I think what you're doing over there is as fascinating as I ever thought it was, and I certainly haven't stopped believing that you have great plans for K&C downtown. My head's just a little fuzzy at the moment."

"I'll take that as a yes. Listen – hook up with Keane as soon as you can. K&C is big on process. That's the part I can't do anything about, and we want to get that stuff out of the way so we can get on to the good stuff."

I suddenly felt very tired. I flopped down on the couch. "I'll try."

"The other thing I wanted to tell you is that Andrea and I are heading off to Europe for the next three weeks. Lots of business, some pleasure. Maybe even some of the business will be pleasurable. Anyway, the house is available and it's yours if you want to use it anytime while I'm away."

"Wow, that's a very generous offer."

"It's nothing. The house is just sitting there. Let me give you Carl's number. He'll pick you up whenever you want and he has the keys."

The thought came to mind that I could pack Daz and Linda up for the weekend and blow them away with a fabulous mini-vacation. Still, in spite of the conversation we'd had about K&C and Daz's assurance that he understood why I hadn't told him about it immediately, the idea of showing him my newfound access to splendor via my new buddy Curt just didn't feel right. On top of everything else, there were some very real practical impediments to simply whisking Daz away at this point.

"I really appreciate it," I said to Prince. "and I'd love to take you up on it. You have a great place there and, believe me, under any other circumstances I'd be out to the Hamptons in a heartbeat. This personal crisis isn't going away in the next three weeks, though, and I'm kind of rooted to the City."

I heard Prince draw in a breath on the other end. "Is this something I need to be concerned with, Rich?"

"It's nothing you *can* be concerned with, Curt."

"Well, I hope you work through it soon. And get in touch with Keane. He has all kinds of theories about why you walked out the other night."

"I'll give him a call tomorrow. Have a great trip and say hi to Andrea for me."

"Yeah, she says hi, too."

When I got off the line, I lay across the couch and looked at the ceiling. Work was hard enough to concentrate on. The little courtship dance I'd been doing with K&C was almost impossible to contemplate. The best I could imagine at this point was just keeping that set of balls in the air. I'd call Noel Keane tomorrow and set up another meeting, maybe for next week, maybe for the week after that. I simply couldn't make myself rush this at this point. Nothing else would happen until Prince returned from Europe, anyway. That bought me time.

Time for *what*, I had no idea. But at least I could purchase some of it relatively cheaply.

The chapter about change happening whether you wanted it to or not

A few days later, Michelle took off on what was reputed to be her sabbatical. We'd had a number of conversations over the past few days, mostly about work and the progress of her projects, but sometimes about how excited her family was that she was coming for an extended visit. Michelle was remarkably unguarded during these discussions. It was so clear that she wanted this and now that I realized how much, it became obvious to me how unnatural living in the City had been for her, even though she'd done a great job of acclimating. As a result, I found myself missing her just a little bit more every time I saw her.

She stopped by my office on her way out the door.

"More rain," she said. "Here *and* in Indianapolis. How much do you want to bet a two-hour flight turns into a seven-hour ordeal?"

"Maybe it's a sign that you're not supposed to go."

"I think it's a sign that I need an umbrella."

"Do you have a good book to read?"

"The iPad is fully loaded. Books, music, magazines – I even brought some knitting."

I squinted, as though Michelle was some kind of shapeshifter. "You knit?"

"It's far down on the list of options."

I never would have guessed that it was even *on* her list of options. Maybe it was time to conduct full-scale interviews with all of my friends so I wouldn't be caught with my chin on the floor so often.

"I guess you're all set then. Sounds like you'd be fine even if you had to stay at the airport overnight."

"Don't even joke about that."

Michelle put down her bags and walked into my office. I stood up and she came around my desk to hug me.

"You're not coming back again, are you?" I said to the side of her head as we continued to hug.

"I'll be back," she said, still holding on.

"Have I told you that I don't completely understand this?"

"Dozens of times." She kissed me and pulled back.

"You really miss it?"

"I think I do," she said with a voice that suggested she was sparing me her true enthusiasm. "You know me, I'll get there and I'll start pining for SoHo and complaining that the bars close too early. But yeah, I think I do. My niece called me on my cell phone about an hour ago. She told me that my sister said she could stay awake until I got there, no matter what time that was. I'm guessing she'll be passed out on the family room couch when I finally show up."

I wanted to be happy that she was excited about this. She was a friend and she was important to me. Therefore, I should be willing to share in her pleasure. I simply couldn't, though. I just didn't want her to go.

"Well, have your little dalliance in the heartland and then come back to us," I said as warmly as I could.

"I will." Michelle was still standing behind my desk. She looked over at her bags, but she didn't move. "I meant to get over to see Daz again before I left, but I never made it. Will you apologize for me?"

I nodded and then took her hand. "I'll tell him you said goodbye."

"I should've."

"He'll understand."

"How can he? I don't even understand it myself."

"Daz will."

"Thanks," she said, looking down at our hands and squeezing mine.

"I have your cell, so I can reach you," I said tentatively.

"Yeah, of course. Everything is in order, though."

"I'm sure it is. But, you know, I might need to call."

She gave me a grim smile and then kissed me again. "I gotta go." She walked over and bent to pick up her bags.

"Our Tuesday potluck suppers won't be the same without you," I said.

She put a hand on her hip. "We haven't done a potluck supper in my family in decades, Mr. Smart-ass."

"Just another reason to come back to New York, I guess."

She arched her eyebrows and then hefted her luggage.

"Send me a postcard, okay?" I said.

She turned toward the door. "I'm not going to Paris, you know."

"Send me a postcard anyway."

"I'll try to find one. See you in a month."

"Hope so."

She headed down the hall. I don't know why I was having so much trouble letting go of her, but it was getting to me. I felt confused and empty and a little abandoned. I walked out of my office, and for a moment

I thought about following after her, though I had no idea what I would say if I did. Instead, I just watched as she turned the corner to head toward the elevators.

I knew I would never see her in this office again.

———

Other than my first drinks date with Noel Keane (I still hadn't called to schedule another one), I always tried to make it to Daz's place by dinnertime. Bringing him dinner made me feel like I was doing something for him, even though I knew nothing I could do would help. However, I couldn't avoid staying late with Vance that night. The Koreans had delayed their trip slightly, but they were coming next week, and we were having more than our share of problems putting a presentation together for them.

We were still working with the themes Daz and I had come up with, but Vance had a difficult time capturing the sense of light that I could picture but not draw. I knew Daz would have pulled it off with both eyes closed and while keeping a soccer ball aloft with his left foot. We couldn't spend the money for elaborate special effects until we had the car company on board, and while Vance was a very talented commercial artist, he just couldn't seem to draw anything that suggested the electrified chrome I was looking for.

"Let's go another way," he said around seven-thirty that night. I assumed that Daz and Linda were eating dinner just about then. I wondered what they'd decided to have, hoping they didn't choose to resort to Ana's cooking. Daz had probably convinced Linda that the diner down the street made great BLT's when everyone knew you needed to go at least a dozen blocks south for that. I realized I probably could have made the run uptown to make a delivery before Vance and I got started, but it was too late to do it now.

"What do you mean?"

"This obviously isn't working. At some point if something isn't working, you need to trash it, right?"

I remembered Daz's early criticism of this idea before he wrapped his mind around it. "It's not time to trash it. It's time to get the image down on the page, to look at it from a perspective we haven't considered."

"And what perspective would that be?"

His lack of commitment to this approach grated on me. "I don't know," I said sharply, "*you're* the art director."

Vance looked at me stiffly and then flipped a page in his sketchbook and started drawing again. The page was facing away from me, so I had no idea what he was drawing. Whatever it was, though, it certainly wasn't making him happy.

"Are you hungry?" I said a couple of minutes later while he was still working away.

"Not particularly."

"I'm thinking about ordering a pizza. Does that sound good to you?"

He continued scribbling and shading. "I'll have a slice if you order it. I'm okay, though."

I gave a moment's thought to simply pushing through, hoping we might make significant enough progress by nine or so to call it a night. Then I could go home and eat alone or maybe even stop by to see Daz and Linda. I realized the odds were against this, though, so I picked up the phone and ordered the pie.

A couple of minutes later, Vance showed me his new sketches and they still weren't close to right. I started to make some suggestions, and he pulled the sketchbook away from me, saying he knew what he had to do.

"So what the hell are we calling this thing, anyway?" he said as he scribbled intently.

"How about *Gleam*?" I said, tossing out my weakest choice first.

"Sucks."

"Yeah, I know it does. What do you think of *Sunburst*?"

"Not much."

"I don't either." I scanned my yellow legal pad, which by this point had pages and pages of nonsense jotted on it. "How about *Beacon*?"

"I don't think so."

I searched the page. "'Flambeau'?"

He looked up from the sketchbook. "You're not serious, are you?"

His attitude rankled me. Did he work this way with everyone? Was he always this completely unengaged? "You know, you could actually come up with a couple of names of your own rather than simply rejecting mine," I said.

He put his pencil down and stared at me. "Hey, *you're* the copywriter."

I threw the yellow pad on my desk. "First of all, I am *not* 'the copywriter.' I am Associate Creative Director of this entire agency, something I shouldn't have to remind you about. And since I'm the senior partner on this team and the guy who could have you bounced off of this project in a nanosecond, you might want to lose the sarcasm."

Vance's eyes narrowed and then he turned away from me and started sketching again. "You got it, boss."

I was extremely pissed off and had to remind myself that it was counterproductive to escalate this disagreement. I could go to Rupert in the morning and tell him that I wanted to work with someone else on this campaign, and he'd give me my pick of any art director on the staff. With so little time left to get anything done, though, I didn't have the luxury of starting over with a new person. I had to gut it out with Vance.

Eventually the pizza arrived.

The good ideas never did that night.

———

The next night, I got to Daz's apartment to find a slim black woman washing things in his kitchen sink. I said hello to her and she nodded and then proceeded to Daz's room. I followed her. When I got there, I saw that Daz was hooked up to an IV for the first time since he'd left the hospital and that he was looking more than a little crestfallen over this.

"Hey," he said when he saw me.

"Hey." I nodded toward the woman.

"This is Harlene. She's the night nurse."

Night nurse? Harlene was intent on monitoring the IV drip, and she didn't even seem to notice that we were talking about her. The drip must have been doing what she expected it to do, because a minute later she nodded and left the room. I sat down at Daz's side. Linda was on the other side of the bed, looking grim.

"Ana tattled on me," Daz said.

"What does that mean?"

"She reported a couple of little instances of incoherence, if you can believe that. A doctor came this morning and recommended twenty-four-hour care. He didn't make it sound like an option."

"Of course it's an option," I said angrily. "If you don't want it, you don't have to have it. You're the one calling the shots, not the doctors."

"I told him that," Linda said, rising to the realization that she had an ally.

"Why exactly should I fight this?" he said, raising his hand to calm the two of us. "I don't think the doctor suggested it to run up the bill."

I glanced out the door. "So she's going to be with you all night? What does she do? She doesn't sit in *here*, does she?"

"I'm not really sure what she does. We haven't had a night yet. I think she hangs out in the kitchen. I hope she has a Game Boy to play with or something."

I turned to Linda. "Are you okay with that?"

She took a deep breath. "I'm okay with whatever Eric is okay with."

I nodded toward the door again and said in a stage whisper, "She's not gonna start cooking for you, is she?"

Daz shook his head slowly. "She's kind of at a different level than Ana. I think her only role is to do nurse stuff."

This mollified me a little. It seemed both reassuring and alarming that she was a first-teamer. The consequences of her presence hardly eluded me, though, and my stomach fluttered a little. I looked at the IV, watching it drip, wondering what Harlene was checking it for and realizing that I wouldn't have a clue if it somehow malfunctioned. I turned back toward Daz.

"A couple of instances of incoherence?"

"You want to know something about those?" he said with a thin laugh. "You really have *no* idea that you're incoherent at the time. I guess that's what incoherent means, huh?" He looked at me with an expression of mock horror on his face. "You don't think Ana was lying, do you? Maybe the stuff in the IV is a drug that will convince me to turn my vast fortune over to her and Harlene."

"I think you're having another one of those bouts now," I said, glad that he was joking about this, even though it was abundantly clear that he was upset. "So I guess the idea of your pinch hitting at tomorrow night's softball game is out, huh?"

He patted the bed. "I'm kinda here."

"I turned the team over to Nick."

"What are you talking about?"

"We're going to have games three nights a week. I don't want to do that right now."

Daz looked at me beseechingly. "We talked about this."

"I know. I decided not to take your advice. What the hell do you know about this stuff anyway?"

Daz stared up at the ceiling for a moment. "Nick is a jerk. The team will hate having him as the captain."

"With Chess and the two of us out, he's the best player. You're right; he's a bit of a jerk. But he'll do okay."

"Hey, you're the one who's going to have to listen to the bitching."

Bob Dylan's *Tempest* album ended, replaced by The Eagles' *Desperado*. The haunting acoustic opening of "Doolin-Dalton" filled the room, and none of us spoke through the first verse.

Linda looked awful, deflated. As though someone told her there was no Santa Claus. Given Daz's ironic responses to my questions, I almost wondered if he hadn't spent the past several hours propping her up instead of the opposite. She saw me looking at her and smiled, quickly averting her eyes. I didn't know what I could do to help her, but I tried to think of something.

"There's a *Wizards of Waverly Place* marathon on Disney tomorrow night," Daz said brightly.

"We're very lucky to be living in this time," I said. Even Linda laughed at that. "Do you need special snacks for such an experience?"

"Barbecue potato chips are the preferred *Wizards of Waverly Place* snack food," he said like this was common knowledge.

"Any particular reason?"

"Adds spice."

I looked at Linda. "Are you also a fan of this show?"

She rolled her eyes. "I've never seen it. It wasn't on when I was a kid and I don't find myself watching a lot of the Disney Channel."

"You aren't going to let me watch it?" Daz said, sounding like a spoiled child.

"Of course you can watch it," she said with the placating tones of a worn-down mother.

"But we're not going to be here," I said impulsively. Both of them looked at me with surprise. "I'm taking Linda out on a little stroll through the neighborhood."

Linda seemed uncomfortable with this. "I don't know if that's a good idea."

"Of course it is," Daz said quickly. "You can't stay in this apartment all the time. And if you think you're just going to sit there tomorrow night snickering at my TV show, missy," he said, pointing a finger at her, "you have another thing coming."

"Missy?" Linda said, a bit of the gleam returning to her eyes.

Daz grinned. "It seemed to go with the sentiment." He leaned his head in her direction. "Go have fun with Mr. Flaccid, baby. The change will be good for you."

Linda nodded and looked over at me hopefully. Daz knew what he was talking about; the change would help, though I would have preferred it if he conveyed these sentiments to her without using my most notorious nickname.

Harlene came back into the bedroom and gave Daz another one of his pills. I wondered if this was a new prescription, if everything had been kicked up to another level. I hated this. I hated that she was here. I hated that she would be present with us every night from here on out. This wasn't how this was supposed to go.

In the NBA, when the game clock winds down to the last sixty seconds, it starts ticking off in tenths, lending a heightened sense of immediacy to the last minute of play. The thought came to mind as Harlene left the room again that her arrival was an indication that Daz's game clock had also begun its frenetic descent. I flung the thought from my mind. Where the hell was the referee so I could call a time-out?

As soon as Harlene left the room, Linda excused herself as well, saying she needed to go get something. She seemed to be teetering from the moment I'd arrived at the apartment, and I wondered if she left because she didn't want Daz to see her cry. I watched her exit and then turned back to Daz. His eyes were still on the door.

"That was really a good idea you had about Linda, Flash," he said, still not looking at me.

"Yeah, she could probably use a little break. I wish I could take you out, too."

He looked at me sadly. "Not as much as *I* wish you could take me out."

I felt my heart in my throat yet again. I found it very difficult to speak and hoped that Daz understood.

"I've been thinking a lot about dying lately, Rich. You know, the whole what-happens-to-you-after-you-go thing. I said a little prayer today after Harlene showed up. I'm sure God thought that was hilarious."

I reached out and squeezed his shoulder, leaving my hand there afterward. I still couldn't think of anything to say.

"It's a pretty cheesy thing to do, isn't it?" he said. "I mean, I haven't even *thought* about religion in a dozen years, and now that I'm coming face to face with the Great Beyond, I start lobbying for a decent afterlife."

"You're going to have a fabulous afterlife," I said, though my voice was practically a whisper.

"What if I don't have *any* afterlife?"

"If there wasn't an afterlife before now, I'm sure they're getting the Grand Opening ready for your arrival."

Daz took several seconds to absorb this statement. Was he trying it on for size? Was he wondering whether this was something he could trust me on? Did he think that I was just telling him something he wanted to hear? Or did he understand that I had just done my own form of praying?

"I don't want it to be a void, Rich. I don't want it to just be now and then nothing. I didn't really allow myself to think about it until today, but now that I am thinking about it, I'm just really, really bummed."

I reached toward him in the bed and he leaned forward until our heads touched. Then I wrapped my arms around him. I was a little concerned about the IV, but Daz was holding me so tightly that I figured this was much more important than any damage I might inadvertently do.

After a short while, I settled back and sat next to him on the bed with my arms around his shoulders.

"It won't be a void. It's going to be someplace where you can watch four TV shows at once while you're playing a video game, becoming air hockey master of the universe, listening to all of the great music ever recorded, and scoring goal after goal against World Cup championship teams. Not to mention the spectacular women and the adoring fans."

He leaned his head against my shoulder. "Do I get to sleep late?"

"That's the best part. No annoying best friends telling you that you have to go to work."

He turned to look at me. Our faces were probably no more than a foot apart. "I'm glad you're not coming on this trip, Rich. Maybe someday when you're a hundred and twenty or something, but I'm glad you're not coming now."

"Sure, you'll have all the fun while I just trudge along down here missing you."

At that moment, Linda came back into the room. I was almost certain she had been crying. When she saw where I was sitting, she stopped short.

"Do you want me to wait outside?" she said.

Daz gave me a little shove and I launched myself comically off the bed. "Jeez, no," he said. "Flaccid was getting all sentimental on me. It's a good thing you're here to save me from that crap."

I looked at Linda and I offered her a guilty shrug. The smile she returned to me would have insulated me in Antarctica.

"I'll protect you, big brother," she said, walking over to him and kissing him on the forehead. I knew Daz wouldn't want Linda to show up in the afterlife until she

was a hundred and twenty or so either, but I certainly
hoped that there was going to be someone there to love
him this much.

The chapter about diversions

It would have been nice if Daz had mentioned that Linda was a foosball pro. That would have saved me the embarrassment of the 11-3 loss in our first game while I "took it easy on her." Or of the 11-7 loss in our second game when I was definitely trying too hard. The 15-13 overtime loss that followed wasn't as difficult to take, but I began to wonder if I was losing her respect. After she beat me 11-4 in the next game, there was mercifully someone else waiting for the table.

We sat back down at our booth. "I obviously misunderstood your earlier references to the wanton thrills of Topeka," I said, feeling a little winded, though getting crushed by Linda had hardly been strenuous. "How did you learn to play like that?"

"Eric taught me so that we could 'play' soccer together."

"But I can usually kick Daz's ass when we play foosball. I mean, I'm *good* at this."

"You must have been off your game tonight." She smiled at me patiently. "I also don't think you fully appreciate just how dull the bar scene is in Topeka. I've had plenty of opportunity to refine my skills."

"Well, I'm impressed," I said, very genuinely so. "And I'm never playing you again."

Linda took another drink of her beer, but she looked at me brightly while she did so. "That would be a shame," she said, putting the bottle down.

"Yes, I guess it would be, and this is probably good for me in the way that flax seed oil is. Hey, have you ever heard of *Search and Destroy?*"

"The video game?"

"*The* video game."

She offered me another patient expression and said, "Yeah, Eric told me how the two of you really get into it. I had no idea what he was talking about. A friend of mine has it, and we played it once. It didn't do much for me. I'm not big on aliens."

Strike one for Linda. She'd clearly never had the full *Search and Destroy* experience, though – the one with the huge TV and surround sound. I decided to forgive her.

This was our third stop of the night. Fourth, if you counted the hour or so we spent with Daz before the Disney marathon started. After the conversation I'd had with Daz the night before, I was a little reluctant to leave him, but the first thing he said when I showed up was "I'm really glad you're doing this for Linda." She'd been shaky all day, and he was anxious for me to "get her away from everything" for a while.

With this in mind, I set about trying to keep the evening light. I thought about shuttling Linda to various New York City landmarks, but that felt artificial and forced, a tourist thing to do. I decided instead to take her to a handful of places I really loved. We started by having dinner at Telepan, definitely one of the top two or three restaurants on the Upper West Side, where Linda had the roast trout and I had scallop and sea urchin stew. She seemed impressed by the room and even more impressed by the careful attention she received. She told me that she was a little concerned about going to a serious New York restaurant, having in her head the haughty attitude that had been expunged from these kinds of places long before I got my first expense account. She was pleasantly surprised that the wait staff was friendly, relaxed, and didn't once make her feel like "a farm girl."

From there, I took her to Java Nirvana. Koren was off for the night, which was just as well; I don't know what I would have done if he'd started asking questions about Daz in front of Linda. We settled in with a couple of cappuccinos (I thought about going caffeine-free like my guest, but I couldn't get myself to do it) and listened to some acoustic music on the stereo by an artist I didn't know while we watched the people go by. The Upper West Side wasn't exactly the crossroads of the City, but a wide variety of types still made their presence felt while we sat there, flitting in an out, standing in corners, grabbing one of the few available tables, or staying just long enough to get their coffee and go. There were young professionals trying to impress each other, students having meaningful conversations at loud volume, a couple talking casually, the obligatory writer sitting in a corner pouring his prose onto a notebook page. It was likely that all of these kinds of people existed in some form in Topeka, but the confluence of them was probably something Linda wasn't accustomed to seeing. Certainly, it appeared to be fresh to her. Whether she did it to be polite or because she was genuinely diverted, she seemed willing to enjoy herself.

An hour or so later, we were out on the street again. Linda stopped and pointed in the other direction. "Isn't Eric's apartment that way?"

"I thought we'd go out for a drink."

"Coffee isn't a drink?"

"*Another* drink."

Linda hesitated. I wasn't sure whether this was over the idea of staying away from Daz longer or over spending more time alone with me, though I wanted to believe it was the former. Finally she held me with her eyes and nodded. We walked over to Jake's Dilemma on Amsterdam between 80th and 81st. It's a place that has plenty of exposed brick and comic-style art on the walls, a huge bar with a half-dozen bartenders, a beer menu with more than fifty beers, and plenty of loud and usually well-selected music on the sound system. They were playing Audioslave when we got there, one of the albums I'd missed during Daz's A-Z rundown.

The Foosball Debacle was still an hour away at this point. First, we had a couple of microbrews each, discussed the relative merits of handcrafted beer vs. mass produced, sang along with the Decemberists song that came on after Audioslave, and tried our hand at darts, a game neither of us were very good at. Linda wasn't exactly a party girl – she was less likely to dance on a table than she was to plot the overthrow of the government – but this was definitely the loosest I'd seen her. And while she sang only marginally better than Daz, she looked a whole lot better doing it.

"What's wrong with aliens?" I said, pretending to be offended.

"They're a little, I don't know, *childish*, don't you think?"

"Are you saying that you don't think there's any possibility that life exists on other planets?"

"I'm saying that if there's life on other planets, I'm pretty sure they won't look like rhinoceroses, won't be dressed like Rambo, and won't talk like Arnold Schwarzenegger."

"You think there's *no chance* of that?" I said with mock indignation.

Linda smiled and took another drink. "You're right, Rich. Anything is possible."

I gestured to accept her concession of my point. "Now you're making sense."

She looked in the direction of the foosball table, which made me look that way as well. A number of people were circled around the contestants and they were making a great deal of noise. Had these people been there when Linda and I were playing as well? Had they all seen me get schooled by the out-of-towner?

"Eric used to tell me all the time about the games you guys played. He could go on for fifteen minutes about some competition or other the two of you had had."

"Our play dates have usually been very enjoyable."

She smirked at me. "This stuff was important to him. Not that it mattered to him at all who won at *Search and Destroy* or foosball or air hockey or anything else you did."

"You wouldn't say that if you saw him while he was going at it."

"Oh, I'm sure he wanted to win. He *definitely* always wanted to win. If I knew you better, I'd show you the little scar on my hip that I got when Eric was a tiny bit too aggressive in a game of three-on-three basketball. But I think the fact that he was playing with *you* was way more important than the outcome."

I could understand that. Certainly during competition (at anything and everything) there was a considerable amount of trash talk and jostling between us, and I always got the impression that Daz was trying very hard to beat me. It never held over, though. I couldn't think of a single time when Daz bore even a moment's ill will over losing a game.

"We've always had a great time," I said. "Right from the start."

"I know you did. I got the recap of the day's events from Eric hundreds of times. They were very entertaining."

I couldn't count the number of times I'd watched Daz speaking animatedly on the phone to Linda. I'd always been curious about her, always wondered what it was like to have that kind of sibling relationship. Not curious enough to go with him on a trip to Kansas, but fairly curious.

"I think it's great the way the two of you have stayed connected," I said. "I have a sister, too. I've seen her exactly twice in the last three years."

"Younger?"

"She's five years older."

Linda nodded, as though this information mattered in some way. "Does she live far away?"

"She lives in Rye. That's about a forty-minute drive from where we're sitting. If there's traffic on the Henry Hudson."

She tilted her head. "Then why don't you see her?"

"She has no soul."

She leaned forward and spoke in a stage whisper. "Did someone steal it?"

"No, it was simply bred out of her."

She sat back and gestured with her right hand. "And yet yours remained intact."

"Depends on who you talk to."

"Rich, you may be lacking in some things, but from what I can see, soul is not one of them."

I toasted her with my beer bottle. "Thanks. I think that's the nicest thing anyone has said to me in weeks."

We let the music play over us for a while. The Decemberists's baroque pop was replaced by Annie Lennox's refined vulnerability. I went to get us another couple of beers.

"How weird does it feel trying to sleep on that airbed with Harlene lurking around?" I said when I returned.

"Pretty weird. I think she's trying to respect my privacy, but it's not a very big apartment. I don't *think* she watches me while I'm laying there." She offered a little shudder.

"You can sleep at my place if you want. I have an actual pullout couch. And I never lurk."

She seemed a little embarrassed by this offer. "Thanks, but I can't. I really want to stay near Eric."

"I'm a couple of blocks away."

"They're a long couple of blocks in the middle of the night."

I knew I couldn't persuade her and I wasn't genuinely trying to do so. As Daz had the night before, I was only attempting to make life a little easier for Linda – all the while knowing there was nothing that could make that happen.

"I'll keep the offer on the table."

"I appreciate it." She cast her eyes downward. "You know what really disturbs me about Harlene? The fact that she exists at all."

"I had the same thought when I saw her."

She worked a fingernail into a crevice in the table made by a previous patron. "Every day it just seems to be getting more and more real to me." She looked at me sadly through the corner of her eye before focusing back on the table.

I hadn't intended the conversation to turn in this direction. This was supposed to be a break, a little side trip off of the road we were headed down. Now that the subject had come up, though, it was ridiculous to try to avoid it.

"It's gonna get a lot more real than this," I said darkly.

She looked up at me face-on now. Her eyes were glistening. "He's having fugue periods. Do you know what that means?"

"I know."

She shook her head and tightened her lips for a moment. "I keep worrying that I'll walk into his room and he'll start screaming at me because he thinks I'm a stranger."

"There's a very good chance that won't happen."

"But it *could* happen. Sometime really soon." Her face collapsed on itself all at once. I think she had been trying hard not to let me see her this way. She had even left the room the night before to keep Daz from seeing her cry. "How do I imprint on his brain that I love him?" she said haltingly.

I found this question devastating, one of the few I hadn't actually considered myself. As Linda held her hands to her face, I wrestled with what she was asking, what she was going through, what we both were going through. I got up from my side of the booth and moved over to her. I put my arm around her shoulders and she buried her face in my neck. We sat that way for several minutes. I knew there was nothing I could say to help her, but I hoped that my just being there offered some solace. It was silly for me to wish this away for her, but I found myself doing exactly that anyway. I wanted a miracle cure to be discovered. I wanted to learn that Daz's diagnosis was entirely wrong. I wanted anything but what all of us were facing.

Suddenly the backdrop of the bar with its loud drinkers and foosball spectators seemed absurdly wrong. Jake's Dilemma had outlived its usefulness for the evening.

"Let's get out of here," I said.

Linda nodded into my chest, then pulled back, wiped at her face and leaned into me, pressing herself against me tightly. "Yeah, let's go."

We walked the eight blocks without saying much of anything. While I wanted to keep holding her, to have her lean into my shoulder while we walked and tried to come to terms with what we were dealing with, once she separated from me, I couldn't think of a graceful way to bring her back. Maybe I should have just reached for her, but I didn't want her to have to handle me in any way.

"Do you want me to walk you upstairs?" I said when we got to Daz's building.

"I'm okay," she said. She didn't seem particularly okay but I got the point.

She reached up and kissed me on the cheek. "Thank you for showing me some of your city tonight."

I looked back up the street and then in her direction again. "It's a big place."

"Yes, it is." She gestured toward the building. "I have to go back to the small place now, though."

I nodded. "Give Daz a kiss goodnight for me. And say hi to Harlene."

She gave me a small smile. "Yeah, I will."

I turned to go and then turned back toward Linda again. The doorman had just opened the door for her. "It was imprinted a long, long time ago, you know."

"Are you sure about that?"

"Absolutely positive."

She held my eyes for a long moment. Then turned and walked through the doorway.

The chapter about the things that stick with you

Dinner the next night was Mexican food from Toloache. Their paella-like Tumbada, their indulgent Rib-eye Cecina, some lobster tacos along with some suckling pig tacos, hamachi ceviche, and their spicy Guacamole Rojo. I knew Daz loved all of this. Linda greeted me at the door when I arrived with the food and Daz's eyes opened widely when he saw what I'd brought. Unfortunately, he didn't wind up eating very much of it. His appetite had been dwindling in recent days, and this was the least he'd eaten yet.

I'd begun to grow accustomed to seeing Daz hooked up and reclining. This wasn't to say that I'd adjusted to it, only that it didn't seem quite as disorienting to me every time I came into the room. It was just part of what Daz looked like now. The same could be said for Harlene, who had a remarkable ability to make herself nearly invisible. I still hadn't exchanged more than a few words with her. Tonight, I asked if she wanted anything to eat and she declined. That was the extent of our conversation.

Daz's sojourn through his music collection had entered the letter g and the Gin Blossoms' "New Miserable Experience" album – a CD copy of which he'd brought with him to college – filled in the background. I'd always loved this album, and there were so many times when we added our discordant harmonies to the mix. Their second album – presumably next up in the queue – wasn't nearly as good, though it had its moments. There were many reasons for the decline in quality, the most prevalent being that the chief songwriter for the band died before the first album had been completed, and the band was completely on its own for the second.

I guessed that Daz had more than five hundred albums in his collection, not to mention a variety of singles he'd downloaded from iTunes over the years. Daz was something of a throwback in this regard, because he tended to buy complete albums, even though most artists had stopped making cohesive works (as opposed to a loose collection of songs) somewhere around the turn of the century. It had always seemed silly to me to buy ten songs when you only really wanted to listen to two, but Daz remained committed to this, just as he was now committed to listening to every one of these albums in their entirety.

"This is almost as good as El Mezecal back in Topeka," Linda said when she tried a taco.

"You have good Mexican food in Kansas?" I said.

"Does that seem impossible to you? There are *Mexicans* all over the country, you know."

We'd had a few of these exchanges the past few days, Linda's acknowledging that the City was the center of the universe while stridently reminding me that it wasn't the *entire* universe.

"Linda's a pretty decent Mexican cook herself," Daz said.

"You cook?"

"Yeah, of course. You don't?"

"That much should be obvious. If you cook, why haven't you made anything for us?"

Linda smiled slyly. "Because you always bring us dinner."

I turned to Daz. "You could have brought this up at some point."

"Hey, I never asked you to bring dinner every night. You seemed to be enjoying yourself."

I chuckled. I *had* been enjoying myself. "I'm getting a premonition," I said, putting a hand to my forehead. "It has something to do with a homemade three-course meal sometime in the next few nights."

We both looked at Linda. She shrugged. "I'll see what I can whip up."

"Daz, I'm counting on you here. I want the ultimate experience. What's Linda's best dish?"

"Well, she has quite a repertoire," he said, beaming at her. "The last time I came to visit, she made this thing with pork and apples that was the most fun you can have with your sister in the room. But if I really had to name one dish, it would be mom's chicken and dumplings."

"I've been making it since I was nine," Linda said. "You get good at something after a while."

The mention of "mom" caused me to wonder for easily the hundredth time why Linda was here but not the rarely-alluded-to Mr. and Mrs. Dazman. It didn't take keen skills of deduction to figure out that Daz and his parents weren't close, but that didn't excuse their not coming to their son's bedside at a time like this. There were times when you put the petty crap aside. It's possible that even *my* parents understood this.

"Hey, where the hell are your parents, anyway?" I said with all the indignation that surged inside of me at that exact moment.

The look that passed between Daz and Linda then was unrecognizable to me. Certainly, my sister and I had never looked at each other that way. I could count on the fingers of one hand – maybe the fingers of one *finger* – the number of times Daz had mentioned his mother and father. I guessed I was about to find out why.

"They don't know," Daz said.

"How could they not know?"

"They're not exactly accessible." Again, Daz looked at Linda and she seemed to understand that he wanted her to explain.

Her eyes flicked toward the bedspread. When she looked up, she looked out rather than at either of us. "You know about my mom having lung cancer a bunch of years ago, right?"

I nodded.

"She recovered. Fully, by all indications. At least physically. But something happened after she came home from her operation. She just seemed a little nervous and sad for a while. I figured this kind of thing was normal. I mean she had just gone through something really, really scary. Who wouldn't be a little shaken up by it?"

"We kept waiting for her to go back to being Mom," Daz said. "I remember coming home from school every day and thinking, *maybe she's gonna be like she used to be today.* After a while, I sorta figured out that I was kidding myself. That she wasn't going to be doing *anything* like she used to."

Linda leaned forward and rubbed Daz's shoulder. "She was clinically depressed. So of course the doctors tried to treat it with drugs. Those just made her manic-depressive. She decided that she couldn't handle it and stopped taking the medication. That's when she started spending most of the day in her room."

"Meanwhile," Daz said, "my father was having just a teensy bit of trouble with this himself. He'd never dealt with anything like this before, and the way he dealt with it now was inconsistent to say the least. One day, he'd hold her and talk to her and try to bring her around. The next he'd rally us and pretend that everything was great and that she pretty much didn't exist. The next he'd be flat-out pissed off. At this point, the rest of our family – and remember, they all had issues of their own to deal with – put as much distance between themselves and us as they could."

"It got a little lonely around the holidays," Linda said.

Daz looked sadly at his sister. In that moment, I imagined some of the tricks he might have attempted to cheer her up at Christmastime. "I almost didn't go to Michigan when I got the scholarship, but Linda told me she'd turn to prostitution if I didn't go."

"I don't think I said that exactly."

"It was something like that."

She swatted him on the leg. "Anyway, after Eric left, Mom shut herself off in her bedroom completely. I tried to convince my father to find someplace for her where she could be taken care of full time but he wouldn't hear of it. He was so damned angry by that point. At her getting sick, at her 'abandoning' him, at just everything about this. I think he was just waiting for me to get out of the house. I got scholarship offers from a bunch of schools, but I told him I would enroll at Kansas State so I could stay home. I even suggested that I would take a reduced course load so I could be in the house more. You should have seen his reaction. He practically threw my stuff out on the lawn. Essentially, he forced me to go to Wichita State. I couldn't understand what he was thinking – after all, *somebody* needed to be with her – until that October."

"That's when he left," Daz said. "Without a freaking trace."

"Your father disappeared?"

"I haven't seen him since the summer between my sophomore and junior years."

Which meant that Daz's father abandoned them while Daz and I had been roommates at Michigan. I couldn't decide which part of this was more stunning to me.

"He just took his stuff and headed off," Linda said. "No goodbye note, no forwarding address, no Christmas cards. The weirdest thing was that he took practically none of their savings with him. I guess that was his last decent act. It allowed us to get Mom into a good mental hospital."

"Where she remains to this day," Daz said, "completely unaware of this little problem I'm having."

Linda glanced down and shook her head. "I saw her just before I left to come here. Eric told me that he didn't want me to tell her anything. I almost did it anyway."

Linda and Daz both looked at me at that point. If they expected me to say something, they were going to have to wait a while.

———

Junior year had been our first living off campus. We had a cramped two-bedroom place about a quarter-mile from school with a refrigerator that groaned every time we opened it for a beer. Daz was convinced the appliance was haunted. I was convinced we were going to open it to warm beer one night.

Daz had an intense two-week relationship with a woman named Hadley not long after school started. I could tell you precisely how intense the relationship was because the walls of the apartment were very thin. Toward the end of the second week, the sounds from his bedroom changed to clipped conversation and sharp exchanges. A couple of days later, Hadley was gone, followed soon thereafter by Daz, who told me he was going home for a long weekend. I figured he must have been pretty upset about his breakup because this meant missing Blotto '05 – a three-day drinking fest sponsored by fraternities all over the university.

Daz didn't come back until Wednesday, and when he did, he was decidedly not himself. He didn't want to talk about his time in Kansas and he didn't want to go out. He didn't even play music from his stereo and he seemed irritated when I put on an album we both liked. This was the first time I'd seen him even come close to appearing sullen. I planned to simply give him space, but when he didn't come out of his room that Saturday until after three in the afternoon, I decided to say something.

When I heard the familiar groan from the kitchen, I asked him to get me a beer as well. He threw it to me where I was sitting on the couch and started heading back to his room.

"She's not worth it, you know," I said to his back. Daz stopped, but he was still facing away from me. "She really isn't," I said to reinforce the point.

He turned sharply and I could see that his jaw muscles were tight. "What the fuck do you know about it?"

I felt a little chill at that moment. I'd never seen this expression on Daz's face before, and he'd never spoken to me in that tone of voice. I truly wasn't sure what he was going to do next.

I held up both hands. "I've broken up with women, Daz. I know *a little bit* about this. Hadley's not worth what you're putting yourself through."

Daz laughed bitterly. He was unrecognizable at this moment. "You're right. Hadley's not worth it." He took a long pull on his beer and then turned, walked into his room, and closed the door.

A couple of hours later, he came into my room. "Where are we going tonight?"

He looked a lot better, which was good to see. "It's Jaegermeister night at the Wretch. I was planning to check it out. You up for that?"

"I'm definitely up for that."

We got ridiculously drunk that night, and Daz seemed more Daz-like afterward. The funny thing was that I thought I'd helped him in some way with my little "intervention." He was letting a woman get to him, and he needed a little reminder that he shouldn't get so hung up.

It wasn't until just now that I realized how little help I'd been. What was bothering him was what was happening back home, but I didn't know that because, for whatever reason, he didn't think he could tell me. The realization of what he must have thought when he'd heard me say, "She isn't worth it" made me feel utterly useless.

———

I'm not sure how long I was lost in that bit of reverie. Linda and Daz were still looking at me and I tried to remember where we were in the conversation.

"You're not going to tell her?" I said at last.

Daz shrugged. "I'm not sure she would understand if I *did* tell her, and I'm worried that it'll just make her crazier."

Linda squeezed Daz's arm. "We've had a few *long* conversations about this. She's pretty far gone, Rich."

I don't know what I would choose to do in their situation. I still had a tough enough time just *imagining* their situation.

I looked down at my plate as though some sense could be made of this from some leftover guacamole and a small piece of corncob.

"How have you guys carried this around all this time?"

Daz smiled at Linda. "It helps if you have someone going through it with you."

Along with someone else to party it out of your mind? I wondered.

"Eric came to visit a lot after my father left to hold my hand and to hold Mom's hand. Meanwhile, I think we used a fair amount of our parents' savings on phone bills. But after a while it just becomes part of you. We all have a family history, right? You have your soulless sister."

"Yeah, I guess I should give her a call and thank her for only *mostly* dumping me."

"You get out of your family what you can," Daz said. "Every now and then they surprise you. My mother somehow remembered my twenty-fifth birthday. That was a pretty big deal. You just build the rest of your life out of what's available."

"I guess you do. 'Families suck,' huh, Daz?" I said, locking eyes with him. He obviously remembered that exclamation from our first night together. At that point, his Dad was still around. I turned to Linda. "Present company excepted, of course."

"Goes without saying."

"Have you thought about trying to get word to your father?"

Daz threw his eyes to the ceiling. "Why would I do that? I truly have no idea where he's living these days. I don't even have any idea *if* he's living these days."

I considered that. "I wonder if he feels anything. Parents are supposed to have some kind of psychic connection to their kids, right? I wonder if he's walking around somewhere with this thing nagging at the back of his head and wondering why the hell he feels so uneasy."

"My guess is that even if he is, he'll never trace it back to me. We are gone and forgotten."

"You don't think that's really true, do you?"

"I'm sure of it."

I found that difficult to believe. While I couldn't imagine what it took to run out on your kids and sick wife like that, and while I certainly didn't believe that my own parents spent much time wondering how their little boy was doing, something told me that you never really put your children out of your mind completely. That just isn't the way life works.

"I hope you're wrong."

Daz just shrugged again. "He's the cutout, by the way."

"What?"

"The cardboard cutout I keep in my office and take out for the April Fool's Day party. It's a picture of my father that I had blown up."

The Dour Man was Daz's father. I couldn't count how many times I'd goofed on that guy in my mind. "I always thought it was some B-movie actor."

"Pretty much the same thing."

Harlene came in at that point to change the bag connected to the IV. I took our dishes into the kitchen to clean up and Linda followed me.

"I don't know what it is about what she does in there that makes me squeamish," she said. "It's not like she's changing the IV itself."

I offered her a little shudder in commiseration. "I try not to think about any of it."

Linda scraped the dishes and handed them to me to rinse and put in the dishwasher. "I didn't realize he hadn't told you about Mom and Dad."

"Amazingly, it never came up in conversation. If there was a feather nearby, you could knock me over with it right now."

"Eric hates talking about it."

"Obviously."

I turned to look at her and she smiled knowingly. "At a certain point, you don't really think about it on a conscious level anymore, you know? Everybody has that kind of stuff."

That wasn't the issue – we were freaking rooming together when it happened – and I think she knew it, but there also wasn't anything to be accomplished by making a big deal out of this with her. Or with Daz for that matter. He didn't need my hounding on this subject. Still, I couldn't help thinking the rest of the night about the dark things that had become part of Daz and Linda's makeup and how these juxtaposed against the vivid images I had of Daz bouncing a ball off his head, or engaging me in an epic *Search and Destroy* battle, or being everybody's best friend at The Creative Shop, or dancing some ridiculous way at Jake's Dilemma or any of the dozens of other bars we'd frequented over the years.

It wasn't that I believed only weeks ago that Daz got off scot-free from the tribulations that all of us face in our first decades. However, if you'd asked me only weeks ago, I certainly wouldn't have been able to tell you what those tribulations were, and I never would have guessed their immensity. Yet he was my best friend. I mean, he really was my *best friend*.

Harlene had finished with her work when we got back, and Daz suddenly looked very tired. I don't know why I hadn't noticed until now that he was losing weight. He had been slim as long as I'd known him, but now he looked gaunt. He was receding.

"You know what I wish I'd done more of?" he said when we returned to the room.

I sat down at my chair. "Everything?"

"Yeah, everything. But specifically, I wish I wrote more correspondence."

"Correspondence."

"Letters. I wish I wrote more of them."

"You wrote me some nice letters over the years," Linda said.

"I did?"

"Well, two or so. Many years ago."

"Did I say anything meaningful in them?"

"Everything you wrote was meaningful to me."

"But would they be meaningful to anybody else in the world?"

Linda seemed a little disturbed by this question. "They weren't written for anyone else."

Daz reached out a hand for her. "No, they weren't, but I wish I'd written some correspondence to *someone* that would be meaningful to everyone. I should have written letters to the *New York Times* or CNN or something."

"Does e-mail count?" I said.

"Nothing digital counts. Except music. And video games. And Pixar movies. And the special effects I used on the third BlisterSnax commercial."

"That's okay, you never wrote anything meaningful in your e-mail messages anyway."

"You must have, right, Flash? I bet you've written timeless letters over the years."

"Not really. I never really had anyone to write to. Do you think I should start?"

"I definitely think you should start. Go home right now and write someone a letter. Make absolutely sure that it's timeless."

"Yeah, I'll think about that. Maybe later tonight."

"When my best friend Becky Centis went to college in Boulder," Linda said, "we wrote these long letters back and forth. Stuff about what was happening and how we felt and all of that. There were people I never met who I felt that I knew personally because of these letters. It was a great thing."

"Are you still in touch?"

"Yeah, of course. She's my best friend. She moved to Houston after college and she's married and has an eight-month-old baby, so now it's mostly e-mail and Facebook, but every couple of months I get a few pages from her written in the tiniest script. I always write her back right away, though I don't always send the letter as soon as I write it because I don't want her to think she needs to get back to me again so quickly. She has a lot on her plate."

"That's a great thing," I said. "And totally foreign to me. Do you say lots of meaningful things in your correspondence?"

"Probably not nearly as much as Eric would like, right?" We both looked over at Daz for his comment.

We didn't get one from him, though, because he was staring dazedly at the far wall. For a minute, neither of us did anything. I felt incapable of action and felt a cold chill of fear that made me shudder. Where had Daz gone? Where was he going?

Linda tentatively reached out to touch her brother, her hand remaining suspended inches away from him for the longest time. Then she moved forward and shook him vigorously. At first this accomplished nothing, and tears sprang to her eyes. Seeing this made me start crying myself. I was so completely not ready for this.

She tried again and Daz startled, a spasm running through his entire body. When he turned to face us, he didn't focus on either of our faces for a moment. Finally, he looked at Linda, saw her crying, and turned into her big brother again.

"What's the matter?" he said, his voice drenched with concern and seeming unawareness of what had just happened.

"Nothing," Linda said, wiping at her eyes.

Daz looked at me for some kind of explanation.

"You just gave us a little scare there," I said.

"I did?"

I reached out and patted his leg. "It's okay. It's over now."

We both turned to Linda. Daz held a finger up to her face to catch a falling teardrop. "Are you all right?"

Linda took a deep breath and nodded her head yes. Then her face crumpled and she said, "No, no I'm not. What am I gonna do without you?"

She collapsed into his arms and Daz patted her back softly. He was visibly anguished. I knew he was thinking that he had to find a way to make things better for her. He'd always been able to do it before.

I sat on the edge of the bed and watched them, my throat throbbing in a way I'd never felt before.

———

The concierge stopped me when I entered the building that night.

"Mr. Flaster, there's a package for you."

I stopped by the desk and he handed me an International Fed Ex box addressed from Switzerland. As I stood in the lobby, I opened the box to find another beautifully decorated box inside. It was from Prince. The card inside read:

Rich,

Best brownies I've ever tasted, Pantry included. Thought you'd like some. Let's catch up when I get back.

Best,
Curt

P.S. I hope your "problem" is looking better.
P.P.S. Andrea says hi.

It was like getting a package from another dimension. I took it upstairs and left it unopened. I couldn't give myself brownies now, and I really couldn't think about Curt Prince, or Kander & Craft, or the fact that Noel Keane was still waiting (or not) for me to set up another drinks date with him.

I would open the box eventually. I would deal with all of this when I could.

Now was not the time.

The chapter about being down home

We hardly needed the episode the previous night to let
us know that we were running out of time. I seriously
thought about not going to work the next day, but I
knew that Linda needed time by herself with Daz. I was
there by four-thirty anyway, sitting with Daz and listening to music while Linda busied herself in the kitchen.
She was cooking for us tonight, even though she seemed
exhausted and distracted. It had seemed like a century
ago that we talked about her doing this.

"You didn't need to make dinner," I said to her when
I got there.

"I did," she said with a faint smile. "Eric mentioned
Mom's chicken to me a half-dozen times this morning.
I'm not going to disappoint him."

An hour and a half later, she brought us our
meal, her face as bright and generous as if she were
serving Thanksgiving dinner. Chicken and dumplings with sides of wild rice, corn, and string beans.
It was about as far away from Toloache, Telepan,
or Gray's Papaya as one could get, but it wasn't
any less delicious. Judging from the expression on
Daz's face when he had his first bite, it was exponentially more so. Linda had come through for her
brother big time.

"This was not the easiest thing in the world to make here," Linda said after accepting our compliments. "For one thing, this is not exactly a well-accessorized kitchen."

"Always worked for me," Daz said. He'd been lucid since I'd arrived, and this meal seemed to rally him. I could tell that this meant a great deal to Linda.

"My point exactly," she said, teasing, seeming to take special joy in being able to do so. "For another thing, I couldn't get White Lily flour anywhere."

"That makes a difference?" I said.

Linda nodded in an exaggerated fashion. "A world of difference. You can tell in the dumplings and the gravy."

"Tastes great to me," Daz said.

"You were always easy to please." She turned to me. "And you don't count because you probably never had this dish before in your life."

"You can grow up in Westchester and still be 'down home,' you know."

"Have you ever had chicken and dumplings before?"

"Not once."

Not counting bowls of cereal, a peanut butter and jelly sandwich I'd made a few weeks back, or that brunch with Curt Prince and Andrea, this was the first home-cooked meal I'd had in months. There was something appreciably different between a meal made in a home kitchen and one made in a professional one. I'd always known this; everyone does, really. For years now, though, I'd convinced myself that having such broad access to the remarkable level of cooking talent available in New York marginalized anything made outside of a restaurant. The meal tonight refuted that theory. As Daz had proclaimed, Linda was quite good at this, and I think I might have felt this way even if the circumstances had been different.

Just like the past few days, Daz didn't eat much. He savored his first several bites and then stopped soon thereafter. When Linda took his plate to bring it into the kitchen, he looked up at her apologetically, and she leaned down and kissed him gently on the cheek.

"I'll do the dishes," I said, moving to get up.

"No, don't be silly, I'll do 'em. Besides, you have no idea how much cleaning we're talking about. I'm a very messy cook. Stay here with Eric."

Linda left with the plates and I followed her with my eyes.

"She's a great cook, huh?" Daz said.

"She is. I guess she got all the talent in the family."

"I'm much better at burping on cue."

"I'm very proud of you."

He laughed and leaned his head back in the pillow. "Sorry I shook you guys up last night, Flash."

"Nah, it's fine. Things were getting boring around here."

"It wasn't fine. I wish I could say it would never happen again."

I took a deep breath. It was getting increasingly difficult for me to maintain my composure for any stretch of time. "Daz, we're here for you."

"I know you are. And just in case I forget to mention this at some point down the road, I appreciate that." He looked off toward the kitchen. "Linda's been kind of a mess all day. I'm worried about her."

"She's very, very strong."

He looked at me and smiled, but he seemed uneasy. Again he glanced toward the kitchen.

"Do you think you could take her out for a while tonight?" he said tentatively.

"Sure, of course," I said, "if she'll come."

"I think that would be really good."

I offered him a little chuckle. "Why? Do you need us to clear out so you can make your move on Harlene?"

"Nah, we already got it on this afternoon," he said with a wry smile. He looked up at the ceiling and his expression changed. "I just think she could use it."

"You're right; she probably could. She might give me a hard time about going, you know. I think we're both kind of feeling like this is where we want to be right now."

"Take her away for a while, okay? Watching her brother disintegrate before her eyes has to be destroying her. I can't help her but maybe you can, at least a little."

I nodded my head in agreement. I wanted to stay with Daz; I didn't want to leave him at all at this point. Still, I knew this meant a lot to him. Therefore, it meant a lot to me.

———

We walked for more than thirty blocks. Into the heart of midtown which was, at this time of night, dormant compared to the neighborhood we'd left. I wasn't sure where we were going; I'd left it entirely up to Linda.

She wasn't in the mood for Jake's Dilemma or any other bar, which was just as well, as I would only have gone if she'd insisted. We spent some time at Java Nirvana, but it was unusually crowded, and we couldn't get anywhere near a table. This time, Koren asked after Daz. I introduced him to Linda and this seemed to make him less inquisitive, because I assume he thought I was on a date. Linda didn't mention that she was Daz's sister, which I was thankful for. I wonder if Koren caught the resemblance. We leaned against a wall while we had our coffee and got out of there right after we were done. There were any number of places we could have retreated to, places that would have been relatively quiet or relatively noisy, depending on what Linda wanted, but once we started down Broadway, she told me she just felt like walking. So that's what we did, sliding over to Seventh Avenue once we passed Central Park.

"This is Carnegie Hall," Linda said, walking up to the building and touching the façade. "Do you ever go here?"

"I went all the time with my mother and sister when I was a kid. Not very often since then."

She looked at the schedule posted outside. "Mitsuko Uchida here tomorrow night."

"Do you know her work?"

Linda nodded broadly again. I wondered if she reserved certain affectations until she'd known a person well enough, and immediately wondered what other mannerisms she might have in store for me as the days went by. "She's a remarkable pianist. She came to Wichita State once."

I walked up next to her. "We could see if there are tickets available."

She held her hand up to the schedule as though she were reading a Ouija board. "No, we can't," she said a moment later.

"We really could if you want. I might be able to get us tickets even if the show is sold out. One of the handful of things I'm actually good for."

She shook her head softly. "I'm not here as a tourist." She offered me a meaningful expression before turning and looking off at the street sign. "Fifty-sixth Street and Seventh Avenue. I guess we've been walking a while. We should turn around."

We started back uptown, and a couple of blocks later, Linda casually looped her arm around mine, leaning her head against my shoulder for just a second as she did so. I wanted to put my arm around her as I had at the bar the other night, to hug her against me, to feel her next to me and have her feel me next to her. However, it seemed better to leave things as they were. I definitely didn't want her to become self-conscious and pull away, and I certainly didn't want her to feel that she couldn't do something like this without it becoming weird. Daz had asked me to try to help her out. In reality, though he hadn't needed to. I would have helped her on my own, if I could only figure out a way to do so.

We passed Columbus Circle, which Daz had defined as the on-and-off switch between work and home. I never really understood why he felt this way; we were still a long way away, a *really* long way if the traffic was bad. For him, though, when we made this turn uptown, we were nearly in our apartments, and when we headed in the other direction, it was time for him to start thinking about the job he had to do that day. I missed taking taxis with him, along with the often preposterous exercise that preceded it in the morning. I was getting to work earlier now, and I rarely had to resort to taking a gypsy cab. It was hardly an even trade.

We took Central Park West uptown. Not that long ago, Daz and I had had one of our worst arguments ever nearby after the softball incident. I'd never truly apologized for my part in that.

Linda and I hadn't spoken for several blocks when she said, "Have you thought about how this is going to end?"

"You mean the actual details of it?"

"I guess that's what I mean."

I tightened my grip on her arm a little bit. "I've been actively avoiding it, if you want to know the truth. That's getting harder to do every day."

"I know it is," she said, glancing over at me quickly before looking ahead again. "He's starting to look so sick, Rich."

"I know. The last few days, it's become impossible to ignore." I hesitated, trying to think of something else to say, not to leave this thought hanging between us. "He's still Daz, though."

I could see Linda smile, though she was facing forward. "He'll always be that, won't he?"

I chuckled. "A legend in his own time."

"I think that's very possibly the last thing Eric ever thought he would be."

"Probably what makes him one."

She seemed lost in a private thought for nearly half a block. Then she said, "I must have given him a thousand pep talks when we were teenagers."

"You were obviously good at it. The Daz I know was *never* insecure."

"That's the amazing thing. I could really see the change in him over the years." She hesitated again. "You know, he was always so impressed that you chose to be his friend."

"Really?"

"Really. A big-time New York guy like you."

"I don't think where I was born automatically qualifies me as 'big-time.'"

"It doesn't. Not by itself. It was everything together that was so impressive to him."

In a different lifetime, I might have pursued this line of conversation in search of easy compliments, but

I couldn't do that now. Certainly not with Linda. "I probably wouldn't have survived my sophomore year without him, you know. Everything had spiraled up to another level, and I really felt like I was flailing between the schoolwork and the totally confusing social scene. But while this was going on, Daz and I were living together and having a kick-ass time and, you know, it was impossible to stress too much over anything when we got together."

"He's really good at that."

"It's impossible to think of anyone who could be better."

When we got to 72nd Street, we crossed over to Broadway. Waiting at the corner for the light to change, I glanced out at Daz's "triangle of bliss": Gray's Papaya to the left, Vinnie's Pizza up the block to the right on Amsterdam, and the Rice Bowl across the street. To Daz, this intersection represented culinary nirvana and he regularly insisted that our cab drop us off here for dinner.

"How come there isn't a significant woman in your life?" Linda said as we crossed the street. I have no idea what had brought this question to her mind. Was it possible she was wondering how I would carry on without Daz?

"There are many significant women in my life."

"Significant in what way?"

"Significant in that they are women and they are significant individuals."

"You *do* realize that wasn't what I was asking, right?"

I glanced over at her and grinned sheepishly. "There are no *significant* women in my life right now."

"That wasn't the question. The question was *why*?"

I shrugged. "Is there supposed to be an answer to that question?"

"Yeah, maybe. I think there is."

It was my turn not to say anything for a short while. "I don't know; maybe I'm not significant enough to have a significant woman," I said, certainly never having thought those exact words before.

"I promise you that isn't the answer."

She said this extremely matter-of-factly, but it still jarred me, and I turned to her to get some sense of her expression when she said it. She was focused straight ahead, though, and I couldn't catch her eye.

"It's gotta be a more deep-seated flaw then, huh?"

"That must be it," she said with a smile. I knew she was kidding me, but I also knew that I didn't want this conversation to be relegated to witty banter.

"I'm not playing around," I said carefully.

I could see I'd piqued her curiosity. "What do you mean?"

"I mean that the reason I don't have a significant woman in my life isn't because I'm playing around, or loving 'em and leaving 'em or whatever the conclusion is that people come to about straight guys in their late twenties who don't have serious female attachments."

She shook her head vigorously. "I didn't think that."

"What did you think, then?"

"I didn't know what to think. That's why I asked."

At the corner of 78th and Broadway, I looked down the block. Liz Painter's apartment was there. Liz and I kissed on this very corner the night she took me home for the first time.

"It's not that I don't wonder about it," I said, stopping halfway between 78th and 79th. "Or that I don't want it. More and more these days, I find myself thinking about wanting it. I would imagine that has to count for something. The cards you're dealt have something to do with all of this though too, don't they?"

"I suppose." She patted me on the arm. "Don't worry, I'm not judging you. I was just curious is all."

"Was I just sounding defensive?"

"A tiny bit."

"Sorry." I started walking again, and she came along with me. I was glad she hadn't let go of my arm. "How come there isn't a significant guy in your life?"

"That's not relevant to this conversation."

"I think it might be."

"No, really, it's not."

"If you don't tell me something, I'll feel like I've just been scammed."

She laughed. "I don't want you to feel that way." She tossed her head to the side. "I go on plenty of dates – I'm *extremely* popular in certain circles, you know – but I guess I have incredibly high standards and none of these guys meet them."

"High standards can be a real problem."

"Yeah, high standards. One of them is that the guy can't turn out to be an absolute jerk like my father."

She said that surprisingly bitterly. I expected her to continue, but she didn't.

"Is another one that he needs to be a legend like your brother?"

Her expression relaxed and she pulled on my arm again. "You've got it exactly."

Neither of us said anything else until we were on Daz's block. It was a great block. If you were forced to live on one block your entire life, you could do much worse than to live on this one. When we decided that we needed to buy, I found my place first and it's in an extremely good location. However, when Daz found this place on 89th, I wondered why I'd rushed into things.

"Would you know?" Linda said.

"Know what?"

"If you were to find your significant woman, would you know that you'd found her?"

I didn't answer right away. There was too much to consider in the question. Had I found my significant woman already and missed her? Did it matter enough to me to keep myself attuned? Did I have any real idea what "significant" meant to me?

I didn't say anything until we got to the building and Linda turned to face me. Her eyes – her luminous eyes – took mine as they had so many times since she'd arrived, and in that very moment, I realized that I knew the answer to her question. It was a stunningly obvious answer, and yet one that might have eluded me forever if I hadn't chosen then to consider it. And doing so now scared the hell out of me.

"Yeah, I would know," I said in a halting tone that surprised even me.

I knew she knew what I meant. She took the slightest step in my direction and said, "That's a very good thing."

One of the truly intoxicating moments in one's life is when you realize that you want to kiss someone. Given everything we'd been through together since she'd come to the City, one could say that this moment had been pre-ordained. However, this wasn't just about the past couple of weeks. It wasn't about Linda and me being thrown together in an emotionally wrenching situation. It wasn't about two people grasping at life in the face of death. It wasn't about her being the sister of my dearest friend.

And of course it was about *all* of that.

As much as I wanted to kiss Linda, as much as I was certain she wanted to kiss me, and as much as I could see that if we did so it would not be an of-the-moment thing, I couldn't get myself to do it. Because in the instant before impulse took over, something far more persuasive stepped in the way.

"Thanks for the great walk," I said softly.

"Thank *you*," she said, a bit of uncertainty creeping into her voice. "I really needed it. I didn't realize how much."

"I'm available anytime," I said casually.

She regarded me with such consideration that I felt at once totally naked and absurdly overdressed. "Is that really true?"

I rocked back on my heels. I don't think she'd intended to make me feel uncomfortable, and I really don't think she was trying to be provocative in any way. Yet I felt very shaky. "Yes, it is."

I looked past her for a second and she obviously saw me do it.

"I guess you have to go, huh?" she said.

"I should. Serious meetings in the morning."

She nodded and then reached out to squeeze my hand, turning quickly afterward. "Thanks again, Rich. I'll see you tomorrow night."

She went into the building and I stood there, ridiculously rooted to the spot where she'd last touched me. The doorman waved to me, and I nodded back to him, now feeling very conspicuous. Yet still I continued to stand there for another couple of minutes.

Eventually, I made my way back home.

The chapter about being brilliant

While I *was* using it as an excuse with Linda, I did have
a serious meeting in the morning. It was the day of the
car pitch to the Koreans, though at this point I found
it nearly impossible to think about work. Fortunately,
we were well prepared. Vance and I had sparred and
scuffled some more after my "I'm the boss" speech, and
our relationship was barely beyond collegial after that,
but we managed to get the job done. The team liked
how things had turned out, I thought we did well, and
Rupert was satisfied, so we figured we were as ready to
go as we could be.

The conference room had a table loaded with breakfast items when I arrived. Rupert always tended to
overdo it when a client was around. That was precisely
what I would do if I were in charge. If Daz had been
in charge, of course, he would have insisted on having
several boxes of Cap'n Crunch at the ready, not to mention that there be a theme not only to the meeting but
also to the setup for the meeting.

The Koreans hadn't gotten there yet, so I
grabbed some granola and went to sit with Carnie.
Uncharacteristically (especially in the conference room),
she leaned over and kissed me on the cheek.

"This is going to go great," she said.

"I hope so."

"Are you nervous?"

I glanced over at her. "Do you think I should be?"

"No, definitely not, but don't they say that great performers always get nervous before a show?"

In truth, I was very nervous, but I had a feeling that if Mick Jagger or Bruce Springsteen got nervous at all before a show, it was for an entirely different reason. "I'm okay," I said, though it was clear even to me that my voice lacked conviction.

Vance walked in and I threw him a smile. He nodded, grabbed a muffin, and sat at the opposite end of the conference table. Our last session had been brutal. I hated the way I sounded when I talked to him, but at the same time I couldn't stop myself from doing it. It wasn't like me to be so impolitic, and it really wasn't like me to get all over the staff the way I did with him. Definitely not my proudest moment, but at least the boards got done. I supposed I no longer needed to worry about Rupert setting me up with a permanent replacement for Daz. I was sure at this point that every art director in the house would respond, "Maybe just for this one campaign" if Steve approached any of them.

The Koreans arrived with Rupert about five minutes later. They were crisp business types in perfectly tailored suits. I wondered what they thought of The Incredible Hulk, Daffy Duck, and the rest of our decor. At the very least, we probably should have removed the inflatable Tony the Tiger from the conference room before they arrived. It was too late to make a better first impression at this point, though.

We shook hands all around and made small talk while everyone ate. I realized as we were doing this that

I felt off, flat. They say that baseball pitchers can tell when they're warming up in the bullpen whether they have their good stuff that day or whether they'll need to improvise. If the same was true of advertising pitchers, I was going to have to call on every trick up my sleeve for today's game.

It didn't help that I had been up most of the night. This wasn't the first time in my life I'd had trouble sleeping before a major presentation. However, it was the first time that my tossing and turning had absolutely nothing to do with the client. Something had happened during my walk with Linda the night before, something entirely unexpected. I already knew that I liked her very much. How could I not? She was fun and thoughtful and caring, and her eyes were just *so* expressive. Still, I hadn't realized until last night that she had gotten to me. It wasn't until we were walking arm-in-arm in the part of the City that I loved above all others while we talked about things that mattered to us in ways that felt new to me, that I fully understood that I wanted to keep doing this; that Linda was making the experience of walking and talking exponentially better. She had become more than Daz's sister to me. With this came two questions that made this morning's meeting all but an afterthought.

The first: *What if this was just part of what we are both going through?* This was a legitimate consideration. Was it safe to give weight to any emotional response under the circumstances? Yes, what I felt for her when she turned to face me in front of Daz's building last night seemed very real. And yes, I truly believed that I could make the distinction between a passing attraction and something more significant. However, Linda and I had been thrown together under extreme conditions – conditions unlike any I'd ever experienced before. It was natural for us to bond around our mutual love for Daz. What if what we felt for each other because of that was nothing more than a byproduct and we discovered a few months down the road that our relationship had no foundation without him?

The second question, though, was the showstopper, the thing that all the tossing and turning the entire night couldn't drive out of my head: *If Linda shared Daz's genes, did that mean she would share his fate?* This was a family that had been marked continuously by devastating illness. I'm sure there were several other cousins and relatives cut down in their primes by heredity whose names had not come up in conversation. If I fell in love with Linda – and I was getting the sense at this point that I already had – and I acted on those feelings, and then she got sick, could I possibly have the strength to go through what I was going through with Daz again? The image of Linda three years from now wasting away on my bed might be the single scariest vision I'd ever conjured. I wasn't at all sure I had the fortitude to withstand it.

I wasn't proud of this response – I was ashamed to even think of it. However, as terrible and as wrung out as I felt about what was going on with Daz, I also knew that I hadn't even experienced the worst of it yet. And this much was already excruciating. While shying away from Linda and what we could mean to each other because of her heredity might mark me forever as an awful person, I couldn't help feeling this way. It hurt enough to make sleeping last night a futile exercise.

Rupert signaled that it was time to get started, and I pressed these thoughts as far down into my subconscious as I could. I stood up and walked to the head of the table opposite the Koreans. I gestured for Vance to join me, but he waved me off, passing over the storyboards instead.

I tried to remember what it was like to put on my game face.

"You asked us to pitch this car to the young professional, the person who hadn't really made it yet, but who believed he was in the process of making it." My voice surprised me with its confidence. "Vance and the rest of our creative team and I spent a good deal of time batting this around, trying to find a way to distinguish this car from the considerable competition you will be facing at this price point. We decided to try to sell the idea that this car would add luster to your life, that not only would you look good driving it, but that it would serve as a calling card – an announcement of your imminent arrival.

"Our recommendation is that you call the car the *Brilliante*." I looked over at Carnie when I said this, and she offered me a smile of encouragement that carried more than a little pathos with it. For just a second, this distracted me enough that I began to feel unsteady, but I got my feet back under me. If I was going to stumble, that was not the place where I wanted it to happen. "We recommend you introduce it with the following thirty-second spot."

I turned the storyboards in our potential clients' direction and took them through each panel. Our proposed spot opens at nighttime on an upscale urban street, the kind of place where an emerging young professional might live. From the right side of the screen, a light begins to emerge and pounding rock music begins to play. The light fills more and more of the screen, nearly drenching the screen in white. Then the angle shifts and we look at the light head on. Slowly, it becomes clear

that there is something in the light. Then we make out
the *Brilliante*, emerging in all its glory. The car comes to
a stop in front of a great apartment building (which of
course has ample available parking right out front) and
a young woman exits the car. She tosses her keys up in
the air once and then flicks the remote, which causes the
Brilliante to illuminate and bathe the screen in its glow
one more time. As she walks into the building, a voice-
over says, "The *Brilliante*. Only your future is brighter."

Vance was never able to make the chrome effects
work well, and we finally settled on this approach instead.
I was uncertain about it right up to the end, but as I pre-
sented it now, it certainly seemed to do the job.

More important, the client seemed to believe this.
They asked a number of questions, suggested that the
actual music (I'd pulled something from our library to
serve as a backdrop to my presentation) have a stron-
ger drumbeat, and recommended that we use a silver
Brilliante (they'd instantly adopted the name) rather
than a red one. Otherwise, they were sold. It was one of
the easier pitches I'd done in the last year.

When the meeting ended and the client left the room,
I walked over to shake Vance's hand. The boards he'd
done were professional and clean, and he had effectively
maintained as much of the spirit of the original concept
I developed with Daz as he could.

"You did a great job with this," I said, "thanks." I
hoped he would see this as an olive branch. I really didn't
want him to bear any ill will toward our collaboration,
though at the same time I had no intention of collaborat-
ing with him again.

"It was easy," he said nonchalantly. "You knew what
you wanted." He smiled thinly at me and walked away.

Fortunately, Carnie and some other members of the team came up to me right after this and I let his gruff attitude pass.

A short while later, Steve Rupert showed up in my office. He was beaming. This account would generate a significant amount of billing throughout the third and fourth quarter, essentially making the year for The Creative Shop.

"You're coming to lunch with us, right?" he said.

"Yeah, of course. I'll be the one ordering the thirty-year-old Scotch."

"Hey, order the three-hundred-year-old Scotch. You nailed it today. Start thinking about the next set of toys you want to buy with your bonus check."

"I assume that means they weren't just being polite in there?"

"They loved it. They told me that we exceeded their expectations. How often do we hear that?"

I was happy for Steve. This was The Shop's first car company, and a successful campaign would be a real boon to their business, not just this year, but for the conceivable future. No matter what happened with me, I always wanted the agency to be successful.

"I know it was a little shaky with Vance," he said. Since I hadn't mentioned anything to him about that, I assume it was Vance who had done the complaining, if not directly to Rupert, then through intermediaries. "You really pulled it off, though. You had every reason to be concerned about how this would turn out, but you made it happen."

Yes, I made it happen. Without Daz. That was the point Steve was too much of a gentleman to make more directly. Other than the BlisterSnax Max sales conference video, which Carnie had essentially directed, this was the first project I'd done since learning Daz was sick – and it was a smash.

"Daz was all over this one," I said.

Steve shook his head. "Then you'll have to let him know you didn't screw it up in his absence."

I smiled. "Yeah, I'll do that."

———

Right after lunch, I left the office to go uptown. These days, Daz always looked much worse when I first saw him than I expected. Somehow, I was never prepared for this. It consistently took me a couple of seconds to adjust, a couple of seconds where I was tongue-tied. I only hope this went undetected by him.

"So did you kill today?" he said. I think he was trying to sound ebullient, but it came off as strained.

"We *killed*," I said brightly. "The Koreans are trying to decide whether to rename a bridge or a shopping center in our honor."

"How about an amusement park?"

"I'll suggest it."

Hot Hot Heat's first album was playing on the stereo. There were still so many albums to get through. I thought about suggesting to Daz that he play only the best songs on each album and maybe even skip a few entirely, but there was no way to say something like that without his taking it the wrong way.

Linda's head had been resting on Daz's arm when I entered the room, and now she sat back in her chair. "Did you accomplish something important today?"

"I pitched a campaign that Daz and I worked on. The client loved it."

"Congratulations. I'm glad your 'serious meetings' went well." She offered me a smile I couldn't interpret.

I wasn't sure how to deal with Linda. I was obviously not the only one who felt what I felt as we were standing outside the apartment last night, but I was certainly the only one who felt *all* of what I felt afterward. Looking at her now, I thought of us on that walk and felt her arm around my arm and the closeness of her body. I thought about the time we went to dinner, and the Foosball Debacle, and the numerous conversations we'd had after Daz nodded off at night. I felt a level of tenderness toward her that I couldn't remember ever feeling for a woman before. It was devastating under the circumstances.

Daz insisted that I call a messenger to bring the storyboards up to his apartment. Over dinner, he prodded me to recount the pitch meeting with the Koreans – he made me do the entire pitch exactly as I had done it in the conference room – and the details of the lunch we had afterward. Linda didn't participate much in the conversation. Neither did Daz. Yet somehow all the spaces were filled.

"You know, I wasn't always great at public speaking," I said after finishing the story. "When I was in third grade, I had to give a report on the three branches of the American government. I did all of my research and even made these really great charts, but when I stood up in front of the room, I got insanely nervous. I somehow managed in the first minute to refer to the Executive Branch as the *insectu*tive branch, and a couple of kids in the back of the room thought that was hilarious and started crawling around the floor like bugs. This was kind of unnerving. I'm pretty sure it was the only time in my life that I stuttered, but

I had trouble even saying the word 'congress.' It wasn't pretty. The teacher reprimanded the kids and got them back in their seats, but I was a lost cause at that point. Finally, she just told me to hand my report in. Hard to believe I ever spoke in public again, huh?"

Daz looked at me with a bemused expression on his gaunt face. I'd hoped that this admission would launch us into a conversation about our most embarrassing moments or flopping in public or some such thing, but he didn't seem up for it.

"Wanna see what's on TV?" I said, reaching for the remote and holding it up for Daz. Though I'd suggested it, I was disappointed when he took the remote from my hand and started flipping through channels.

He was asleep not long after. Linda gestured for me to join her in the living room, and she settled on the couch while I took the massage chair. Neither of us said anything right away. I looked toward the dining table to see Harlene making her best efforts not to look at us. For each of us, this experience was conjuring its own set of demons.

"He didn't know where he was for a couple of hours today," Linda said, drawing my attention back to her.

"He seemed okay after I got here," I said, not needing to add that "okay" was a relative term at this point.

"He did," Linda said, dropping her eyes as she did so. I wished she would look at me, but I also wasn't sure what I would do if she did.

"He remembered the presentation."

"That was practically the only thing he remembered all day. The doctor came again this morning and upped his medication. He told me it would make Eric groggier and less responsive." She hesitated, then added,

"I'm not sure how many clear stretches we can expect in the future."

I looked back toward the bedroom. I wanted to shake Daz awake, tell him that we had too much to do for him to sleep the day away. Didn't he realize that every moment counted? "I'm not ready for this," I said, realizing as I did that Linda didn't need to hear this from me.

She looked up and I saw that her eyes filled with tears. "Neither am I. It doesn't matter whether we are or not, though." She reached out a hand and I leaned forward to take it. I wanted more than anything to hold her, but at the same time, I was so ridiculously afraid of what would happen if I did. I hated that I could even think like this at this point. At the same time, though, I realized that it was *this point* that was making me think this way. Again, I thought of going through this with Linda a few years from now, and found the notion unbearable.

The position we were in wasn't comfortable, but I couldn't will myself to go to the couch any more than I could make myself let go of Linda's hand. I have no idea what she thought of this. Given what she must have been thinking about her brother, there was a very good chance she hadn't even noticed.

"I'm scared to death of speaking in public," she said.

It was difficult to believe that she wanted to pick up on my monologue from Daz's room. Then I realized that this wasn't what she was doing at all.

"You'll get over it," I said. "You always can if it's important enough."

"Will you help me?"

"In every way I possibly can."

The chapter about admissions

I tried going to work the next day, but I only lasted until about ten o'clock. Rupert was great about letting me take off, and I knew it had absolutely nothing to do with my having just secured a big account.

Daz fell in and out of sleep most of the day. Like yesterday, there was a period where he seemed almost entirely incoherent, and even when he was relatively sharp he seemed to be having a tough time maintaining the thread of any conversation. I didn't want this to be painful to him, so for the most part, Linda and I just sat on either side of his bed and the three of us listened to music. Daz hadn't spoken for a couple of hours at this point, and Linda and I did little to break the silence.

When I was sure she couldn't notice, I watched Linda's face. Even as shadowed as it became as Daz faded further and further, it was still so luminous. So much genuine concern for her brother. I felt this at times when she looked at me as well. It was remarkable that she could give it and a truly remarkable thing to receive.

Sitting here, with my best friend disappearing before my eyes, I continued to struggle with my feelings for her. Maybe this was just a way to avoid thinking about what was happening to Daz, about the fact that the inevitable was very much upon us. Probably not, though, since it didn't serve that purpose anyway.

We had been sitting almost trance-like for an hour or so when Harlene came in and shook us from our joint reverie. As we did almost automatically at this point, we got up to go into the living room while the night nurse did what she needed to do.

"I slept by his bed last night and I've been sitting there all day today," Linda said as we stood waiting for Harlene to come out of Daz's room. "I think I really need to get out for a while."

I nodded, but didn't otherwise respond.

"I was thinking about going to a movie or something," she said. "Do you want to come?"

I tilted my head to the side and said, "I think I'm going to stick with Daz."

"There's a really good chance he's out for the night. The drugs and all."

"I know." I allowed myself to be distracted by the sound of Harlene tinkering in the bedroom. "I just think it might be better if I stayed."

If she knew that at least part of the reason I was saying this was because I didn't know how to be when I was out with her, she didn't push the issue. "Do you mind if I go? I really need a few hours away."

I gestured with both hands. "No, of course not. Go. There's a multiplex on 84th street. Are you okay going out by yourself?"

Her face held the barest trace of a smile. "I think I can handle it."

"You have your cell with you, right?"

Now she seemed a tiny bit alarmed. "I shouldn't leave."

"No, go, really. We'll both be here when you get back."

She hesitated for a very long moment, and then shut her eyes tightly. When she opened them, it seemed that she had made up her mind. She went back into Daz's room for a minute, and then came out and headed toward the door. When she got there, she stopped.

"Hey Rich?"

I turned to her.

"This is the hardest thing in the world. It would still be hard if we were doing it together but maybe not as hard."

I nodded. It was all I could think to do. She offered me another half-smile and walked out the door.

When Harlene was done, I went back to see Daz. Harlene had turned off the music, and the room was quieter than I could remember it being since Daz had gotten sick. In fact, it was quieter than I could ever remember. Certainly, there was no noise in the apartment on those many mornings when I rousted Daz out of bed to get to the office, but even then it *felt* like something was going on, even if it was nothing more than me making a racket to get him in motion.

I sat next to Daz in this silence for maybe fifteen minutes. As I did, the futility of what I was doing set in. I was literally sitting here waiting for my best friend to die. Whatever comfort I had been able to offer him in the early stages of the disease had been minimized recently by his long periods of unconsciousness. I had absolutely no value beyond this. I couldn't do a single thing for him. I couldn't even bring him great take-out anymore, because he'd stopped eating. Whatever nutrition he got now came through his IV.

The quiet became too much for me. I walked over to his phone. The album Harlene had turned off was the

Indigo Girls' live recording, *1200 Curfews*. We'd played it often in our junior year of college, especially when our female dorm-mates next door convinced us to drink dark rum and make ragged attempts at four-part harmony. There were twenty-seven songs in the set, the best of which were in the second half. The album had only begun when Harlene shut it down. I wondered if I would upset all of Daz's plans if I skipped ahead. I knew he intended to listen to every album in order, but since, if he really was down for the night, I technically shouldn't play any album at all, I guessed it really didn't matter what I put on.

I jumped to "Galileo," one of the truly great songs ever, and I leaned back into my chair and closed my eyes. I envisioned Daz belting out the chorus with a slightly inebriated Tracy and Roxanne, missing at least half of the notes and not being the least bit self-conscious about this.

"You're moving on without me already."

I opened my eyes to see Daz with his head tilted in my direction. I could almost kid myself into thinking that he was looking somewhat alert.

"Sorry, I didn't think this would wake you up."

"I missed half of this album?"

"I didn't play the first half."

He offered me the closest approximation of a frown he could muster. "And my body's not even cold yet."

I stood up. "Do you want me to switch back to the beginning?"

"Yes, I do."

I got his phone to make the change. As I was doing so, the duo was singing, "If we wait for the time till all souls get it right / Then at least I know there'll be no nuclear annihilation in my lifetime."

"I really didn't mean to wake you," I said as I sat back down.

"That's a first."

"Yeah, I guess it is. Do you want to go back to sleep? I can turn the music off and leave you alone."

"I'll probably nod off during the next song anyway." He turned his head in the other direction. "Where's Linda?"

"She took off for a while. She figured you were going to sleep right through until morning. She went to a movie."

"I'm glad. How come you didn't go with her?"

My first thought was to invent a story for him. There were so many easy answers available, so many things that would have been better for him to hear than the truth. I couldn't do it this time, though. I needed not to do it. I guess in some way, I believed that he needed to hear what I was thinking. I knew I really had to say it.

"Listen, there's something I kind of have to tell you about me and Linda."

His eyes met mine. This was the most life they had shown in days.

I continued. "I think I'm starting to have feelings for her."

He chuckled thinly. He was doing everything thinly at this point. "I probably should have kept the two of you apart."

"Yeah, well don't worry about that. I think I'm doing a good enough job of it myself."

His eyes narrowed. "You screwed up with my sister?"

"Not yet. Not officially, anyway. I'm just in the *process* of screwing up."

He seemed very uncomfortable. I couldn't tell if it was the subject matter or the need for him to say more than he felt he had the strength to say. When he did speak, it came out slowly.

"What's the matter? Too beautiful, too smart, and too giving for you?"

"She's too *Dazman* for me," I said abruptly.

When Daz looked at me, I could swear he reached right down into my soul, pulled it out, and sneered. "Want to explain that?"

"I hardly know what to say," I said quickly, beseechingly. "And you're probably the last person in the world I should be saying it to; except that you're also the *only* person in the world I can say it to." I paused and tried to find some sensible way to explain what I was feeling. I realized that there was none.

"Daz, I think I'm in love with Linda. Yeah, she's beautiful and smart and giving. She's much, much more than that. There's probably stuff you don't even realize about her because she's your sister and you've known her for her entire life. She makes me feel important. She makes me want to protect her, even though I'm pretty sure she can kick my ass. It's great, Daz. I mean, it really might be the first time I've truly felt this way about a woman.

"But there's one gigantic problem: I don't think I can go through this thing we're going through now twice."

Daz didn't speak for an extended period. I knew he understood what I was talking about and I knew it had gotten to him.

Finally, without looking at me, he said, "Everybody dies, Rich."

"Not in their late twenties. Not because of some genetic family curse."

He cringed, and I wished I could stuff that last sentence back into my mouth.

"Linda's not gonna die young," he said at last.

"How do you know that? Is she somehow immune to all the shit that goes on in your family? Is she part alien? Is she *adopted*? How can you say what you just said with any sense of confidence at all?"

"I can't. I just know it."

"Can I get that in writing?"

He laughed, though it came out more like a puff of air. "No guarantees, Flaccid. But you're an asshole if you pass this up."

I slumped down in my chair. "This has been the single most terrible month of my entire life."

His eyes narrowed again and he made what seemed to be an almost involuntary gesture with his chin. "It has? I thought we were having fun hanging out."

I was about to tell him how gut-wrenching it had been to watch him deteriorate. I was about to tell him that I had never experienced anything anywhere near as difficult as it was seeing him slip away. I was about to tell him that there was no doubt in my mind that this was the absolute most horrible stretch of time I'd ever experienced.

I didn't do that for two reasons. The first was that this wasn't something he needed to hear. I had already dumped more on him than I should have – probably much, much more – and what I was "going through" was nothing compared to what he was dealing with.

The other was that I wasn't sure it was true.

"Daz, me and Linda, that wouldn't be playing around. That would be real."

He turned his head to face me straight on. He didn't move his body and I wondered if it was because he couldn't. "What's your point?"

In that moment, I realized I didn't have one. Not a single one. Not a single one that would make sense to anyone, least of all to me. I was still feeling all of it, but I didn't have a point. "I think I just figured out why lots of people find it easier not to care about anything."

He looked away from me. "Is that what you just figured out?"

I ran both hands through my hair. "That or something else."

"Something else," he said, almost dreamily.

I didn't want him to fade back out just yet. "Daz, what can I do for you?"

He looked toward me again. "You can skip this song. I hate it."

It was the Indigo Girls song "Pushing the Needle Too Far." I never liked it either. I reached across his body for the phone.

"Go to 'Midnight Train to Georgia,'" he said.

This required jumping more than halfway through the album. I did what I was told and sat back down.

"Maybe it's time to switch to greatest hits," he said.

"Either that or stop being such a lazy slug."

He smiled a little. "That's it."

We let the rest of the first verse of the song play in silence.

"Daz?"

"Yeah?"

"This hasn't been the single most terrible month of my life."

"Really? What was?"

"That wasn't really what I was going for."

"I know."

Then he was out again. Just like that. Without ever bothering to mention that we'd just had our last conversation.

The chapter about trying not to say goodbye

I stayed next to Daz the rest of the night, nodding off at some point, slumped forward in the chair with my head on his mattress. Midmorning the next day, I went back to my place to shower and change my clothes. When I returned to Daz's apartment, Linda told me that he'd awakened for a few minutes to talk about babysitting her when he was eleven after their uncle died.

This was the last thing he would talk about. After that, he lapsed into a coma that lasted eight days, passing away in the early morning while both Linda and I were sleeping in the room with him. We kept the stereo going the entire time for this last stretch, even while we ourselves slept. During this time, I thought about playing another album out of order, hoping it would wake Daz up again the way the Indigo Girls album had, but I think part of me knew it wouldn't work this time and it seemed more important to maintain his wishes. When the doctor pronounced him dead, R.E.M.'s *Automatic for the People* album was playing. I turned the machine off right after "Man on the Moon," a song about Andy Kaufman, another brilliant artist that died much too soon. And then I just lost it.

Linda was right; there was absolutely nothing we could have done to prepare ourselves for this moment. We could have known the precise time it would happen and exactly where we would be and what we would be doing, and it wouldn't have made any difference.

Linda and I said separate goodbyes to Daz's body before it was taken away and then we sat together quietly for a few hours before we called people to let them know. Steve, Carnie, Chess, and several other members of S.U.L.K. came over not long after, and we suspended membership requirements and just let ourselves react. At one point, Carnie called Michelle and several of us pretended to catch up. Michelle said she'd be back for the memorial service. She then informed me that afterward she would be going back to Indiana to stay.

The next several days passed in a haze. Unbeknownst to me, Linda and Daz at some point had a conversation about burying him in Kansas before deciding that he was meant to stay in New York. I don't know why I was so glad they'd made this decision. I never bought into the notion of a cemetery plot being someone's "final resting place," but I felt better knowing that Daz wouldn't be all that far away. As though such a thing was even conceivable.

The funeral was intentionally a small one, attended only by Linda, me, Daz's closest friends, and Daz's father's brother. Linda still hadn't told her mother, believing that the only proper way to do so was in person and knowing that the woman didn't have the constitution to handle coming to New York herself.

The memorial service, on the other hand, was huge. It seemed that every under-thirty advertising person in the City was there, as was staff from Java Nirvana, Jake's

Dilemma, and the Rice Bowl, along with the executive team from BlisterSnax. Some of Daz's teammates from his Michigan soccer team flew out, as did his high school coach. I would have loved to have seen his old art teacher or any of the people who had ever suggested that he was wasting his talent, but none of them showed.

Curt Prince and Andrea came. They were such an anomaly in this group that for a second I couldn't place them. Curt and I hadn't spoken since that phone call before he'd gone to Europe. I guess he now knew what my personal problem was. I appreciated his coming and especially appreciated how sad he seemed to be there. He shook my hand before the service and asked me if I was okay. I nodded, probably unconvincingly, and introduced him to Linda.

The room at the Society for Ethical Culture was decorated with tear sheets of Daz's best work, and we had a video monitor in the corner alternating some of his commercials with tape of his soccer days and a home video Chess had taken of Daz doing an Eminem song at last year's birthday party. Several people from The Shop spoke, and one of the women in Daz's bullpen performed a song on acoustic guitar that she had written in his memory. After that, Linda told some of the funny stories about Daz's childhood that I'd only heard myself in the past few weeks. In spite of her concerns about speaking in public, she did a great job of holding it together until the very last story.

Then it was my turn. I'd started and rejected a dozen attempts to memorialize Daz over the past couple of days. I wanted to say something that Daz could have tolerated listening to while at the same time saying something that reflected how I felt about his being gone. As

I stood at the podium, I still wasn't entirely sure what that would be.

"I don't need to tell you about Eric Dazman. The people who spoke before me have done a wonderful job of capturing who he was and why we care about him the way we do. More to the point, I don't need to tell you, because if you ever met him, if you were ever even in the same room with him, you got a piece of him, and that piece almost certainly had a huge impact on you.

"Maybe the best thing I can say about my life to date is that I don't need any introduction in a room full of Eric Dazman's friends. It would be wrong to say that I defined myself by Daz. But it wouldn't be wrong to say that I defined myself with him. I've come to understand that you grow up in stages. When Daz and I met a couple of days before our freshman year at Michigan, I was already grown up enough to be able to survive an Ann Arbor winter. But I think the rest of my quantum moments happened with and because of Daz. Right up to a few days ago.

"Daz and I usually had a great time together. That in itself is an impressive thing to say about someone you saw nearly every day for almost a decade. And for the longest time, I thought that this was the special thing about our friendship. We always had a great time. I was kinda missing the point.

"No cliché about friendship is appropriate to describe the kind of friend Eric Dazman was and will continue to be. At the same time, every cliché is appropriate. Fortunately, I don't have to explain what that means to any of you, either."

I looked out at the people gathered. As my eyes touched upon several of them, many of whom meant a huge amount to me as well as Daz, I came perilously close to losing my composure. Still, I had one more thing I wanted to say.

"In Daz's memory, I'm going to sit in front my television tonight and stream several episodes of *Duck Tales* in succession. I'll eat Cap'n Crunch cereal directly out of the box with a milk chaser and I'll have the Fatboy Slim album he insisted I download playing in the background. Then, before I go to bed, I'll brush my teeth first with strawberry toothpaste, then wintergreen, and finally bubble gum.

"I implore you all to do the same."

———

Eventually, Linda and I were by ourselves in the apartment. Ever since we'd started making calls, people had been focused on not leaving us alone. However, after the memorial service and after several hours here where many had come back to reflect on Daz, the support teams dissipated. Michelle and Carnie stuck around longer than everyone else, but then it was time to get Michelle to the airport. At least we didn't kid each other this time when Michelle and I said goodbye. She showed me some pictures of her with her niece, the little girl's arms wrapped tightly around her neck. If I hadn't gotten the point before then, I finally did.

There was a huge number of practical issues to address. Daz had drawn up a will not long after he bought the apartment – something else I'd only learned recently. Not every little thing was detailed, but it wouldn't be difficult to figure out who should get what. Linda told me I could have the massage chair and the air hockey table.

We picked out something from the apartment for each of his closest friends. Linda would keep his memorabilia and the rest of his stuff, and of course the proceeds from the sale of the apartment, which I would help her put on the market tomorrow.

"This place will sell fast," I said as we sat on the couch together. "Things are going really quickly in Manhattan right now in spite of the economy."

"That's good," she said. "I don't think I can handle months of realtors parading people in and out of here."

"That won't be an issue, I'm sure of it." I shifted slightly to face her more directly. "What happens after that?"

Linda turned to look out the window. "Back to Kansas for me, I guess. I have to go see my mother and take her through this. Then I'll go to Topeka and find a job. Get myself up and running again."

I leaned toward her, even though she still wasn't facing me. "I wish you wouldn't."

"Get myself up and running?"

I reached out for her hand. "Return to Topeka. At least not permanently."

She turned back to look at me and I took her other hand. She looked down at our interlaced fingers. "What do you mean?"

"I mean I would love it if you didn't go back. I would love it if you stayed here with me."

She tilted her head gently. "That's an awfully dramatic thing to say."

I shrugged. "I was going for significant."

She looked up at me and through their red rims there was that singular brilliance in her eyes.

"We aren't meant to be a thousand miles apart," I said.

"I'm not as easy to get along with as Eric."

"I'll keep that in mind."

"And I don't do anything halfway."

"Then we should be just fine."

She came into my arms then and we stayed that way for I don't know how long. It wasn't the first time that I'd held her, but it was the first time that I held her knowing I would hold her this way for as long as I possibly could.

As Daz said, there were no guarantees. But when did life ever give you guarantees? There were approximations of certainties, though. As I kissed her hair and pulled her a little closer, I was absolutely convinced that Linda was one of them.

———

A few days later, I thanked Curt Prince and Noel Keane for all of their attention and told them that I wouldn't be going to K&C. As much as I admired Prince and knew I could learn from him in so many ways, making a move like that no longer made any sense to me. Prince seemed genuinely upset about this and asked me to stay in touch. He told me to call him in a few weeks to set up a time for Linda and me to come out to the Hamptons house.

A month later, I resigned from The Creative Shop. Steve Rupert was stunned and even recommended a long vacation and a grief counselor before I made things official. I knew that my decision had nothing to do with grief, though. Linda and I had talked about it at length before I did anything. She's a really great sounding board. I had a tremendous number of friends at The Shop, the support of my superiors, clients I truly enjoyed working for, and a welcome future. But I couldn't be "Flash" there without "Dazzle," and no amount of adjustment on my part or The Shop's could change that in any meaningful way.

However, I could open the Flaster/Dazman Agency, which I did the next week. It's a tiny office with only two other full-time employees, which means I'm outsourcing just about everything right now, including art direction. Still, it'll grow over time, and I'll do everything I can to make it what it was meant to be.

Both my name and Daz's are on the company's letterhead. This sometimes confuses prospective clients who haven't heard the stories about Daz and are curious about the co-president they've never met.

If they ask, I simply tell them he's the world's greatest silent partner.